I0578098

Run
with it
ML NYSTROM

For information, contact the publisher, Hot Tree Publishing.
WWW.HOTTREEPUBLISHING.COM

EDITING: HOT TREE EDITING
COVER DESIGNER: BOOKSMITH DESIGN
FORMATTING: RMGRAPHX

E-book ISBN-13: 978-1-925853-88-9
Paperback ISBN-13: 978-1-925853-89-6

Dragon Runner MC Series

Mute
Stud
Blue
Table
Brick

MacAteer Brothers Series

Run With It

This book is dedicated to all the single moms struggling to be the breadwinner-teacher-coach-counselor and all the other hats worn by a parent. You are super rockstars! Also, to those special men who come to love and support those single moms and are unafraid to take on an instant family.

Chapter 1

His deep hazel eyes bored into mine as he handed me a perfect single red rose. Words weren't necessary, as he easily swept me off my feet and carried me into the candlelit bedroom. I ran my hands through his shiny blond hair as he gently laid me down on the soft coverlet. He caressed my face before leaning over to straddle my hips with his muscular legs. I watched as he slowly undid the ties that held his billowing white shirt closed, and in one swift movement, he whipped the fabric over his head, revealing his gleaming rock-hard abs and perfectly formed pecs topped by copper-colored nipples. My breath left me at the intensity of his gaze, need and want reflected in those beautiful orbs. I gasped, and the scent of sex and male musk coated my tongue. He wanted me. He wanted me badly. Slowly he bared my beautiful, svelte body. Peeling the silvery gauze dress from me, he revealed my firm, lush breasts and smooth feminine curves. I was his and his alone. His hands moved to his black leather pants, and he popped the first button, revealing more of his glistening six-pack. He leaned back and his golden hair gleamed in the candlelight. I heard his moan when he traced his fingers over the lines of hard muscle around his navel. His eyes glowed with fervent want. My own want rose in me, and I grew breathless with anticipation of his heated touch. He popped the second button, revealing the paler skin of his groin and the outline of his mouth-watering package. He popped the third button and—

"Mom! Abby won't get outta the bathroom!"

The yell pierced through my dream like a hot knife through butter. I sighed as I opened my eyes to the pale early morning light. Gone was my beautiful sexy body and fantasy lover, and here I was, back as my thirty-eight-year-old self, short, round, and slightly overweight. Maybe a little more rounded than I should be.

Okay, I'll say it. I'm fat. I'm just fat.

My bed squeaked as my feet hit the wood floor. It was old, and the mattress seriously needed replacement. I kept meaning to get a throw rug for my room, but that and several other wants had to go behind the needs and wants of my kids.

I have four—Abby is my oldest at fifteen, Jacob is twelve, Sarah is ten, and Matthew is my baby at eight.

Where is Dad? The short answer is he's not here. Last year he traded me in for a younger model just before his fortieth birthday. What a twentysomething girl sees in an older married man with four kids I'll never figure out. I was sure it was the money. My husband—ex-husband—has loads of it. He received the bulk of an inheritance from an uncle just over a year ago. Enough money that we could have paid the college costs for all four of our kids and still had a small fortune left over. Instead, my husband—*sigh*, ex-husband—decided he was done with his aging wife and kids and found himself a perky blonde trophy, a fancy new house in a fancy new neighborhood, fancy new friends at a fancy new golf club, and of course a fancy new Porsche convertible.

I get angry when I see that red car zipping around town. That one car could've paid for the entire four years of college for Abby and two or three years for Jacob. Meanwhile, I still have my old, falling-apart Ford minivan.

What did the kids and I get from this windfall? Nada. Nothing. Zip. I can't prove it, but I'm 100 percent sure he knew about the money he would get and left us before he claimed it. Filed the separation papers one week and was collecting his bounty the next. My lawyer said it sucked, but the dates worked out that his newly found riches weren't considered a marital asset. He did have to pay child support, but that was based on his previous yearly income, which didn't amount to squat in comparison. I didn't have the means for a long court battle, as every penny I made went to support myself and the kids, and getting free legal help would take years. Social services was backed up *that* far. He got a big fat bonus. The rest of us got the shaft.

I couldn't pay the mortgage on only my salary and next-to-nothing child support, so I had to sell our nice big house and cram us all into a three-bedroom duplex. I barely broke even on the sale, despite my husband—*dammit!*—ex-husband not arguing for his portion. My bedroom looked like a converted closet, but the kids needed the bigger spaces more since they had to share. Bunk beds, shared closets, and the worst of all, one bathroom for everyone.

"MOM!" The yell was louder now, accompanied by the hollow stomping of feet to my bedroom and followed up with hard pounding against the door.

"All right, all right, I'm coming," I grumbled, reaching for my robe and belting it around my waist. "Abby? Get a move on."

The bathroom door muffled her teenage whine. "I'm doing my hair!"

"Yeah, well, the rest of us will flood the place soon. Finish primping in your room."

She complained a bit more while she made a mad dash to her room before the curling iron cooled.

I made Jacob wait as I took a two-minute pee; I could hear him huff and puff at the door. Privacy was a luxury I no longer had. Sarah was up, dressed, and sitting in the kitchen, which was separated from the living room area only by a long breakfast bar that served as our dining table, school project desk, laundry folding station, utility spot, and anything else that needed a flat surface. I sighed and moved several backpacks—for the bazillionth time—off it to make room for the cereal bowls.

"Morning, Mom!"

Mattie ran in, barefoot, and grabbed spoons out of the drawer. He wasn't born with an off switch, and he was always in motion. Climbing on everything, swinging from anything that held his small weight, and constantly running.

I wasn't sure that kid knew how to walk. I used to be critical of those mothers who put child leashes on their kids, but that was the only thing that kept my miniature tornado from getting hit by cars when he was younger. No fear, my little Mattie!

Jacob had finished up in the bathroom and slipped back to his room, which meant I had about three minutes to take a lukewarm shower. Between Abby and Jacob, most of the hot water got used up, and more than once I'd had to deal with cold. I rushed through my routine, staying mindful of the clock, quickly towel-drying my hair and pulling the dark mass back into a damp ponytail. I didn't keep a style per se, just trimmed the ends occasionally. Long hair was easier to maintain, as all I needed to do when I was in a hurry was tie it back. Hurry was the norm these days. I threw on clothes and dashed a little moisturizer over my face. No time for makeup. Routine done.

Jacob had made coffee for me, and the two youngest were eating cereal as they gabbed about their upcoming day. I knew eggs, bacon, and sausage were better for a longer-lasting protein-filled breakfast than sugar-filled corn puffs and colored marshmallows, but time dictated the cooking while money dictated the weekly grocery list.

"Abby come down yet?" I poured a to-go cup of the precious caffeinated elixir of life.

"Nope." Sarah crunched a spoonful of Lucky Charms. "She's putting her face on."

I yelled up the steps, "Abby! Get down here now! We're behind already, and you need to eat something!"

She yanked open the door and stuck her head out. Sculpted curls adorned one side of her head. "I'm still doing my hair."

"Then hurry up. You still need to eat."

"I'm not hungry."

"You're—"

She stomped back into the bedroom.

I growled under my breath and then yelled out loud, "Don't make me come up there."

She yanked the door open and glared down at me.

"You are not leaving this house without breakfast."

She flicked back a lock of hair that slid into her eyes. "I said, I'm not hungry."

I glared. She glared. We could go on like this for days. The clock on the wall read quarter 'til eight. I moved back into the kitchen, then heard the bedroom door slam shut. A picture on the wall slid sideways on the nail with the force. I still needed to get through the morning schedule of "where's-my-backpack-I-need-my-shoes-find-my-homework-I-need-lunch-money" and whatever else my kids forgot to get together last night.

Twenty minutes later, I herded the kids to the door relatively on time. I thought maybe, just maybe, we might make it to their various schools without any drama.

Too bad I lived in a fantasy world.

Mattie opened the door and grinned at Jacob. "Losers are last."

"Wait a min—"

The screen door slammed shut behind Mattie, knocking

the top hinge loose, again.

Jacob ran after him. "Hey, that's not fair."

I caught the screen door before it could slap shut and take the whole thing off the frame.

Sarah cut around me and followed her brothers.

Abby stopped beside me and rolled her eyes.

I looked at the mass of waves she had lacquered into place on her head and followed behind her as she walked out. "Don't be so smug. You were just like that a few years ago."

"No I wasn't." She spoke the words over her shoulder. Her creative coiffure barely moved.

"I got here first." Mattie had one foot pressed against the edge of the passenger door and a death grip on the armrest while Jacob yanked on his other foot.

"Because you cheated!"

Sarah opened the side door on the van and tossed in her bright pink backpack.

"Both of you, move. I sit in the front seat." Abby crossed her arms, and both boys fell quiet. Then Mattie laughed.

Abby twisted up her mouth and looked at me. "Mom."

"All of you in the back."

"But I got here first!" Mattie kicked at his brother.

"Back, now. All of you. No one is sitting in the front."

The boys moaned and clambered from the passenger seat into the back. Abby started to get in the front.

"All of you means all of you." I put my purse in the passenger seat just in case she needed a hint.

"What? Why?"

"Don't argue. You used up all that time to do your hair. Now get in and buckle up."

Abby huffed and slammed the door. She slid into the rear seat next to Sarah. Jacob had Mattie in a headlock in the third row.

"Hey, you two. Knock it off."

"But he kicked me!" Jacob tightened his hold.

Mattie's cheeks turned redder. "No. I. Didn't."

"If you two don't stop, you'll be riding on the luggage rack." I dug in my purse for the keys. "Now put your seat belts on."

I glanced up to the mirror and spotted Mathew pulling at the side door. "What are you doing?"

"You said we could ride on the luggage rack."

My hand automatically pinched the bridge of my nose. "Mattie, sit down and put on your seat belt."

"But I want to—"

"*Mattie!*" I met his gaze in the rearview. His expression fell, and he threw himself back into the seat next to Jacob.

I started the van. At the end of the drive, I remembered the Pop-Tart I'd grabbed. I took it out of my purse and handed it to Abby. She opened her mouth.

"Do. Not. Argue. Just eat it." It might not be the most nutritious breakfast, but it was portable. She rolled her eyes at me but opened the silvery foil and munched while I drove to the elementary school. Mattie and Sarah got out and bounced into the brick building. Jacob was next at the middle school, and Abby was last at the high school. The afternoon pickup route varied depending on who had soccer practice, science club, drama club, study group, etc.

"Still heading to the library after school with Phoebe? Don't forget to call me when you get there," I directed as we parked behind the main campus building. The high school was old and looked more like a prison. Regardless, it was a good school with great teachers. The colorful homecoming banners looked out of place, but at least they attempted to take away some of the gloomy look.

"I know, Mom. I call you like every afternoon." Abby rolled her eyes at me again. I supposed I should say something to her about being disrespectful, but right now, I needed her out of the car so I could get to work.

Where do I work? Right here. I was the chorus teacher and school pianist of Asheville High School, in the mountain city of Asheville, North Carolina. It wasn't the glamourous job I thought I would have when I was in school. I had dreams of becoming a great jazz musician or getting my name in lights on Broadway as a famous headlining singer. Instead, I had Abby, and that dream turned into sleepless nights of diapers and baby vomit. I had no regrets. Being a mom was the best thing I'd ever done in my life, and I cherished every moment of it, even when I had a kid who was planning on me buying her a car next year. Did a Hot Wheels die-cast Mustang count?

Abby rushed ahead of me, trying not to be seen hanging with Mom. I didn't mind. A lot. I knew most of the kids in these classes would rather not be with their parents. It stung, but I was used to it.

Thankfully, my first period was my planning hour, and I

took a few minutes to finish getting myself together. I kept a stash of makeup in my desk drawer for just this reason. After a quick primp job, I ran to the teacher's lounge for my second hit of caffeine for the day. Melanie Miser, one of the algebra teachers, was there with her perfectly coiffed blonde hair and immaculate clothes. She may have been my best friend, but sometimes I hated her.

"Morning, Beverly!" she trilled as she stirred fake sugar into her cup.

I growled at her as I filled my own cup with the strong dark brew. "You are way too perky to be a teacher at this school. You look like you walked off the cover of a fashion magazine."

She laughed, showing off her perfect white teeth. "Life's too short, baby. You never know when Mr. Right or Mr. Right Now will show up."

"I'll settle for Mr. Fix-it. My landlord doesn't put maintenance high on his priority list." I inhaled my much-needed caffeine fix.

Some people were addicted to drugs, drinking, money, and fame. I was addicted to coffee, and I didn't plan on stopping.

"My kitchen sink is dripping and backs up constantly, the fan in the living room wobbles in circles like it's unscrewing itself from the ceiling, my lawn mower is making this weird noise, and the toilet runs so much it flushes itself several times an hour. I'll trade Mr. Right for a handyman any day."

"A hot and hard man with the right tool for the job. Yum!" Melanie practically drooled.

"More likely a beer gut and butt crack man with serious bad breath and sweat stains, but it might be worth a date or two to get my plumbing fixed." I swallowed the last of my coffee and got a mouthful of grounds. *Bleh!* "You've been reading too many of those romance novels you like so much. I hate to tell you, but hot vampire lovers and alien warriors are not going to suddenly appear and sweep you off to Neverland."

Melanie pouted and pointed a French-manicured nail at me. "You're such a spoilsport! It's called fantasy for a reason. Don't let that ex of yours keep you from dipping back in the pool. Not every man out there will be a Chris Hemsworth or a Jason Momoa, but there are plenty of good-looking men who would love to be with you." She gasped. "I know what you need! I'll make you a profile on Meet-n-Match. They have a six-month special price deal going on. Merry Christmas early!"

I rolled my eyes with such precision that even Abby would be proud. "Don't you dare. I'll worry about that later when my life doesn't revolve around child drama and a falling-down duplex to hold together. Right now, I need to get my happy ass to my classroom and get ready for the kiddies to show up."

Melanie laughed and put on her sassy friend look. "You and your happy ass are excused. Talk to you at lunch?"

"Sure. Go torture some freshmen."

I exited the lounge and continued to the classroom I shared with the band and orchestra teachers. Jim and Joe Kirkpatrick were the husband-and-husband team for instrumental music and were already in the rehearsal room. They shared the big office; I got the little closet one that had just enough room to hold a desk and a file cabinet. I waved to the couple as I settled in and booted up the computer. Immediately, I was tagged with an urgent email from my ex.

Sorry to spring this on you, Bev, but I can't take the kids this weekend after all. Mandy wants to go out of town for a weekend in New York and already bought plane tickets for the two of us. I haven't told the kids yet, and I don't have time, so I'll let you handle that. Have a great weekend!

I read the email twice just to be sure I was reading it right. This was the second weekend visit recently that he'd made plans that didn't include our children. His precious Mandy didn't like it when he brought the kids home with him. Mattie told me she called them noisy and messy. To keep her happy, the last few times Doug got the kids, he took them to a local hotel but only for an overnight. He was supposed to have them every other weekend, yet even four days a month were too much to plan his life around. Other than a few minutes on the phone, he hadn't seen or spoken to his kids in over a month.

I was furious at my ex.

I was hurt for my children.

I was disappointed that my plans for the weekend suddenly had to change.

To top it all off, I wasn't surprised.

I closed the program and took a deep breath. Time to put it away and compartmentalize. I had students coming in, a fall concert to prepare, lesson plans to make, paperwork to file, and later today I had to tell my kids that their father wouldn't be seeing them this weekend.

Oh joy.

Chapter 2

The kids took it better than I thought. Abby shrugged and stated she wanted to go to the Friday night football game. No problem, since we usually went to all the home games anyway. Asheville High was a large school with a winning football team, and even in this eclectic little mountain city, football was king.

Just like every other Friday night when I took my family to the game, it started off in total chaos.

"Mom! Where's my blue shirt?" Abby encamped herself back in the bathroom again, this time doing game primp instead of school primp.

"Laundry!" I yelled back as I dumped a load into the washer, including said blue shirt.

"I need it *now*!"

"You should've put it in yesterday's load!"

I didn't have to be a mind reader to know that got an eye roll from my eldest daughter as she flounced out of the bathroom. The other kids made a rush for the open door and crowded in the tiny room.

"*Mooooom!* Sarah's hogging the sink!"

"Jacob threw his toothbrush at me!"

"Because she made that face at me again!"

"Mom, I'm hungry!"

That came from my little Mattie, who was always hungry.

"We'll get hot dogs at the game." I punched the button on the washer and heard the water gurgling as it filled.

"Ewww! Those things are nasty." Abby appeared in a light pink, off-the-shoulder sweater showing a cream-colored tank top. "I saw a YouTube video on what they're made of. Absolutely disgusting."

While I agreed with her, I was running out of time. "Do not argue if you want to make the kickoff. There's peanut butter in the kitchen. Go make yourself a sandwich."

"You made that for lunch today! I don't want another one!"

"I want jelly on mine!"

"Most hot dogs are made from animal by-products like hearts and lungs and stuff."

"Can I still have a hot dog if I have a sandwich here?" That came from Mattie.

Gah! My brain was ready to explode.

"Abby, you can either eat here or there, but you *will* eat something. Jacob and Sarah, stop bickering, and unless you gotta pee, share the bathroom. Mattie, you can have a hot dog if you're hungry at the game, but you must finish it before I get you any other treats. Now, I'm getting in the van in fifteen minutes, and I swear if you're not in there when I pull out of the driveway, I'm leaving all of you here and driving to Disney World!"

"Jeez, Mom. You don't have to be so dramatic." My fifteen-year-old flipped her hair over her shoulder as she sauntered past me to the kitchen.

I could hear my teeth grinding away.

The sun had started its downward arc as I finally got my group corralled and out the door. An old beat-up pickup truck pulled into the driveway, blocking my van. The other side of the duplex had been vacant since we moved in, but it looked like it would not be empty anymore. A tall figure climbed out of the cab just as a moving van appeared and parked behind him. I vaguely remembered a message my landlord sent that the other half had been rented along with the work building behind the property. That must be him.

"Mom! We're gonna be late!" Abby wailed.

"She just wants to see Ashton before he goes on the field," Jacob tattled.

"Shut up, Jacob!"

The man turned and looked at the wide front porch where my kids were holding the welcome wagon. Just my luck to have them squabbling loudly when our new neighbor was moving in.

As we moved to the driveway, I noticed he was a large man, broad and solid. I wore mom jeans with elastic at the waist, sneakers, and an oversized hoodie with a picture of our school mascot peeling from age. My hair was scraped back in its usual ponytail, and any scrap of makeup I had on from earlier today had worn off hours ago.

Please don't be handsome too. Please don't be handsome

too, I prayed. It would be more of my luck to have a real hottie move in when I looked every bit of my age.

"I blocked you in, didn't I?" His voice was deep and slightly accented with something European. Irish maybe? *Ya ain't from around here, are ya?* floated through my mind in a deep Southern twang.

"Um… yeah. We were just leaving for the football game, and you're makin' us late," Mattie told him. Not a shy bone in that kid's body.

"Mattie, don't be rude."

The man didn't seem to mind my son's bold statement. "Sorry about that, lad. I didn't realize you were leaving. Get on in your car there, and I'll move my truck for you, yeah?"

As I got closer, his dark hair came into view. The lower half of his face sported a short beard of the same color. He wasn't classically handsome, but he certainly wasn't bad to look at either. His bright green eyes had small lines that radiated from them, making him around my age. He was definitely rugged, and his tanned skin made me think he worked outdoors a lot.

"Oy! Owen! Back out! These people have somewhere to be!" The man's powerful yell made me jump.

The moving van jerked once as it reversed and backed into the street.

The man turned back to us. "I'll park my truck on the street tonight, and we'll figure out how to make it work later. Fair?"

"That's very fair, Mister…?" I hedged.

"MacAteer. The name's Connor MacAteer." He held out

a giant paw. Lord, the man was a bear!

"Beverly Archer." Heavy calluses scratched against my palm as his hand swallowed mine in a firm handshake. "Nice to meet you."

"Moooooooom! We gotta gooooo!"

He let go of my hand after a light squeeze and hurried to the driver side of his truck. "Be out of your way in a bit. Enjoy the game," he grunted, not looking back.

The heat from his broad palm lingered, and I hadn't seen a wedding band.

I hurried to my huffing, impatient children, backed out of the driveway, and drove off with a wave. So we had a new neighbor or neighbors. The duplex wasn't terribly big or new, but it had a nice big fenced-in backyard and a huge empty workshop in the back. I had chosen the smaller side mainly because the rent was affordable on a teacher's salary, and it was in a good neighborhood close to the schools.

We got to the high school and the only spots left open were in the back of the parking lot. I managed to shuffle my brood to the gate, buy tickets—teacher discount, of course—and get us settled on the cold metal bleachers. Immediately, Abby ran off with a quick I'm-gonna-go-find-my-friends-and-ignore-all-of-you wave, Jacob asked if Mr. Barnard, the robotics teacher, would be there, Sarah stuck her lip out at being abandoned by her older sister, and Mattie asked about food. Melanie sent me a text asking our location and joined us, looking like she'd just stepped out of the pages of *Vogue*.

"You're wearing designer jeans and heeled boots at a high school football game? How did you manage not to get mud on them when you walked through the field to get here?" I groused while pulling another twenty out of my wallet.

"I'm talented like that," she trilled with a big smile, then plopped her custom stadium chair next to me. No cold ass for her.

I handed the money to Jacob and told him to take Sarah and Mattie to the concession stand. This would be the first of several trips, as the athletics department worked the food stand, the marching band had a bake sale going, and the cheerleading squad had a coffee and hot chocolate station. A fund-raising wine bar would attract a lot of people, but I guessed that wasn't a good idea at a high school. Pity, as I would have dropped money on a glass of wine right now. Perhaps two. Or three.

The marching band loudly made its way to the track around the football field, the drums pounding out a dancing cadence and the flag girls twirling their long poles of glittering silk. As the chorus teacher, I knew most of the music students in one way or another, and even though I was not part of the band program, I loved the spectacle of the massive colorful marching shows.

"What's happening for you the rest of the weekend?" Melanie asked as we stood for the national anthem.

I put one hand over my heart, the other holding an invisible microphone to my mouth, and assumed a game show host's tone. "The usual. Tomorrow morning will be a titillating time of housework and the drama of making four kids clean their two rooms. A luxurious afternoon shopping trip to Walmart for groceries, followed by a wonderful session of grass cutting provided the mower works well enough. We will top the night off with an argument from Abby about hanging at the mall with her friends. But wait! There's more! It's a night of Redbox for the kids while I hide in the bathtub for a hot minute and ponder life's inequities. We're not done yet! Sunday, I'm subbing at the big Baptist church on Fifth Ave in the morning, then rounding out this exciting weekend with laundry in the afternoon. It's bedsheet week." I finished my presentation with a hand flourish, bugged-out eyes, and a wide-open smiley mouth.

Melanie rolled her eyes and let out a loud huff. "Such excitement in your life!"

"Here's something you'll find exciting. I have a new neighbor now. He was moving in just as we left to come here. A guy named Connor MacAteer. He's a big fella, and before you ask, that's all I know."

She blinked at me. "Damn, Beverly! You could've invited him to the game."

"Did you miss the part where I said he was just moving in? He pulled up in a pickup truck and had a moving van right behind him. He was probably ready to get his bed set up and jump in it, not come to some random high school football game in a city he just moved to."

"How do you know he just moved here?" She was like a dog with a bone sometimes.

"I just got that impression. Plus the plates on the truck said New Jersey."

I watched as she fluffed her hair—a useless gesture, as

she had on a pretty cream knit beret and scarf. "Well, that's a missed opportunity. Anyway, I'm surprised you're here. I thought you were kid free this weekend and going to do something fun, like say, go out with me to the Saddles and Spurs club."

"Yeah, well, I wasn't supposed to have the kids this weekend, but Doug bailed on them again. Mandy booked them a trip to New York and didn't include the kids."

"Bitch" was Melanie's response. "Think your ex will ever grow a set of balls and stand up to Little Miss Silicone Boobs?"

I laughed as I wiggled my freezing behind on the cold bench. *I love my BFF!*

"Honestly! What if you had plans, or a big date, or a weekend out of town yourself? Doesn't he ever think about anyone but that bimbo he's dating? I swear she snaps her fingers, and he jumps. I'm so glad you're not with him, girlfriend, but at some point, you really do need to get a life of your own."

"I was saving up for one, but the state insurance didn't cover all of Jacob's braces, and I had to spend my single's cruise money on his mouth."

"I'm serious, Beverly. You spend your life being a mom and a teacher, and that's great, but you gotta be you too. When are you going to start dating again?"

"What year is it?"

"Ugh! You're impossible!"

Melanie was gearing up to lecture me some more but got interrupted by the kids returning with hot dogs and drinks.

I took a bite of the soggy red-dyed health hazard and promptly dropped a big splodge of mustard and chili on my chest. I wiped it off as best I could with the flimsy napkins the school provided, but it didn't do much more than smear the mess around.

The first quarter ran well, even though the opposing team scored first. The cheerleaders bounced around, and the band blared out "Eye of the Tiger" anytime the team got close to the goalpost. Our mascot was a cougar, but no one cared about that detail in the song.

Mattie wanted hot chocolate, and I sent him and Sarah off to get three of the overpriced cups. Jacob had found Mr. Barnard and was talking animatedly to him. Melanie played on her phone and started asking me a bunch of questions.

"When were you born?"

"What are your interests? Hobbies?"

"Where is your favorite place to go on vacation?"

"What are your pet peeves?"

I gave her random answers as I intently watched the game. I was one of those anomaly women in that I loved the arts but also loved sports. Our team was getting closer to the goal, all of them crouched in a line, ready for that final push before halftime, and I was so ready to jump up and cheer for a score. The band had emptied their spot in the stands and was lining up for their show.

"I like Disney World, and my biggest pet peeve at the moment is a nosy friend asking me questions when I'm watching a football game! What the hell are you doing?" I blasted in irritation.

"I'm making you a Meet-n-Match profile. Look, see? I used your picture from graduation last year. It's the best one I have on my phone."

She turned the screen toward me and showed me the app with my pic and profile. I'd admit the pic was a good one, showing me in a partial profile, my hair styled for once, and wearing full makeup. I was smiling and relaxed, as that ceremony completed the end of school year, and my students were moving upward to bigger and better lives.

"Are you nuts? I don't have time for that, *and* I'm not that desperate!"

"Really? When was the last time you went out on a date since the dirtbag left?"

Bleh! I love my best friend, even when I could just smack her. "So I haven't been out much. It'll happen someday." I spotted Sarah and Mattie returning with white Styrofoam cups. I also spotted something unexpected, and my belly threatened to send back my hot dog.

"Daddy!" Sarah yelled, dropping her cup and sprinting toward the couple that was walking away from the home side bleachers. Doug looked around sheepishly and quickly put a grin on his face. I didn't think he expected to run smack into his ex-family.

"Hey, pumpkin, how ya doin'?" She jumped into his arms, not giving him a choice but to catch her.

"Momma said you were going out of town."

"Um, yeah we are, but not 'til tomorrow morning. Mandy's sister is a cheerleader on the visiting side, and we came for a bit to see her. We have to get home to pack."

Sarah blinked, her exuberance gone in a heartbeat. She released her grip and dropped to stand in front of her father and the woman he was with.

Mattie didn't show any such restraint. "You came here to see Mandy's sister and not us?"

Doug faltered. "Uh, I didn't know you'd be coming to the game. I'm glad you did."

Mandy rolled her eyes but stayed silent, like it was beneath her to say any words to my son.

Me? I saw red, and my little-ears filter turned off. "I cannot believe you, Doug. You could've had the kids tonight, at least, instead of canceling completely. Showing up at the game anyway? How could you?"

Doug waved his hand in a dismissive gesture. "It's not what you think, Bev."

"Then what is it?" Melanie quirked an eyebrow.

Have I mentioned I love my BFF?

"None of your business, really. Come on, Dougie! They're gonna do the big dance routine soon, and we'll miss it!" Mandy's whine cut through my head.

"Okay, Dee-Dee. We'll make it in plenty of time." Doug turned from his children and put his arm around Mandy. "Great to run into you. I'll call next week."

Dougie? Dee-Dee? Really?

Doug looked good. His styled blond hair shone under the stadium lights, and he was wearing nice pants with a sharp crease, a white dress shirt, and a tailored blazer. Mandy was dressed to the nines in designer everything, even more so than Melanie, and looked every bit the fashion model. I sat there in my mom jeans and mustard-covered hoodie, with a bare face and sloppy hair.

Mandy lifted her left hand to Doug's shoulder as they walked away, and I noticed the big rock she had on. Neither of them glanced back to see the looks of hurt on my kids' faces. The fight bled right out of me.

We walked back to our spots on the bleachers and sat down. Sarah and Mattie stayed quiet as they drank the two surviving hot chocolates, and I watched the halftime show, keeping the tears in my eyes from falling. Melanie made a few snarky comments about Barbie dolls and trolls, but when I didn't respond, she left me alone. I was feeling all sort of feels and thinking all sorts of thoughts. I flew from angry to hurt, depressed to enraged, decisive to irresolute, over and over again. The love I had for the father of my children had been trampled flat and thrown out like garbage. The years we spent together building our family and making our home became meaningless to him at the recitation of a few sentences denoting his fortune. Now with his bright shiny new toy and bright shiny new life, he had no time or consideration for any of us, not even the four precious lives we made together. I wondered if he'd ever loved me at all.

The band finished its show and, with a swirl of flags, left the field as the football players came back out for the second half. Jacob wandered back and sat next to Melanie, gushing about the robotics project Mr. Barnard would help him with. Sarah and Mattie lost their quiet mood and began to squabble over something. I saw Abby hanging with her group of girls, flipping hair and gossiping, probably about boys. I wiped at my eyes and shook myself off. Time to put it away—again. I was getting really good at this. I greeted my students as they walked by with nods and waves, asking about weekend projects and other school-related bits. At the end of the game, I gathered my ducklings and ushered them back to the van, even the oldest one, who was arguing and stalling in order to see her latest boy crush.

The duplex was quiet and dark when we got back home. The moving truck sat on the street in front of the pickup truck. I pulled into the driveway, making a mental note to talk to my new neighbor about how to work out our vehicle situation. The kids were loud, pumped up on too much sugar, as we clattered up the steps to the porch, and I shushed them several times. Jacob was jumping off the walls to work on his robot thingy, Abby disappeared into her room to text her friends and use up more than her share of cell phone data, Sarah turned on the TV, and Mattie was hungry again. I sighed and waved a hand, telling them to do their own thing, just don't burn down the house. I retired to my room with a sigh and flopped on my bed.

Now I could let it out.

I curled up as close to the wall as I could and jammed a pillow over my mouth to muffle the sobs. Even though the divorce was final a few months ago, my heart still hurt. I cried for my failed marriage. I cried for my kids' pain. I cried for me, my age, my looks, and all the what-ifs I had built up in my head.

"Mom! Mattie took the last Little Debbie oatmeal crème pie!" Jacob yelled up the steps.

I ignored the cookie crisis for a moment. It was a good thing my makeup had worn off so the kids wouldn't see me with raccoon eyes. I blew my nose and dabbed at my eyes. *Not too swollen. I can hide this,* I thought as I picked up my phone.

"MOOOOOM!"

"I'm coming! And quit yelling! We have new neighbors!" The irony of my volume was not lost on me.

I sent a quick text to Melanie.

Me: Did you really make a profile for me on Meet-n-Match?

Melanie: Absolutely! Looks nice. I just have to make it active and then the dates will come rolling in!

I hesitated over the buttons for a moment, but then the vision of that big fancy rock on Mandy's finger flashed before my eyes again.

Me: Post it.

Melanie: Woohoo!!

I'm glad someone's happy tonight, I thought as I made my way into the crème pie fray that was happening downstairs.

***

Connor relaxed back in his bed and sighed. His younger brother Owen snored in what amounted to the guest room and would leave in the morning for a jobsite in Florida. He was the only brother who had time to help him move. Owen's twin, Garret, was already in the southern state working. His other two younger brothers, Patrick and Angus, still worked with their father, Fergus, up in New Jersey.

The youngest of his siblings, his sister Eva, lived with her husband and children about an hour or so away. A few years ago, she broke from the family construction business and settled in the small North Carolina mountain town of Bryson City. The Dragon Runners motorcycle club had hired the Irish Pub Builders to rebuild their bar that burned down. While they were there, Eva met and married one member, a man named Stud. Connor had his doubts about the biker, as he'd earned his name from his reputation with the ladies, but after seeing the man's total devotion to Eva, Connor was okay with him as a brother-in-law.

He threaded his fingers together and placed them behind his head. Eva and Stud were only about an hour's drive from Asheville. Connor thought about moving to Bryson City but decided that was too close and his business venture needed the larger, more urban setting.

Shortly after rebuilding the Dragon Runners' bar, Connor left the family business. He didn't plan it, but the break was necessary. For years, he had done nothing in his own life but keep the business together, working from dawn 'til dusk and then some. Fergus had been screwing up supply orders, double-booking work dates, making poor decisions about safety, and other concerns. Connor became the one to fix everything and clean up the messes his father left behind. His life had become nothing but hard physical work during the day at a jobsite and hours of paperwork at night until the words blurred before his eyes. Days off and vacations didn't exist for him.

The breaking point came when Fergus's negligence ended up ruining the tiny house Eva built for herself during their travels. Fergus had double-booked the crew again, and the family split up for a few weeks to cover both sites. Some stayed in Bryson City to finish up the new River's Edge Bar, and some traveled to Wilmington for a pub rebuild in a hotel. Connor asked if he could borrow Eva's tiny house on wheels to help offset the cost of hiring extra crew members and housing. She didn't like it but agreed. She didn't allow smoking in her tiny house, but Fergus did it anyway, and one of his forgotten burning cigars started the fire that burned down everything Eva owned.

Her stricken face when she saw the blackened remnants of her home was the last straw for Connor. He quit the business and would have left that night but for the reputation of his family. Fergus stepped down and retired back to New Jersey, where the rest of the extended family lived. The brothers stayed to complete the job in Wilmington and finish out the booked contracts for the rest of that year. Afterward, Patrick and Angus stayed with their father, working odd handyman jobs and spending all their free time drinking and partying. Owen and Garret joined with other construction work crews. Connor did the same for a time, but moving from jobsite to jobsite was getting old, and he wanted a permanent place. He gathered his tools and equipment and moved to Asheville, hoping to start a new life.

The rattle of an engine in need of a major tune-up hit his ears. His neighbors were home. The kids' excited voices penetrated the walls as they entered their half of the house. Connor frowned at the noise. The landlord told him when he rented the apartment that the other side was occupied, but he didn't know it was a single mom and four kids. Loud kids.

He sighed. This was still the best location for him for the rental price. The landlord agreed to let him use the large workshop in the back for his own business purposes, and Connor agreed to do some handiwork for the building in exchange. He hoped the woman next door was good with that.

Her harried, frazzled look was unsurprising, as keeping up with four energetic kids could drain a person. He should know since he had done it for most of his life. Only now, when he was looking at his forties, could he finally claim his time as his own.

He heard clearly, "Mom! Mattie took the last Little Debbie oatmeal crème pie!"

"MOOOOOM!"

"I'm coming! And quit yelling! We have new neighbors!"

Connor chuckled at the woman's ironic yell. Beverly. Nice name and probably a nice woman, but she'd best not get any ideas toward him. More than once at the various jobsites he'd worked, women hit on him for handyman jobs and sometimes just sex. He discovered it was more trouble than it was worth and stayed away from relationships that could get complicated. He'd already had enough complications in his life and didn't have time or the inclination to take on someone else's problems. His solitude had become precious to him over the last few years, and he was determined to keep it that way.

With that, he rolled to his side and closed his eyes. He heard Owen shift and resume snoring in the other room. As he drifted, he briefly wondered who won the crème pie fight.

Chapter 3

I pulled up to the front of the house with Sarah and Mattie in the back seat. Abby was out with friends at a Saturday movie matinee, and Jacob had opted to stay home and work on his latest "invention." I had a van full of groceries, a Redbox movie, and a precooked rotisserie chicken I'd picked up for dinner along with a premixed salad. I'd spent the morning scouring my kitchen and was in no mood to mess it up any more than I had to by cooking a full meal.

It had been a week since the home football game, and I'd offered for Doug to get the kids since he missed his time last weekend. He had plans for golfing with Mandy at some fancy country club, so I kept them yet again this weekend. That really didn't change my Saturday routine, and the kids hadn't said a word about missing another weekend with their dad.

Mattie flew out of the van just as soon as I put it in Park. Sarah was right behind him.

"All right, you two hooligans, get back here and take a load with you!" I yelled, not bothering to look and see if they heard me. I had a fifty-fifty shot that one of them would come back to help. I raised the van's rear hatch and jumped back as a long, tanned arm reached in to grab several plastic bags in a single move. I looked up into Connor's bright green eyes.

Our daily schedule during the work week was almost the same. We left the duplex about the same early time every morning with a "have a nice day" greeting. He came home later in the evenings and usually went to the workshop in the backyard. My kids had watched from the window as Connor and his brother—I assumed—moved a bunch of stuff into the building. There were some huge pieces of equipment and machinery. I couldn't tell what the stuff was, just that there was a lot more of that being unloaded than there was furniture. The moving van left a day later, and only Connor and his pickup truck remained. He told me he would park his truck on the street but would need access to the back workshop from time to time. That was no problem, since we left for school and work by seven every morning and got back around five every night. If we had to play musical parking spaces, all he had to do was ask. Aside from that, we hadn't had any real interaction other than a few hello/goodbye waves.

"Hi." I cringed at how lame that sounded. "Um… you don't have to do that. The kids should be helping."

"It's no problem, Ms. Archer." He lifted a mass of bags in one hand and reached with the other to grab more, leaving only two for me to carry. The man was strong! Carrying this many bags would normally be four or five trips, yet we were getting them all in one go.

"Ms. Archer is my ex-mother-in-law. You can call me Beverly." I bumped open the door with my hip. The latch didn't work unless you lifted the knob and made the effort to force it shut. My kids had been—ahem—*thoughtful* enough not to close it completely.

Mattie and Sarah had plonked themselves down on the couch and were already bickering over a video game. Jacob sat at the bar with his latest project spread over the speckled Formica. I didn't smell any questionable fumes, so I guessed we were safe for the moment.

"Jacob, you're going to need to move that stuff soon. I need the space for dinner."

"But, Mom!"

"No buts."

He grumbled but moved his bits and pieces.

"Building a radio?" The deep voice got everyone's attention including mine.

Jacob looked at Connor with something like adoration. "Yeah! How did you know?"

"I've done some electrical work from time to time. The black one is backward. That's why it's not working."

Jacob scratched his head. "Oh! So that's why. It's really a radio robot. I want to make it so it moves from room to room, kinda like one of those robot vacuums, but instead it plays music. If it bumps into a wall, it changes stations, but I haven't figured that part out yet."

"Tough job, but a cool idea." He held up two armfuls of plastic. "Where do I put these?"

I gestured to the small counter space. "Here for whatever fits and the rest on the floor. Thanks for your help, Mr. MacAteer." I was proud of myself that I remembered his last name.

"If I'm calling you Beverly, you can call me Connor." He set the bags down with a quiet rustle. "Here, lad. Let me see what you've got so far."

Jacob's eyes bugged out so much, I thought they would burst from his head. "Well, I attached the *blah blah* to the *bliggity blah…*"

"Not a bad design, but your *blah blah* has to line up with the *bliggity blah* or else it will *blah-dee blah…*"

I tuned them both out as I put away the groceries. My educational background was artistic, so there was only so much science-y, electronic-y stuff I could understand.

The rotisserie chicken filled the air with its mouthwatering aroma. As if on cue, Mattie's food radar kicked in.

"Mom! When's dinner gonna be?"

"Sooner rather than later, thanks to Mr. MacAteer helping get the groceries my ungrateful progeny forgot."

"What's a progeny?"

"Children."

"Oh. When's dinner again?"

Water off a duck's back. Gotta love my kid!

I added Alfredo pasta to the menu, as it would be easy to make and wouldn't add that much mess. Boil noodles. Open sauce jar. Dump and done. Cooking from scratch was just not possible anymore, as I usually had thirty minutes or less to get something edible on the table at night before homework and other activities commenced. Mattie and Sarah were still pounding away on the controllers, and Jacob and Connor were still engrossed in the pile of gadgets spread out in front of them. I watched my oldest son ask questions and babble at our quiet neighbor like he'd found a kindred spirit. Clearly, the ginormous amount of tooling now residing in the workshop denoted Connor to be a tradesman of some sort, and apparently he knew a thing or two about wiring. If he were some sort of handyman, that would tell me the stars had finally lined up in my favor for a change. I hoped he had good rates or would barter.

I started to fill a pot with water. As if the universe heard my thoughts, a rumbling sound came from the faucet and a huge arcing spray flew out, covering me and the floor. I screamed at the face full of cold water and tried to turn the knob to stop the water flow. If anything, the spray got worse. I wrapped my hands around the knob and grabbed a dish towel to jam against the spewing leak, like that would do any good.

The water suddenly shut off, and I opened my eyes. Connor had crouched down and reached under the cabinet. I could see a big patch of tanned skin where his shirt had ridden up and exposed his lower back. No butt crack visible, but it was close.

"I shut off the main to the kitchen sink only. You'll still have water in the other parts of the house."

Somehow, he had stayed dry while I was squelching in my sneakers. Water from my soaked hair dripped down my back, and my sweatshirt clung uncomfortably. Mattie and

Sarah had stopped to watch the show and were now rolling on the sofa in loud peals of laughter. Jacob was looking in horror at the water that had sprayed across the breakfast bar and his robot gadget pieces. I looked at Connor as he tried to stifle his own laughter.

"I'm sorry to say this, but you look madder than a wet hen right now."

I think I growled. That sent my kids into further hilarity, and Mattie fell off the couch.

"Ha, ha, ha, very funny!" I looked at him as he flopped on his back and held his stomach. "Just for that, I'm withholding dessert!"

That changed the little bugger's attitude. "Aww, Mom!"

Connor whistled through his teeth. "That's pretty extreme, Ms. Beverly. If you'll keep dessert on the menu, I'll go get my tools and fix this up in a jiffy. Do you need more water?"

I shot him my best stink eye.

He chuckled again, telling me he was either immune to it or my stink eye needed some serious work. "Don't get your dander up, *a chara*. I meant for cooking."

"Ah car what?"

"It means friend."

My anger disappeared in a heartbeat. "You can fix this?"

He shrugged. "It's one of two problems. It shouldn't take long. I'll go get my tools. Jacob, do as your mother says. Mattie and Sarah, can you find some towels or a mop and clean up some of this water? That would be a big help and might get your mom to have dessert after all."

The kids rushed to comply. I rolled my eyes. Telling my kids to clean their rooms or do any chores was a long-drawn-out process that involved whining, bargaining, and occasionally one of them faking sickness. With one soft-spoken sentence, my kids were bending over backward to do Connor's bidding. The little snots!

He left for his side of the house, and I slopped up the stairs, leaving a long trail of water behind me. I changed into my favorite faded sweatpants and another sweat shirt, then bundled up the wet clothes and brought them back downstairs to put in the dryer.

Connor had the kitchen faucet in several pieces, and Jacob was watching avidly. "See here, lad. There's buildup pluggin' the aerator. Makes the water pressure rise, and it has to go somewhere. This gasket is bad, and that's the weak spot."

Jacob nodded, totally enthralled with the process of taking something apart and putting it back together.

I filled the cooking pot with water from the bathroom sink and set the pasta on to boil. My phone dinged with a text from Abby telling me she planned on eating dinner at the mall's food court with her posse and would be home later. I sighed and texted back a reminder of her curfew. I didn't get a response.

I was dumping the sauced noodles into a bowl when Connor cleared his throat. "All right, Jacob, show your mother."

Jacob grinned at me when I turned to look. He turned the faucet knob with a grandiose flourish, and water easily poured from it, no leaks, spews, drips, or any other problems. I clapped my hands. "Wonderful! You can have two pieces of dessert tonight."

"Aww, Mom!" That was from Mattie. "We helped too."

I put my hands up, palms out in surrender. "Okay, okay. Everyone can have extra tonight. Happy?"

"Yay!" chorused through the room.

I turned to Connor. "Thank you for your help. The sink would still be spewing and we'd be swimming all night if it hadn't been for you. Can I pay you something?"

"You don't owe me anything. The landlord gives me a break on rent for maintenance. I'm guessing that means your side too." He was putting away his tools in a long metal box. "But I'll take some of that dessert if you have enough to spare."

"Stay for dinner too. We have plenty, and it's the least I can do for you rescuing me from a huge emergency plumber's bill."

Jacob and Mattie both jumped at the impulsive invitation.

"Yeah! Please stay!"

"Dessert is apple crumb cake with ice cream! Mom makes the best!"

Yeah, I make the best. Assisted by Betty Crocker and instant pie filling, but my kids don't know the difference.

Connor didn't have time to refuse as Sarah grabbed his hand and tugged on him to sit at the bar. Jacob moved to put another place setting out. I pulled apart the roasted chicken and poured the salad and pasta into serving bowls. I knew it would be more dishes to wash, but I insisted that, in my house, we would sit and eat at a table as opposed to balancing plates in front of the television. The kids argued with me over it from time to time, but tonight they were too curious about our new neighbor to complain.

"You talk funny."

I turned to admonish Mattie on his rude statement, but I kept my mouth shut and just listened to my handy, cute neighbor as Connor answered him.

"I suppose I do."

"How come?"

"My da was born here, but my grandparents are from Ireland. They immigrated to New Jersey many years ago and kept a lot of the traditions and Gaelic language. I spent a decent amount of my early childhood around them and picked up a lot of their words. I'm sure growing up in New Jersey also has something to do with it."

I had wondered myself about his speech pattern. The kids continued to pepper him with questions. The man's patience was astounding.

"Whatcha got in the back building?"

"A lot of big power tools. There's a couple of wood and machine lathes, a big drill press, a band saw, and a few others."

"What's a lathe?"

"It turns wood really fast, and I use chisels and other tools to form it into something like table legs or spindles for plant stands."

"How did you learn to do that?"

"My da taught me a lot. The rest I learned on different

jobs I worked."

I brought the food to the table and sat down at the head of the bar. Connor was on my left side. I passed him the platter of chicken, and then the real fun started as my kids' focus shifted from being interrogators to ravenous horde.

"I want a leg."

"I want one too."

"Me too!"

"You can't have one. Chickens only have two legs."

"I want both wings, then."

"Can I pull the wishbone?"

I glanced up at Connor's amused face. He looked like he was taking it all in stride and happy to be there, watching the chaos. By now, Doug would have been snapping at the kids to sit still and behave like humans instead of savages. Connor didn't seem to mind the noise at all.

He caught my look and smiled. "This reminds me of my own family at dinnertime. I have four younger brothers and a younger sister. The table was always full of noise and arguments."

My stomach turned over once. He really was a good-looking man.

Jacob dropped his fork and his mouth dropped open, showing a mouthful of half-chewed food.

"Wow, that's a lot of brothers!"

Jacob was right. *Five boys? At the same time? And one sister? Connor's mother must be a saint.* "Jacob, chew with your mouth closed. Mattie, sit on your bottom, not your knees. Sarah, use your fork. Let's show Mr. MacAteer that we have a few manners."

Connor served himself some noodles and passed the bowl to Sarah. "Yes, it's a lot of brothers. I've worked alongside them with my sister and my da for nearly all my life. We had a family business, Irish Pub Builders, and traveled most of the year, all of us living in a giant RV. We moved from job to job, sometimes building, sometimes remodeling, but we all worked and lived together."

The kids peppered him with more questions, all of them rapid fire and asked at once.

"Me and Jacob share a room, but that's only two of us. You mean you were grown-ups and still had to share a room?"

"Why did you move here?"

"Where are your brothers?"

"Are they coming to live with you again?"

"Can I see your workshop?"

"Do you have a dog?"

I offered the chicken platter to Connor again, and he took the other thigh.

My only sibling was my much older sister, who had little or nothing to do with me growing up. She was eighteen years older than me and off to college before my first birthday. That age gap ensured that I was more or less an only child and that we would never be close. My parents were in their forties when I was born and referred to me as the "oops" child. The one they hadn't planned to have at their age. They were still alive at a retirement village in Florida, but other than the occasional phone call and obligatory Christmas card, they kept to themselves. The last time we saw them was over a year ago when I took the kids to Disney World for spring break. My mind was a little blown by the idea of living in even closer quarters than my half of the duplex.

"Kids, leave him alone and let him eat in peace."

He set the platter back on the bar. "I don't mind. It's nice to sit at a table again." He turned his attention back to his plate and continued answering the kids' questions.

"The business broke up some years ago, and I've been making my own way ever since, doing a lot of freelance work. My brothers aren't here and have no plans to move in. At least I hope not. The oldest two are still working freelance, and the younger two are making trouble back in New Jersey. My sister is settled in Bryson City, not too far from here, with her husband and kids. I got a call for a remodel here at the Beer Kettle store and remembered the city from a past job. It's a nice place, and I decided to move here for now and stay in one place for a change. Start my own business and see how it goes."

He looked at Mattie directly. "And no, I don't have a dog. Might be I'll get one someday."

"Coolio. Mom, can we have cake now?"

My little Mattie. One-track mind always on food.

Connor ate well and had two pieces of apple crumb cake. He even helped with clearing the table afterward. The kids bounded off in their various directions, delighted they got out of dish duty for a night.

"Very nice, Ms. Beverly. Thanks for the meal. It's been a long time since I've had home cooking."

"I'm not sure that Walmart chicken and jar sauce count as home cooking, but the crumb cake was"—*sort of*—"my recipe. By the way, it's not Ms. Beverly. Just Beverly, or Bev to my friends."

Connor smiled, the faint lines around his eyes crinkling up as he did so. "Okay, then. Bev it is. I'll leave you to your evening. Jacob, if you need any help with your radio robot, I have a soldering iron and some other components you might find useful. If it's okay with your mother, you can come over sometime and I'll help you put it together."

Jacob radiated pure joy.

Connor left to go back to his side, and the kids and I spent the remainder of the night on the couch, watching the latest Disney movie available on Redbox and throwing popcorn kernels at each other's mouths. Abby came in just before curfew, huffing and fuming over some new teenager crisis, and refused to talk to me about it. She passed straight to her room with a long dramatic sigh. I wasn't too worried yet, but I was still keeping an eye on her. Abby would talk to me eventually, which I was forever grateful for, but lately she was getting more and more secretive. Too many of my students hid stuff from their parents, and more than one had gotten into messes they couldn't handle. I hoped I would never be one of those parents, and I made the effort to keep the line of communication open with my eldest daughter, even when she resisted it.

My thoughts drifted to my new neighbor. Connor was a nice man, built solid, and not bad on the eyes. It was nice of him to help me out tonight with the sink emergency, and feeding him was not a big price to pay for that help. He didn't look at me with any interest, other than perking up when he heard I had apple crumb cake. His manner was polite, and he didn't push anything. I wasn't real sure what I thought about Jacob's sudden infatuation with our neighbor, but since Doug took little interest in Jacob's inventions lately, having a male figure understand what he was doing meant something to him.

The kids wrapped up and went to bed, surprisingly without protest. We had to be up and out in the morning, as I had another substitute piano job this weekend. My kids would have to stay at the church the entire morning, but I'd promised them a treat with the earnings. My piano accompaniment skills brought in quite a bit extra. Some months, that extra made the difference in paying for groceries or charging them on the credit card. Sometimes I picked up extra work accompanying local music majors at the university during the jury and recital months. That was usually enough to help finance Christmas or when the next big expense appeared. There was always something that came up.

I lay in my own bed, tallied up a few bills, and divided that by paycheck and gig money. The credit cards still carried a hefty balance, but there would be food on the table, and lights would still burn in the house. I guess it could always be worse.

My phone dinged, and I absently looked at the message.

Melanie: **You got one, girlfriend!** ☺

Me: **One what?**

Melanie: **TAG!**

Me: **What in blazes are you talking about?**

Melanie: **OMG! You are sooooo out of touch! A tag on Meet-n-Match! Someone liked your profile and wants to meet you! Woohoo!**

I tapped the link she sent me, and a picture of a man appeared. He wore a yellow hard hat over his long blond hair, bib overalls, and no shirt, showing off a very impressive pair of hard pecs and bulging biceps. He looked every bit like one of the fantasy lovers I imagined from time to time, and I would be lying if I said I wasn't intrigued. Men who looked like that generally didn't need a matchmaking site to find women.

Me: **He looks nice.**

Melanie: **Nice! He's *hawt*!! I've read his profile, and he's perfect for you! I'll message back and set up a time to meet next weekend.**

I cringed.

Me: **So fast? Don't I get to think about this a bit? Maybe I have plans next weekend.**

Melanie: **If you have the kids, I'll hang with them so you can go out. Come on, Bevvie!!! You can't stop living!!**

I knew from experience that once Melanie got an idea in her head, it would take a mining blast to get it out. I might as well give in, as she would badger me to death unless I followed through.

Me: **((Sigh!)) You're such a pain in the ass!**

Melanie: **You love me!**

Me: **We'll see how I feel about you after this date happens.**

***

Connor brushed his teeth and spit white foam into the chipped sink. The bathroom needed updating badly. So did his kitchen. The cracked linoleum floor and patterned Formica countertops were outdated by at least two decades. There was a lot of work to do if he planned on making this place a home.

He rinsed the sink, then put his lone toothbrush in a plastic cup at its edge and stared at it. He still wasn't used to seeing only one. All his life, his toothbrush had shared the cup with a jumble of others that belonged to his brothers. The only way to tell which one belonged to which brother were the colors. Even then, he figured they probably ended up sharing a few times.

He looked up at his reflection and scolded himself again for taking Beverly up on her dinner invitation. When he saw her struggling to get the grocery bags in her house, it wasn't his nature to sit back and watch. Helping people had been ingrained in his DNA from birth. The thing with the sink? What else was he supposed to do, let it keep spraying? That was simply being a good neighbor and part of the deal with the landlord. Right place, right time.

The old medicine cabinet squealed when he opened the door. He spotted the slot in the back where older generations dropped their used shaving razor blades. A lot of houses in the fifties had this feature, which told him when this place was built and how long it had been since it got updated. Connor expected if he pulled out the cabinet, he would find a small rusty mountain of the metal rectangles resting in the interior wall space.

When he pulled, not if.

Connor pushed off the sink and went into his bedroom. His unit only had two, but they were spacious. He guessed that Beverly's three were small. If his calculations were right, his two bedrooms and her three occupied the same square footage amount. Not a lot of room for five people, but he'd lived in cramped quarters for more years than not. Tough way to live, but survivable.

Beverly's side of the duplex needed a lot of work. The plumbing he'd fixed showed some serious wear, and the whole faucet unit needed replacing, not just the gasket. Her floors needed refinishing, the walls painted, counters, light fixtures... *ahh!* He needed to turn off the construction mode in his brain so he could actually sleep for a change. Besides, it wasn't his job to reconfigure her part of the house, just do the upkeep for a break on the rent.

He climbed in the queen-size bed and stretched out his arms and legs. He wasn't used to having this much space to himself, having crammed his large frame onto a twin-size RV berth for years. Even the brief time he had freelanced, he still shared minimal housing accommodations with other workers.

A thump followed by a muffled "dammit" caught

his ears. Beverly was in her bedroom. He figured out last weekend during the crème pie fracas that they shared a wall. Throughout the week, he watched the family come and go in their daily routine. The woman moved constantly, taking the kids to school and working her teaching job. After school must have been a flurry of activities, as he saw the youngest boy in a soccer uniform, the oldest boy with armfuls of gadgets, and the youngest girl carrying a pile of library books. The oldest girl seemed aloof and argued with her mother a lot. He guessed that was what teenage girls did.

Connor empathized with the woman, but he didn't need to rescue her. She was cute—real cute—but he needed to keep his life simple.

What about the lad? You opened your mouth and offered to help him. You gonna turn him down after you said you would?

He took a deep breath and let it out slowly. He did make the offer to Jacob and would keep his word should the boy come and ask, but hopefully the kid would forget about it. *I won't get involved. Just be the good neighbor. That's it.*

Connor sighed and got out of his too-big bed. Sleep was going to be elusive, and he knew he would pay for it tomorrow, but he could sleep in late.

He chuffed. Rarely did he stay in bed past six, even on his restless nights.

He walked barefoot down his creaking stairs to his kitchen and got a glass of water. The generous slice of apple crumb cake Beverly gave him earlier sat on his breakfast bar. Connor looked at the plastic-wrapped piece as he sipped from his glass. He settled in his single kitchen chair and ate the whole piece.

50

The church was one of the biggest in the area but not so mega-big that it gave an impersonal impression. This was a long-term sub job, and the contract was for the next six weeks, as their normal pianist was out of the country for an archaeological dig in Turkey. It was a lot of extra work and a lot of extra time, but at a hundred bucks per service, and two services per week on Wednesday night and Sunday morning, I would make it work. Christmas was coming, and I had four kids to budget and buy for.

Even with the obligatory morning bathroom fight, I still managed to get us all in the van on time. Abby was the last one out, grumbling about how Dad didn't make them go to church anymore and how tired she was.

My sympathetic nature was lacking this morning. "Yes, dear, and I'm sure staying up half the night texting with your friends has nothing to do with your energy level."

One of these days, her eyes were going to roll so hard, they'd end up with a view of her brain.

"Shotgun!" Mattie took off running across the front

porch, making as much racket as possible.

"Mattie, keep it down. Mr. MacAteer's still sleeping."

"How do you know?"

"His lights are off, and you hooligans probably wore him out with all your questions."

Sarah sauntered by. The look I got was a perfect imitation of her older sister's. "Nuh-uh. He was tired when he got here."

Jacob scrambled after Mattie and smeared dirt on his clean pants. "Yeah, Connor is an über-awesome dude!"

Über awesome, eh? I guess Jacob would think that seeing as he's found a kindred spirit.

"Think he would help me with my science fair project?"

I swallowed the flood of saliva that suddenly erupted in my mouth. Doug had not done a lot with the nightly homework routine, but he had insisted for years that he should be the one to help the kids with their big middle school science fair projects. He cited that, as a musician, I didn't have the skill set needed, and I had to agree. It spoke volumes that Jacob was ready to give up that father-son bonding moment and ask his new hero, Connor.

"We can talk about you asking Mr. MacAteer later. Right now, we need to get going."

Miracle of miracles, we got to the church with time to spare. The kids got sorted to their various Sunday school classes, and I took a quick tour through the sanctuary to check out the piano. I'd not played here before, so knowing a little more about what I'd be facing for the next six weeks was top priority. I sat down at the keyboard and ran through a set of warm-up scales. The action was great, the key weight balanced under my fingertips, and the tuning was flawless. I recognized a well-cared-for instrument when I played one. Some churches I had subbed for in the past had pianos on their last legs or so out of tune that nothing sounded right. This one would be a dream to play.

"You must be the new key tickler."

I turned at the voice to see an older man with a cane leaning on the railing that separated the choir from the congregation. A spiffy safari hat sat on his head with a kangaroo emblem on the side.

"Name's Mike Hodges. I'm one of the church deacons, and I'll be singin' in the choir this morning. You a sprinkler or a dunker?"

I was taken aback. "I have no idea what you're asking."

"A sprinkler gets baptized by a finger flick of water. Just a little sprinkle on top. A dunker holds their breath and goes all the way under. So which is it?"

"I guess I'm a dunker."

He nodded in approval. It seemed like I'd just passed a critical test.

"Saw you have some kids. It's nice to have new young people join in. Any of them sing?"

"My oldest does when forced. Sarah is starting to make some noise. The other two don't really have an interest, but they still like music."

We chatted as I warmed up my hands. I supposed this would creep out some people if a random stranger started asking questions about your kids, what you did for a living, and where your husband—ex-husband—was. But Mike was friendly, and I didn't get a bad vibe from him. In fact, he was one of the most charming and welcoming people I'd met. I found myself opening up to him and telling him about my divorce.

Mike clicked his tongue. "That sucks. Makes no sense why a man would leave a perfectly good woman for a young chippie he don't have a prayer of keeping up with. Them youngins is a lot o' work."

"Yeah, well, it is what it is. The kids and I are fine. It's a struggle, but we're making it."

He sighed and shook his head. "Hmph, I bet that new chippie is—" He paused for dramatic flair and wrinkled his nose as if smelling something really bad. "—an alto!"

I couldn't help myself. I burst into laughter. It had been a while since I had the option to let loose and just enjoy. I didn't think Mike had any idea how much that moment meant to me.

I spent some time with the minister of music, running through the order of service and working with the organist to coordinate everything. They were friendly and easy to work with, and I found myself relaxing in their company. This was a good gig, and I looked forward to the next six weeks. The schedule would be rough, but I could handle it. I had to.

My kids lined up on the front pew where I could keep an eye on them. Abby had been huffy all morning but was now cajoling, as she had found several of her high school friends were members, and she wanted to sit with them.

"Please, Mom. All my friends are sitting over there."

"All your friends?"

"Yeah."

"If all your friends jumped off a cliff, would you jump to join them at the bottom?"

"Maaooum!"

I counted four syllables in that one drawn-out word. "Never mind, I understand why you want to go over there."

Her blank stare meant she hadn't seen him yet.

"Ashton Fordham apparently goes to this church. He just walked in."

The blood drained from her face, and she whirled to spot the object of her attraction strut down the center aisle.

"Ohmigod, ohmigod!" She turned and sat down hard. "Did he see me? I hope he didn't see me. My makeup's all gone, and I didn't finish my hair. I have to hide. Ohmigod!"

Sarah plopped herself down on the pew. "I don't think you're supposed to say that here."

"Mom! They had snacks!"

Mattie and Jacob showed up. Both seemed to have forgotten the difference between inside and outside voices. Time for me to take control.

"Abby, you can sit wherever you want, but you can't go hide somewhere in the building. Sarah, Jacob, and Mattie, sit right there on the first pew where I can watch you. No arguing, whispering, touching, poking, sleeping, slumping, burping, farting, picking your nose and wiping it on each other, or any other movement for the next hour. If I forgot to list something, then just know it's implied. I'm glad you had snacks in your class, Mattie. That should hold off starvation for a while. Now I have work to do, so sit. Abby, what are you going to do? Stay here or go with your friends?"

The conflict in my eldest daughter was obvious. Her friends were beckoning, and Ashton sat two rows behind them, chatting with several other boys from the school. Abby was biting her lip, both wanting to get noticed and yet concerned about it. She finally put on her game face, straightened her spine, flipped her hair over her shoulder, and raised her chin. No runway ever had a better and steadier model walk than that church aisle. I looked long enough to catch Ashton glance up at my daughter. She waved at him, and he waved back. A frisson of panic hit my stomach, as I knew Ashton's reputation, but this was still just a schoolgirl crush, and to my knowledge, he had a steady girlfriend.

You of all people know that doesn't mean much.

I wanted to argue with the voice in my head, but I didn't have time. The service was beginning, and I really did have work to do.

It ran smoothly, the transition from event to event seamless, and the choir pieces were flawless, if I did say so myself. The piano was one of the best I'd ever played.

It felt good. It felt right.

Mike came up to the piano while I was packing up after the service. "Ya done good, kid. Never missed a note even when the altos messed up."

"I didn't hear the altos mess up."

His nose wrinkled up again. "They're altos. They always mess up."

I laughed. "So tell me exactly what it is you have against altos."

Before he had a chance to answer, three-quarters of my brood showed up.

"Mom, Jacob drew pictures on all the offering envelopes."

"I had an idea for my science fair project, and I had to write it down so I wouldn't forget."

"Not all of those pictures were science projects."

"I had a bunch of ideas."

"Mom, I'm hungry."

I sighed. "Mike, meet my kids, Sarah, Jacob, and Mattie, otherwise known as the bottomless pit. My eldest is somewhere with the youth. Speaking of which, Sarah, go get your sister, and if she argues, tell her you have my permission to embarrass her unless she gets over here now."

Sarah scurried off on her quest with a "nicetameetchamistermike." Jacob stuck his hand out for a handshake, and Mattie did the same.

Mike pumped each kid's hand twice before letting it go. "Might be some donuts left in the back prayer room, if you want to grab one."

"Donuts!" Mattie nearly left skid marks on the carpet before he realized he didn't know the location of the back prayer room.

"Um… Mr. Mike?"

"Down the hall, last room on the left. Better get two. The secretary bought cheap this week and got those itty-bitty ones from the grocery store. I'm gettin' 'em next week. Krispy Kreme, baby."

"All right!" Mattie was off and running.

Of course my little egghead Jacob had to stop and analyze. "I like Krispy Kreme, even though it's kind of an oxymoron. You know, like jumbo shrimp. Are we coming back next week?"

"Yes, and for the next five. I told you this already."

"I forgot. Can I please get a donut too?"

"Yes, but hurry back. I have a butt ton of papers to grade and log before tomorrow morning, and I still need to get my planning done."

"Okay." Jacob left at a slightly slower pace than his brother.

I flopped my music bag over my shoulder and braced against its weight. "Thanks a lot, Mike. I just love sugared-up kids in the car." I winked at him to say I wasn't serious about the rebuke. He was fast becoming one of my favorite people here.

He grinned at me. "No problem, key tickler. I'll get some of those fancy donuts with the extra-sweet puddin' in the middle for your bunch next week. Welcome to the church family."

"Thanks. Thanks a lot."

He wandered off, and my daughters appeared.

"He looked at me," Abby said breathily, then sighed as she walked up, followed by Sarah.

Walked? Floated seemed more appropriate, as she had this ethereal look on her face.

"He even waved back. I waved first, and he waved back. It was the most perfect wave ever."

Sarah looked at her older sister with concern. "I think Abby's broken."

"I think you're right, Sarah."

"What's wrong with Abby?"

Jacob and Mattie came back, both with white powdered rings around their mouths.

"Puppyloveitis."

"Huh?"

"Don't worry, it's not contagious unless you're a teenager."

I got my kids loaded and home in record time. As a treat, I took us through the Arby's drive-thru for roast beef sandwiches. Feeding all five of us at a restaurant would cost me nearly one service's pay, but the "five for five dollars" deal was something I could afford. I got fries for everyone as well, but no drinks since I had plenty of those at the house. I pulled up, and the kids piled out, making as much noise as possible.

"I wanna play Mario Kart."

"You always wanna play Mario Kart."

"I like it."

"But you lose like all the time."

"I still like it."

"Shhh… what's that noise?"

A loud screaming sound came from the backyard. It stopped for a moment and then started again. It sounded like an animal was being torn apart in sheer agony. I panicked. Bears coming into residential neighborhoods was rare, but it happened from time to time. Call the police? Absolutely, but not until I could find out what it really was. Melanie had made a call once about someone she thought was an ex, who she found sitting in her front yard, stalking her. The thought of the officer's condescension to her was enough to make me hesitate making that phone call.

"Get in the house and lock the door."

Abby was my drama queen. Tears flowed down her cheeks, and her face bunched in on itself.

"Mom. No. You can't go back there."

"Get in the house, now."

"Mom?"

"Now!"

I picked up one of the tomato plant stakes I'd bought when I'd toyed with the idea of growing a few vines. That dream never happened, but I still had the stakes sitting on the porch. I hefted the flimsy piece of wood over my shoulder like a baseball bat and crept through the backyard.

Someone had cleared the jungle of debris, and the grass showed a recent mowing. I already knew who that someone had to be.

The sound was coming from the open woodshed, and I sighed in relief when I saw Connor just inside. He was wearing goggles and big headphones on his ears and was using a fancy electric saw to cut into a block of wood. He was pulling down on a big circular spinning blade, and the screaming noise was the wood being parted, not some unfortunate animal.

"Awesome!"

I jumped three feet in the air. The wood torture stopped

as Connor lifted the saw and turned it off.

Jacob stared wide-eyed into the shop. I saw big industrial machines capable of ripping arms and legs apart from little bodies. He saw wonderland.

Connor pulled the headphones from his head and lifted the goggles from his face. A heavy shop apron covered his chest and thighs. "I'm sorry. Is the noise too loud? I'm almost done with this part if you can stand it just a bit longer."

"Um, yeah. That's fine. I just… I didn't know what it was, and I'm glad it wasn't anyone or anything getting hurt."

He looked at me with a sheepish grin. "I guess the noise does sound pretty bad. I promise I'll only do this during the day when no one is at home and I'm not on a job."

"What are you doing?" my little egghead asked, his eyes glowing with the desire to touch the cutting machine.

"I'm prepping wood blocks to go on the lathe so I can spin them down into table legs and spindles. Remember? I mentioned that tool at dinner last night?"

"Is that what you're planning to do for your business? Make table legs and spindles?"

"Eventually. I'm taking handyman jobs and some interior remodels for now, but I hope to start making and selling more of my custom furniture. We'll see how that goes."

"Coolio!" Mattie ran full tilt into the shop, and I reached out to snatch him back from all those metal jaws of death.

"Mom, I wanna see the stuff!"

"Not without a Kevlar vest."

"What's Kevlar?"

"Bulletproof. Keeps you safe."

Mattie's eye got big. "Oh wow! Is Connor making guns?"

Connor came closer to us. Wood chips decorated the apron, his hair, and even his beard. "He won't get hurt in here, Bev. Mattie, do you see these ear cans?"

"Uh-huh."

"And these goggles?"

"Uh-huh."

"And these work gloves?"

"Yup."

"No one, not even me, is allowed in the shop until they put on all this stuff. Your mom's right about being safe. These tools can be dangerous if you use them wrong or don't protect yourself. Running in here when I have a machine turned on is an absolute no. You might get hurt, or you could get me hurt, and some of those hurts may be permanent."

Mattie hung on every word and then abruptly changed the subject. "I'm hungry."

I laughed. "Food's in the house. Go. And wash your hands before you eat!"

Both boys took off running.

I looked back to Connor, who was wiping his hands on a shop rag. "Jacob got a look in here and started drooling. You may have a rabid fan."

Connor grunted an affirmation and lifted another piece of wood to the cutting machine. I turned to go back to my side of the house.

"Bev?"

I glanced over my shoulder at his summons.

"You look really nice today."

My stomach fluttered at the compliment. "Thanks. I better get going before the kids hog all the horsey sauce."

* * *

Connor slipped the cans back on his ears and the shield on his face. Just a few more cuts and he'd have enough stock to turn two sets of table legs and two spares in case he needed them.

Beverly did look nice today. He didn't know about styles and fashion, but the dress she wore fit her well in all the right places. It was just impulse that he had to tell her.

The saw slipped, and the piece of wood shattered. Fragments flew at him, and he stepped back. The safety on the spinning blade kicked in and stopped the machine automatically.

Fuck, Connor thought with disgust. *Make that two sets of table legs and one spare. Get your head off your pretty neighbor.*

Maybe he needed to rethink letting the kids in the shop with him, but he had been younger than Jacob when his father started him running these type of machines and without the extra safety gear. He wondered about the kids' father. He made the connection that Beverly was divorced, but so far, he'd not seen anyone else come around to pick up the kids. She was with them every day and every night.

The only break she had was when she was at work. Maybe he could—

Not your business. Don't go there. Don't start. You don't need anything to complicate your life.

Connor picked up a shop broom and swept up the wood scraps and dust from the floor, then dumped the debris into a bin he kept in the shop. Sawdust was great for absorbing oil spills on the floor or making wood putty to fill in cracks and other defects in his furniture pieces. He bet Jacob would enjoy that bit of woodworking trivia.

Stop it, Connor. That kid is not gonna be allowed back here. Too much.

He put the broom back in its spot and picked up one of the cut pieces of wood, mounting it between centers on the lathe and setting the tool rest at center. The machine started spinning the piece in a blur. Connor lifted a long chisel and laid it on the rest, carefully setting the sharp tip to the whirling wood. Long, clean shavings peeled away as he shaped the first table leg.

Beverly likes horsey sauce, eh? Arby's sounds like a good place to pick up food later.

Chapter 5

A week after the discovery of the screaming woodshop, I stomped into the teacher's lounge on Monday afternoon, dumped my lunch bag on the table, and gave Melanie the evil eye. It had been nearly three weeks since she put up that blasted profile, and already I was regretting my moment of weakness in letting her do it. She took one look at the scowl on my face and dropped her spoon back in her yogurt cup.

"I take it Saturday noon didn't go so well?"

I flopped into a chair and let out a huff. "How in the name of all that is holy on this planet—no, the entire *universe,* did you *ever* consider that man and I would be a match?"

She shrugged and lifted her spoon once more. "I read his profile. You both have kids, divorced from bad marriages. He's a carpenter looking for an intelligent woman. You're a woman looking for a hardworking handyman." She licked the spoon clean with an exaggerated swipe of her tongue. "Besides, he's *hawt.*"

I huffed again. "Yes, he's hot. Real hot. Best-looking man I've ever seen. If the date would've ended when I saw him in the gym parking lot where I picked him up, it would've been perfect. But then he started talking."

Melanie dropped her spoon again and raised a sheepish eyebrow. "Ooh, this isn't going to be good, is it?"

I tore open my sandwich bag and fished out my smushed-up peanut butter sandwich. "First off, I found out the real reason I had to go pick him up instead of him meeting me somewhere." I dropped my sandwich and ticked off each point finger by finger. "He claimed his car had been impounded for having an expired license plate. He didn't know this as the time, but that plate belonged to a previously stolen vehicle. It wasn't his fault, though, as it was a favor he was doing for a buddy of his. This buddy said he needed to hide something from his ex-wife in the trunk. Therefore, he needed to switch license plates. His buddy got the stolen plate from another friend 'cause he didn't have the money at that time to renew his own plate. Does any of that convoluted mess make any sense whatsoever to you?"

Melanie grinned and tried not to laugh as she shook her head.

"He took me to a restaurant for lunch. It was a pretty nice place until he asked the waiter about his employee discount. He works there as a part-time dishwasher and gets *his* meals at half price. I understand the need to save money, but he argued with the waiter over getting half price for *my* meal as well as his. This wasn't policy, and I just smiled and agreed to go dutch. I don't mind paying my way, but that was pretty embarrassing."

"Oh no!" Two other teachers had come into the lounge

and were laughing at my words.

"Then we got into talking about work and kids. Yes, he has kids. He has *seven* kids by three women, and *four* of the seven are in foster care. He told me he works under the table for cash because if he doesn't report all his income, he can avoid paying child support. I suppose that little tidbit of information doesn't go over very well on a Meet-n-Match profile!"

"Jeez, Beverly, I'm so sorry!" My best friend continued to cackle at my expense.

"Oh it gets better."

"There's more?"

I ripped into my sandwich and talked around the sticky wad in my mouth. "He told me he grows his own pot and is immensely proud of the hydroponic garden he keeps in his mother's basement. In case you didn't hear that right, he lives with his mother. Why? Because it's free. He's a forty-three-year-old man who mooches off his mom. I was thinking about hiding in the bathroom or faking a sick stomach until he left, but since I drove us both, I decided it was too rude."

An "oh, crap!" came from behind me as one of the other guffawing teachers nearly fell off her chair.

"I made it through the date, but I would love to get that two hours of my life back. I got to hear all about his exes, how he wants a smart woman because he's a smart man. I listened to 'I got me a genius-level IQ' over and over again so many frickin' times I was ready to throw something at his head."

Crumbs fell on the table as I ate and talked. Teachers only got about fifteen to twenty minutes to choke down food, and I had a lot to share about this disaster of a date.

"He wanted me to drive him home, but thankfully I managed to only take him back to his gym parking lot. I thanked him for the date and was waiting for him to get out so I could escape. That's not even the highlight."

"It gets worse?"

I nodded and swallowed the lot in my mouth so I could speak clearly. This was the most important part.

"Even if the pot, the child support, the genius IQ, and the cockamamie story about his car weren't enough, he turned to me in the car and said, and I quote, 'You're bigger than the other women I date, but I guess I can work my way around it.'"

My colleagues erupted in uncontrollable laughter at my low, gruff imitation of the man's voice.

Melanie gasped and wiped tears from her face. "Holy shit! He didn't really say that to you, did he?"

I bit off another chunk of sandwich. "Yup. Like I said, the best part about the date was the first part, seeing him across the parking lot. He was great to look at, but once he opened his mouth, he got butt-ugly real fast."

"What a loser!" I heard from behind me.

"Well, all the men on Meet-n-Match can't be that bad!" Melanie opened her laptop and started rapidly clicking around on the keyboard. "Here's one who likes kayaking, camping, and rafting, no kids, works at a car dealership as a mechanic. Nice-looking. Right age. Never been married.

What about him?" She flipped the screen around to show me a picture of a medium-build brown-haired, brown-eyed man.

I sniffed at her and shoved the last bite of bread into my mouth. "I'm not doing this again, Melanie. Please take my profile down."

Her face fell. "Oh, come on! One bad date doesn't spoil all of them. Just go on one more. I'm sure this is it."

"You said that about the one I just had, and look how that turned out," I said wryly, sipping from my water bottle.

"I know, I know, but this one is different. Just try one more." She tossed her empty yogurt cup in the trash. "Not all my ideas are bad. You have to admit the Saturday lunch date idea was a winner even when the guy was a loser. The kids finally spent some time with their dad, and that perfectly freed you up so you could do something for yourself for a change. It also put a time limit on the date, and you got to duck out when you discovered he was a douchebag."

I nodded in agreement. "Yes, that was a good idea. That good idea balances the bad one; therefore, we're all squared up. Please take down my profile."

"Please not yet, Bevvie. I mean, look at this new guy. He looks like a big ol' teddy bear, nice and steady, and cuddly. And he's a mechanic! If nothing else, he can give you a discount oil change or something."

She waggled her perfect eyebrows on "oil change," and I decided to ignore her innuendo. "By the way, what's up with your new neighbor? Has he killed any more trees this week?"

My weekly schedule had become vise-tight with little to no wiggle room. Between school during the day, supervising nightly homework, the kids' activities and clubs, chores like cooking-cleaning-laundry-grocery shopping, and the now obligatory Wednesday rehearsals, my life revolved around the calendar with only razor-thin segments of free time. I practiced when I could at the school between classes and my brief planning period.

I knew Connor still existed as our neighbor, but that was about it. We left for work and did our have-a-nice-day wave, and that was the extent of our contact. Jacob saw him a little more than the rest of us, as he'd visited the woodshop Thursday night for a bit. I saw him through the back window getting decked out in safety gear while Mattie and I studied for the Friday spelling and vocabulary test. This was the second time Jacob had gone back to the woodshop at night when Connor was working. He said Connor was really careful about him being there, and he had to wear a set of ear cans and goggles.

Friday night, I had all four kids at the football game. This was supposed to have been a full weekend for Doug, but he said he only had time to take the kids to lunch and shopping Saturday afternoon. At least I had been free enough for this first attempt at an internet date.

I pulled a juice pouch out of my bag and jabbed the flimsy straw at the opening. "Not that I've heard. He and Jacob have formed a boys-only club in the back, and no one told me the secret knock to get in the building."

"Is he nice?"

"You've met Jacob."

"You know who I meant."

"Connor's nice too."

"Is he hot?"

"Gee, Melanie. Obvious much?"

She gave me a sly smile. "Close and convenient, wouldn't you say?"

I thought about Connor, his easy smile, his polite manners, his patience during the times he was around the kids. He was a handsome man, but it seemed he had as much on his plate as I did. Every time we crossed paths, he was either heading to work or back to his woodshop. He certainly didn't need to go through a dating website to find potential partners, but from what I had observed, he wasn't really interested in that part of life.

Too bad.

"Connor's a nice neighbor, Mel. That's it. He's not interested in me." *Even though I kinda wish he was.*

"But didn't he fix your sink? If you go out with him a few times, he might take care of the plants that are sprouting from your gutters."

"Melanie, I'm not going to date someone for oil changes, gutter fixing, or anything else like that. When I go out with a man, it will be for him, not for his work skill set."

"Okay, then. I'll get it set up for next weekend. You can do a dinner date this time. I'll be on standby for the kids." Her fingers flew over her phone's screen. "Done. I'll let you know when he responds."

"Wait, what?"

"You said 'when,' not 'if' you go out on a date with a guy, and that means you really do want to meet him. Tom is his name, by the way."

"Did you—?"

"Absolutely. I've been studying up on all your potential matches and made your top pick list for you. There are a bunch of them, but I believe this man Tom is the one for you. I just know it this time!"

"GAH!"

Banging my head on the table sounded like a good idea.

***

"Hey, Connor."

Connor turned from the lathe and removed the new table leg he'd just finished detailing. Jacob stood in the open doorway, waiting patiently for the machine to turn off. Connor only had to tell the boy once not to come into the woodshop without gear or disturb him when he was working the lathe or the saws. Jacob's quick understanding of the safety rules was impressive. The young lad was smart as a whip, and Connor was fascinated by the boy's fertile mind.

He looked at the beaming face. "Isn't it Monday? I thought you'd be at soccer practice."

"That's for Mattie. It works out 'cause Sarah has her school drama club at the same time."

Connor frowned. "Who's supposed to be watching you?"

"Abby, but she's up in her room being mad about it. She

wanted to go to her friend's house, but Mom said she had to stay here with me. I told Mom I could just hang with you, but she said Abby needed to stay home and get her work done. Mom told Abby to empty the dishwasher and reload it. She hasn't done it yet, and Mom will probably get mad at her about it. My job is to put the meatloaf in the oven at six thirty so it will be ready when they get home. Can I do something?"

Connor hesitated, but the joy in the kid's eyes made him give in. "Hmm. Here, boy-o, start sanding this for me." He handed Jacob a square of sandpaper and the freshly turned table leg. He usually did the sanding underpower on the lathe, but eager-boy needed to have his hands occupied.

"Mom had a date this weekend."

That took Connor by surprise. "A date? I saw her at home with you guys all weekend."

Jacob grinned. "Nah, she went to lunch with some guy on Saturday. He called her fat."

Connor picked up a Flexcut knife and began to run it along a sharpening stone. "Your mother is not fat."

"She says she's fat."

"Well, she's not." *She is the perfect size for a healthy, beautiful woman.* The knife slipped and cut a perfect slice in Connor's palm. *Shite! Where did that thought come from?* Yes, Beverly was a beautiful woman. He could acknowledge it, but it didn't mean anything more than that.

Jacob chattered as he industriously sanded the table leg, getting the paper folded and into each groove. "It doesn't matter. She's not going to go out with him again."

Connor placed a clean white shop cloth square against the cut. "How do you know all this?"

Jacob shrugged. "It's hard not to hear what everyone is doing when you live so close together."

Connor had to agree. He knew more than he cared to about his brothers' business when they were crammed into the RV together for months at a time.

Jacob started humming as he worked. Connor spread a Band-Aid on his hand and proceeded to cut the underside bracing for the table legs on the miter saw.

It wasn't any of his concern if the woman next door had a date. He wasn't interested.

At least not much.

Right?

Chapter 6

A teacher's life is simple to define. There isn't one between the months of September to June. School hours always extend into home hours. I was no exception. I had a full load of classes to plan for and instruct. There was the underclassmen chorale, the girls' chamber choir, a few madrigal groups and quartets, and the top mixed chorus that went to competitions and did most of the school musical production that I directed in the spring. Add in my general music classes and my personal practice time for my supplementary piano gigs, and, well, let's say some things got neglected.

I was referring to my house and my yard. I could barely find time to mow. Trimming and planting flowers? Cleaning the gutters? I thought my landlord was supposed to do that sort of thing, but apparently the contract I signed—but didn't read—stated I was responsible for day-to-day upkeep. If any damage occurred due to my negligence, that was on me too.

I sighed as I looked up at the sagging gutter on my side of

the duplex and wondered if I actually had a ladder. Melanie was right in that several green shoots growing from the dirt-filled channel looked a lot like mini pine trees. Could I get away with leaving them there and calling them bonsai? Getting up on the roof was not on my list of priorities, but the fear of a ginormous repair bill was enough to make me do it. Not tonight, though. Tonight, I had to mow the jungle that was my half of the front lawn. If I hurried, I would have enough time before the sun disappeared to take care of it.

I kept the mower under a tarp at the back of the house. It had been there long enough for a colony of spiders to take up residence. I snatched off the tarp and hoped if there were any eight-legged demons lurking around, they were flung far away. The mower was old, but it still worked. At least I hoped it did.

The first yank on the T-pull did nothing but make the engine sputter. Prime. I had to prime it. I pressed the button on the side several times and tried the starter again. Something popped in my elbow on the second pull. I jerked again, and pain radiated down my arm. *Dammit! Why don't these things come with keys like cars?*

I wanted to give up. Then I looked around at everyone else's evenly striped mown lawns, flower pots and beds bursting with color, neatly trimmed edges, and other yard décor. The neighborhood was older and definitely a working family place, but it seemed everyone else had time to keep up their yards, and mine was the biggest eyesore. It was Thursday night, the weather was clear, and I had an incredibly full weekend to get through. This was my only shot at getting it done. I sighed again and jerked at the cord, hoping it would start and I could mow my weedy patch. At least it was green.

Connor's truck pulled around the corner and into the driveway. I waved at him, but I didn't think he saw me as he drove straight in the backyard to park at the giant shed. I hadn't seen him in several days. Only the different placement of his truck on the street and the lights on in the workshop at night told me he was home. Last time we had spoken was last Sunday when we came home from services. He said I looked nice, and I kept my Sunday clothes on during lunch. Now he was home, and I was wearing some torn yoga pants and a baggy T-shirt with a faded "Here Comes Treble" on the front. It figured the moment we were in the same time zone he would catch me looking my worst. At least my jiggly butt was covered. I didn't do shorts. Ever.

I yanked the cord again. And again. My frustration level rose higher, but I was determined to get my yard cut.

A large dirty hand covered mine, keeping me from trying yet again.

"Take it easy, *a chara*. You're going to dislocate your shoulder. I can tell you from experience, it's not a fun time at all."

I leaned back, already sweaty from exertion.

"Hi, Connor. Good day at work?"

"More or less. You?"

"Yeah. That is until I got to this part. I haven't started cussing yet, but I'm sure that's next."

He chuckled lightly as he fiddled with the mower. "I hate to tell you this, Bev, but this machine isn't gonna run tonight. You're out of gas."

My face heated up. I should have thought to check something so simple. Did I even have any fuel? The look on my face must have been completely readable. Connor stood up and dusted off his hands. "I'll grab my can from the back and have this done in a jiffy. You go on in the house. I'm sure you have stuff to do with the kids."

"I always have stuff to do with the kids. Dinner is beef stew that's been cooking in the crock pot since this morning. Lots of vegetables, and I'm making homemade biscuits. Do my lawn and I'll feed you. Deal?"

He seemed hesitant. I wasn't sure if it was food he didn't have to cook or the fact that the lawn looked like the set of a Tarzan movie. "Deal. I'll shower before coming over."

The boys were at the breakfast bar, their papers strewn all over, finishing up homework. Sarah was at the front window watching Connor push the mower back and forth across my half of the lawn. Abby was upstairs ignoring everyone and burning through phone data.

"Connor's cutting our grass."

"Yes he is. He's working for food. Speaking of which, how much more homework do y'all have?"

"I need help with math."

"I have to write an essay."

"I need another three-ring binder."

I opened the cabinet while my brain sorted tonight's tasks in order of priority. "There are some in the closet."

"Mrs. Elseworth says we need ones with three-inch rings.

Those are only two-and-a-half inches."

I gritted my teeth at Mrs. Elseworth's demands and my Sarah's quest for absolute perfection. I contemplated my weekly schedule. The kids were supposed to go with their dad and Mandy for dinner tomorrow night before the game. He wasn't going to take them for the whole weekend—again—because he and Mandy had some sort of golf thing they were attending. I was taking advantage of the little window of time to go practice at the church before meeting them at the football field before kickoff. I mentally recalculated the time to add in a trip to Walmart. Tight but doable.

"If you can wait, I'll get you one when I'm running errands tomorrow night. Mattie, we'll work on math after dinner. Jacob, clear your stuff. Sarah, get the dishes out."

"Connor's got the Weedwacker out now."

Trimming as well? I was going to owe this man more than beef stew. I started my homemade biscuits. At least it said "homemade" on the tube before I poomphed it open on the counter.

"He works a lot. Like all the time." Sarah's commentary continued, and I glanced out the window at the man taking care of my lawn.

Oh my! How can a mouth go dry and droolly simultaneously?

Connor had his shirt off, showing a set of big shoulders and heavily muscled arms. A thin patch of dark hair stuck to his sweaty chest. His stomach was flat and lined, but not a gym-defined super six-pack. His strength and build came from good, old-fashioned hard physical labor, and it showed. He turned around and was close enough to the window that I spotted a large, flat dark spot in the middle of his back. Birthmark or mole? I had the urge to fine out.

Down, Bev! Stop perving on your neighbor!

"Yes he does."

"Dad doesn't cut his own grass. He gets another man to do it. Think he'll hire Connor?"

Jacob dropped several papers on the floor and bent to pick them up. "Nah. He don't do landscaping. He builds stuff."

I filed away the luscious sight of Connor and assumed my mom mode. "'He doesn't,' not 'he don't.' Jacob, what's your essay topic?"

"The breakdown of social norms in the arena of a capitalistic society."

I almost dropped the pan of bread dough. "Do what?"

The little imp had the audacity to grin at me from his position on the floor. "Nah, I'm kidding, Mom. I have to pick a day or an event in my life and write about it like I was giving a newscast. Lame."

I shook my head out of my trance. "Thank God for boring. That first topic sounded more like a doctoral dissertation than a seventh-grade essay. What event are you planning to write about?"

"I dunno yet."

Mattie ran into the kitchen and slammed his feet onto the linoleum like a surfer. He glided smoothly to the fridge and yanked at the handle.

"Do we have any string cheese?"

"Dinner will be on the table soon. You don't need string cheese."

He grabbed his stomach and whined in his best voice. "But I'm starrrrving."

"Well, when you shrivel to nothing in ten minutes, I'll take you outside and use you for a lawn ornament. I could use some nice decorations."

"Mom! That's so mean."

"Yup. I'm the mean mom, and don't you ever forget it."

"Connor's hosing off the mower. Are you supposed to do that?" Sarah hadn't moved from her spot at the window.

I sighed and pulled out the plates and bowls. "I have no idea, but if Connor is doing it, it must be okay. Get the table set."

"He's going in his side now."

Shit! I still looked like a ragamuffin. Did I have time to change? Not really. I also didn't want him to get the impression that I cared what I looked like around him. Then again, I didn't want to look so sloppy that he thought I didn't take some pride in my appearance. Why was I even worried about it? It wasn't like I didn't have a bazillion other items on my to-do list. *Get your mind off your hot neighbor, Bev!*

Mattie swung through the kitchen again, this time missing the fridge and banging into the counter. "Ow!"

I wasn't even fazed by this anymore. "What is it this time?"

"My elbow."

"Are you bleeding?"

"No."

"Did you break something?"

"Not on me. The drawer handle fell off, though."

I turned from the oven to spot the sheared-off knob on the floor and Mattie fingering the newest of his bruises with interest. I sighed and tore off a paper towel to load with ice for the swelling.

"I don't want any ice."

"Do it anyway."

"It's cold."

"Correct. That's what ice is."

Abby flounced down the steps. "You're such a brat, Mattie."

"Am not."

"Are too."

"Am not!"

"Are too!"

"MOM!"

I guess sneaking away to put on real pants and a shirt wasn't an option. "Cut it out, both of you. Abby, get the biscuits out of the oven and in a serving dish. Jacob, get your stuff out of here. Sarah, get your butt out of the window and get the table set, now!"

"Chillax, Mom. Connor's here."

I felt it. I actually felt more gray hair erupt out of my head. I turned to Connor's concerned face. He was cleaned up and dressed in his usual uniform of jeans and work shirt. His hair was freshly washed and combed back. He even smelled good. My head warred with *how in the hell did he shower so fast* and *damn, I look like a grubby troll* and *oooh! He smells really nice!*

"Is this a bad time?"

My teeth gritted into a smile that I was sure was less than reassuring. "It's fine, Connor. Welcome back to the house of perpetual chaos. This is our normal."

He grinned. "Mine too, for more years than I care to admit. Anything I can do to help?"

I glanced behind me and saw a miracle occur before my eyes. Sarah had the table set, and Abby was putting the golden-brown biscuits in a serving basket. Jacob's papers were in order and stacked to the side, and Mattie was sitting quietly, holding the dripping paper towel to his arm. Whatever he had that made my kids behave like this, I wanted to bottle it.

"Nope. We got it under control."

For the second time, Connor put his feet under my table, and I served him dinner. Dare I admit I really liked the feeling? I dipped stew from the big pot in the center and handed the bowls around.

"How's school going for everyone?" Connor's query opened the door.

"I don't like my math teacher. She's old and smells funny."

"Mr. Barnard is the coolest! I love robotics."

"I wish we had a debate team."

"I want to try out for cheerleading next year."

This was new from Abby, who had never been interested in making any effort to do anything physical beyond styling her hair. "Why do you want to do cheerleading all of a sudden?" I asked.

"I just do."

"It's so she can see Ashton at football practice."

"Shut UP, Jacob!"

Mattie had to pipe up at that moment. "Abby and Ashton, sittin' in a tree! K-I-S-S-I-N-G!"

The chant was cut off when Abby stuffed a biscuit in Mattie's face. My always-hungry kid chomped at it, making his cheeks bulge with effort to inhale the whole thing and not let the tiniest crumb drop. Sarah looked on and shrugged. Debate team in an elementary school? She'd be the one to organize and promote it.

I was embarrassed. There was no other way to put it. Nevertheless, I had to say something smartass to lighten the mood. Or should I say lighten *my* mood?

"Connor, I have a confession to make. These aren't my kids. They are experimental robots the government sent me for behavioral observation. You'll be expected to fill out a survey later."

Connor smiled wide and laughed out loud. I could hear the thump in my lady parts. "This is perfect, Bev."

His eyes shone, and I think he meant it. Maybe I imagined the hesitation from earlier.

After dinner, the kids scattered to their various evening activities either in their rooms or the den. Connor thanked me for a fine meal and announced he was heading home. Jacob stopped him with a question.

"Connor? Would you please help me build my science

fair project for school?"

Connor stopped moving and cut his eyes to me. There it was. He didn't want to get involved. I guessed I really couldn't blame him. My kids were a handful and were sometimes more than I could take. He was a good-looking single man, and hanging out for hours with a middle schooler wasn't high on the list of stuff a good-looking single man wanted to do.

"Jacob, I think—"

A loud knock on the door interrupted me. "Bevvie? You home? I meant to run these new test stats by you earlier, but the department meeting ran late. Janice is the chair, and I swear that woman can talk longer than— Oh, hi! I'm Melanie Miser, teacher of Algebra One and Two at the high school. And you are?"

"Connor MacAteer."

"Ah, the handsome handyman guru who fixes water emergencies."

Melanie looked every bit the professional, dressed in fitted black slacks and a rose and periwinkle V-neck top that brought out the color of her eyes and emphasized her firm feminine shape. Her heeled boots made her almost as tall as Connor. She stuck out her hand for him to take and shake, and I had the sudden urge to slap it away. That surprised me a bit. I had never been particularly possessive or jealous of women around Doug. Perhaps I had just been too naïve about my marriage. I used to think that once the vows were taken, that was it, and I didn't need to concern myself with my husband's fidelity or values. I couldn't prove it, but Miss

Silicone Boobs moved in with Doug awfully quick after we separated.

Melanie and Connor didn't look that bad together as a couple. They were both very attractive and tall, but where Melanie was outspoken and only looking for fun, Connor was a quiet workaholic and very private. I would almost call him shy, but he'd been pretty open with me and my family.

Friends and neighbors, I reminded myself. *That's it.*

Connor smiled. "I know a thing or two about plumbing and construction."

"I'll just bet you do."

Melanie's breathy reply made me think about the consequences of throat punching my BFF.

"Ahem. You have something for me?" I asked her.

She dropped his hand and pulled out a thick sheaf of papers from the bottomless pit she called a handbag.

"Uh, yeah. The school board sent these down with recommendations for the standardized test exams at the end of each semester. They've already been approved, but we're supposed to get them out for the faculty to go over."

I sighed. More paperwork on top of an already overloaded system. "I'll get to it as soon as I can. I still have grades I need to upload tonight and a calendar to update."

"I hear you, sister, but you have to read and sign these tonight. They have to be turned in tomorrow by noon, which is why I'm dropping them off now."

I looked at her with dismay. "You're kidding? Of all the foolish…."

I bit off my diatribe. This wasn't Melanie's fault. It was

just another day in the life of an underappreciated teacher. I sighed. "Thanks, Mellie. I'll get it done."

"Thanks for understanding, Bevvie. Look at the bright side. You get first crack at these papers. Most of the teachers won't get this until tomorrow morning."

I supposed that was an advantage.

"Um… Mom?" Jacob was still next to me, waiting for an answer about his science project.

I sighed again. "Jacob, sweetheart—"

"I'll help you." Connor's rough voice cut through my thoughts. "I'll be home early next Thursday night, and we can make a plan. Good deal?"

Whole cities could stay lit from the bright energy shining from my son.

I had to be the spoilsport. "Are you sure you want to take that on?"

Connor's eyes came to mine. "No trouble, Beverly. I gave the boy my word, and I'll keep it. He's welcome anytime, provided he follows my safety rules, and he has your permission."

"Awesome sauce!" Jacob enthused as he bounced up the stairs.

I made mental plans to include a bigger grocery order. I had the feeling I'd be feeding Connor a lot. "Well then… uh… thanks for being so good to Jacob about his science project. This is the happiest I've seen him in a long time."

He paused for a moment, and his expression was unreadable. Maybe I'd gone too far or said something wrong?

"No worries at all, Beverly. Good night, Ms. Miser."

"Call me Melanie."

He nodded and left. She turned and mouthed, "Oh my God," dramatically fanning herself as if she was on fire. "*That's* your neighbor? Damn, girlfriend! I'd be breaking shit every day."

"Have I told you lately how annoying you are?"

"Just as many times as you love me."

I snorted. It wasn't very elegant sounding, and I was glad Connor wasn't around to hear it. I shook the sheaf of papers in my hand. "Is this really necessary?"

Melanie became all business. "I know, I know. It's redundant as hell, but someone higher on the food chain thinks they know more about what should happen in the classroom than we do."

This was a recurring complaint among those of us in the trenches who dealt with students. I often thought the "people higher on the food chain," as Melanie called them, were oblivious at times to the fact that students were people and not columns of statistics and numbers. She, I, and other teachers dealt with seeing their faces on a daily basis, getting involved in their personal lives, knowing their home circumstances, and learning what made them individuals. In some cases, we spent more time with them than their parents. This handful of graphs and charts seldom showed that side of my profession. "Ugh, another layer to add. Just what we needed."

"I hear you, sister, but until I get to the top of the ladder, all I can do is hang on and keep pushing."

I nodded. Melanie had been making noise about running for the school board or higher administration, as she was just as fed up as the rest of the teachers with the system. She was in a good position, armed with firsthand knowledge in her head, a healthy bank account from a well-to-do family, and a fire in her gut to do something about it. Guilt filled me for my throat-punching fantasy a few minutes ago.

"You totally should break something else."

Guilt trip over.

"All right, Miss PITA, time for you to get going and me to finish my workday."

"Pita? You're calling me after bread?"

"No, smartass. P-I-T-A. Pain. In. The. Ass."

She made a kissy noise at me. "You're still on to meet Tom this weekend, right? Early dinner date Saturday while I hang with the kids?"

I huffed a loosened piece of hair from my face. "Yeah, I guess. Why are you so determined for me to date someone?"

Her face softened. "You're my best friend in the whole wide world, Bevvie-levvee, and I want you to be happy. I know you were happiest when you were married, and I want that for you again. Maybe not marriage, but at least a good man who can appreciate the treasure you are."

My nose tingled. Melanie had stood by me and had been the anchor I needed these last few years.

"And if Tom doesn't work out, you so totally need to start breaking more shit."

"PITA!"

She left with a laugh and a finger wave. I cleaned up

and worked with Mattie on his math homework while Sarah played games. She was the only one of my kids who I never had to prod about schoolwork, and she usually got it done early. Hmm, could there be something to my idea of a government robot experiment? Abby had already sashayed upstairs to text her friends, probably mooning over Ashton.

"Hey, Jacob? What's your project going to be?" Sarah called out from her perch on the couch.

"I dunno yet, but whatever it is, it will be totally epic."

Jacob skipped off to bed, and Mattie's battery finally ran out. Sarah soon followed, and that left me alone in the living room. I carried the sheaf of papers upstairs and opened up my ancient laptop while settling back in bed. The Wi-Fi in the house was spotty, and this was the best place to hook in. As the computer chirped through its booting up beeps and whistles, I heard some faint movements behind my head on the other side of the wall. Connor was settling in for the night as well. Damn, it was really nice of him to help Jacob. My little egghead boy was so happy I decided not to mention his father's usual role. Sometimes I got tired of defending Doug to the kids, and frankly, I didn't have the time or the energy to keep it up. Especially when my workload carried into the wee hours of the night.

I clicked open the teacher's portal and started adding grades. I had a lot of students, and this would take a while. Fatigue hit me suddenly as I pulled out the papers Melanie brought over. The document was written in the language of legalese and hard to decipher. Noon tomorrow? I swear the board did this last-minute shit so teachers would sign these documents without reading them. I wasn't one of those teachers. It was gonna be a long night.

***

Connor flipped over and punched his pillow several times. He couldn't find a comfortable position and rolled over again. Dammit, it had been a firm decision that he would stay away and not get involved with his pretty neighbor and her family. So what if he mowed her part of the lawn? It wasn't that big, and it made his part of the duplex look better too. People bartered for centuries, so accepting a meal for work wasn't out of line. Nothing he did implied he was interested in being anything more than a good neighbor.

But what about the science project?

It was the look on Jacob's face when Beverly started to speak. He knew by the look on her face that she was about to tell the boy no. Jacob's expression started to fall in disappointment, and not just mildly. The fascination this kid had with the tools and other equipment in the shed was deep. Based on what he observed and the few snippets Jacob told him, Connor knew the kid felt rejected by his father. Connor didn't want to be a substitute role model for the young lad, but when faced with either hurting him or helping him, there was only one decision he could make.

Connor rolled to his back, tangling the sheets around his bare legs. He lifted his hands behind his head and stared at the ceiling. He said he would help Jacob, but that was all.

Well, he'd still mow the lawn too.

His eyes followed a long crack in the Sheetrock overhead. Shite, he was too stirred up to sleep. He got out of bed and padded down to the kitchen where he'd left the spackling compound and spatula. He'd noticed Beverly had some ceiling cracks as well.

Jesus, Mary, and Joseph, Stop thinking about your neighbor! You can be friends and that's it.

He climbed on the bed and stretched his arm high to press the white filling into the crack. Maybe sleep would come after he finished this task.

Gonna be a long night.

CHAPTER 7

"I'b sorry, Bevvie! I dinnit bean to ged sick!"

Early evening Saturday, and I was supposed to meet Tom at Olive Garden in twenty minutes. Somehow, I had managed to feed the kids, take a shower, style my hair, put on a full face of makeup, and was still on time. I had on one of my nicest dresses that was actually flattering and a bit slimming to my full figure. I had been thinking my luck had changed after all, but then I got the call from Melanie about her contracting the plague that had been running rampant through the school.

I held back a sigh and tried to comfort my friend. "Not your fault, Mellie. Stuff happens. I'll just call Tom and cancel."

"Ohhhh nooo! Cand Abby stay homb for a bit? Jacob iz almost thirteen. Cand 'ee helb oud?"

I cringed a little at the whine in her voice, as if her most desired dream had shattered. I picked up the full garbage bag and walked out onto the porch in my fabulous clothes with fuzzy sock slippers. I planned on wearing my high, spiky black pumps but didn't want to kill my feet until the absolute last minute.

"Abby is already out spending the night with a bunch of girls at Phoebe Baker's house. It's no biggie. I can cancel and try again another time."

Abby and her posse planned makeovers, so no telling what my eldest child would look like when she came home tomorrow morning. I prepared myself for blue hair and hoped no piercings would occur. If it was just Jacob by himself, he might be okay without a sitter, but all three left alone together would spell epic disaster. A night without adult supervision may result in Jacob's room exploding from the nuclear reactor he made from paper clips and laundry detergent, or a trip to the hospital for Mattie with injuries from the obstacle course he created in the living room for practice to be on the ninja warrior show. Sarah would have spent the time with Melanie, safely painting her nails and playing with hair curlers, but for the fact that Melanie caught whatever bug was making its way through the student population. My friend sounded miserable, both for getting sick and for bailing on me.

I dumped the garbage bag in the big rolling container at the street when the deep *lug-lug-lug* of Connor's truck came down the street. He pulled into the driveway just as I climbed up the porch steps.

"Wass thad?" Melanie's whine was back.

"Just Connor coming home."

"Mebbe he can wadjuh the kidz?"

"What? No, Mellie!"

"Why dot?"

"Because… well… because…." I really didn't have an answer other than I didn't want him to know I was off to meet a man. That made no logical sense, but it bothered me anyway. "Because I can't ask him to do that."

"Bud why?"

"Because."

"Becauz why?"

"Just because!"

"Bud *whyeee*?"

I rolled my eyes at the grade school dialogue. "Melanie, I cannot ask Connor!"

"Ask me what?"

I whirled around at the deep voice to see Connor standing behind me, wearing a construction work shirt and holding a box of random stuff in his hands. He smelled of dirt, wood, and outdoors. It wasn't bad. In fact, I kinda liked it.

"I… ah… I have a date, or rather I *had* one. Melanie is sick and can't come sit the kids tonight."

"You have a date?" His face was unreadable, but I got the impression it took him by surprise.

"Ummm… yeah. Melanie signed me up for this internet dating site. I'm supposed to meet someone for dinner tonight, but I need to call him and cancel. I'm supposed to be there in twenty minutes, and I don't have time to make other arrangements." I shrugged. "It's no big deal."

Connor got quiet for a moment. "You don't have to cancel. I can stay with the kids, no problem. I've got some odd parts here that Jacob might like to mess around with and see what he can build with them. Might work for his radio robot."

I looked at the tangle of wires, doohickeys, and gizmos and admitted defeat. "Okay, just don't let him build a moon rocket in the backyard," I let out in a huff.

"Yippee!" came from my phone as I deliberately clicked it off.

The kids were surprisingly cool about hanging out with Connor. Apparently, my tall neighbor was more popular in my house than me. It thrilled none of them that I was going out on a date, and I'd been getting dirty looks from Sarah most of the night. Jacob's attitude made a one-eighty when he saw the box of thingy bits Connor brought to him.

"Dude! Super cool!"

I blinked. Since when did my son speak like a teenager?

Mattie ran in from the back room and executed a perfect dive roll over the back of the sofa next to Sarah.

"Mom! Make him stop!"

That was my cue to get moving. I plopped down on the other end of the sectional, stripped off my socks, and slipped on my heels. "Right. Connor, everyone's been fed, but if you're hungry, I have leftover turkey tetrazzini in the fridge if you want some."

"We'll be fine. Have a good time on your… date."

"I won't be out long. It's just dinner, and then I'll be home. I have two services to play for tomorrow morning and have to be up early like a normal workday."

"Services?"

"Yeah. Tomorrow we're going to be Baptist. In fact,

we're going to be Baptist for a while until the regular guy gets back from his trip."

"What are you normally?"

"Methodist mostly, but I've worked at Lutheran, Episcopalian, several other Baptist churches, one gig at a Catholic Mass, and a bar mitzvah a few years ago. I'm not sure it matters how you believe, just that you do."

I stood up and teetered a bit. Connor reached out and grabbed my elbow to steady me. "Easy, Bev. You don't want to break an ankle."

Damn, my arm zinged where he touched me, and I laughed to cover it up. *It is wrong to go out on a date with one man while thinking of another, right?* "I don't wear these shoes often. They're a pain but they're the only pair I have that will go with this dress. I'll be fine as long as I don't have to run or hike."

At least I hoped so. The ache had already started in my feet from the black strappy spikes.

"If the shoes hurt your feet, don't wear them. You look good just as you are."

My cheeks heated up as they colored. I didn't know why his compliment meant so much to me, but it did. He let go of my elbow, and the heat from his palm lingered.

"Thanks, Connor. I'm still going to keep the heels, but I… well… thanks." *Bleh. I'm such a wordsmith!* "Okay, I really have to go. My cell number is on the fridge if you need it."

I picked up my purse. "Kisses, kids, and don't give Connor any trouble!"

"Love you, Mom!" Mattie was the only one who responded. Jacob was face deep in the gizmo box Connor brought over, and Sarah gave me a glare from her stiff position on the couch.

Whatever!

I made it to the restaurant a few minutes late, and Tom was already there. He hadn't been seated yet and was waiting for me. I thought that was a nice gesture. He was big and tall with longish dark hair brushed back behind his ears and a neatly trimmed mustache and beard. He looked strong but did have a slight gut, very much like the teddy bear Melanie had described. Not overly handsome but certainly not bad-looking either.

"How d'ya do? You must be Ms. Beverly. You're even prettier than your picture. Really nice to meet 'cha." His southern accent was thick as he thrust out his hand for me to shake. I noticed the heavy calluses on his palm, and my mind wandered to Connor sitting in my home with my kids.

"Sorry 'bout my rough hands. Been workin' on cars most a' my life, and it takes a lot out of 'em."

"I understand about working with your hands for a living. I do that too, so to speak, as a performing musician."

"The site says you're a chorus teacher. Never knew that was a real job. Oh, I 'pologize, ma'am. That was a rude thing to say."

"Don't worry about it. There are a lot of people who don't think being a musician is a real job, but it is."

He grinned. "I ain't met no one before who plays from sheet music. My mama used to play old Conway Twitty 'n some Hank Williams by ear, but that's 'bout it. You must be real smart 'bout music."

The hostess seated us before I could continue. Tom held out my chair for me, and again I was impressed by his manners. "So where do you work?"

"I work over at Ronnie's Auto Barn out near Weaverville. He's my daddy's uncle's wife's brother, and I been workin' for him since high school. Never went to college but I make a good livin'. Did you go to college for music, ma'am?"

"You can call me Beverly."

He shook his shaggy head. "My mama'd turn in her grave if I forgot my manners. Said you're a mama with four kids. I come from a big family and want one myself someday. I go kayaking with my cousins on weekends a lot of times. Does your kids like to kayak, ma'am?"

"We did a rafting trip once in Bryson City but haven't really tried kayaking."

"We can do that sometime, if that's something you wanna try. Nothin' more fun than showin' a kid how to do somethin'. Bein' a teacher is somethin' real special and takes a special person to do it right."

Hmmm. He had said all the right words so far. I had to admit, I was enjoying myself. He was a country boy, nice and very polite, the kind of man a mom would want her daughter to bring home. The more he talked in his thick accent, the more I learned about him. He seemed to be steady, hard-working, and I was starting to think this dating site found a potential match.

I should have known better.

The waiter had just brought us coffee at the end of our meal when the first shoe came hurtling down.

"Hey, Beverly, lemme ask you a real important question."

I looked up, expecting he was going to ask me on a second date. Thoughts of picnics and kayaks filled my head, and I imagined that would be a great plan for him to meet the kids.

"Do you believe in aliens?"

I blinked. That was so far from what I expected, I wasn't sure about how to respond. "Umm… I've never really given it much thought."

He leaned forward in his chair and assumed a demeanor that meant he was going to let me in on a big secret like the truth behind the Kennedy assassination or the burial location of Jimmy Hoffa.

"You know, they really are on this planet conductin' experiments. We cain't see 'um, but they're here. Them movies 'bout extraterrestrial life-forms? You know, like that *ET* or the *Body Snatchers*? It's real. I got some friends that say we ain't got no really bad ones yet. They's here just lookin' at plants and stuff right now, but I know better. I found a website that has evidence them aliens are what's behind a lot of them kidnappin's and other people disappearin' we see on TV. I cain't sleep at night sometimes 'cause I start thinkin' 'bout all the experiments 'n stuff them creatures are doing on us humans."

And just like that, my evening took a nosedive, and I hoped I could finish my coffee quickly and get out of there. No words came to my mind. I sipped at my cup and wished for a fire drill to interrupt. Tom took my silence as an indication to continue.

"I think it was them rockets we sent up to the moon. Some folks say it was faked, and we didn't send no one up there. I say we did. When them astronauts brought back the moon rocks 'n stuff, the aliens hid inside them crystals so's they got here undetected-like. Maybe not the whole body, but just the spirit. Once they got here, they infected some people an' started reproducin', an' now they're here to slowly take over our planet while no one is lookin'. You know what else? There's more than one kind of alien. There's ones that look like lizards, and there's ones that look like trees and ones that look like dogs. That's how they git 'cha. You know them stories 'bout whole families gone missin' an' the only thing left in the house is the family dog? Them's the aliens. I bet we can go down to the shelter and find a whole mess of 'um."

I almost choked. Surely this guy would sit back, laugh, and tell me he was pranking me.

"You told me your son likes to play with radios and science and stuff. Well, out at the house, I put up a couple o' fifty-foot antennas and got me a ham radio operator rig I built m'self. Me and my buddies got a network, an' we take turns every night to monitor signals so's we can alert people to a possible invasion. Your boy can come over one night when it's my turn, if he wants to."

Visions danced in my head for a moment of a creepy log cabin deep in the dark woods at night. Tom, with a maniacal look on his face, hunched over a radio messing with dials and microphones. His zombie minion, Jacob, by his side. Nope. Done.

"Jacob is more into robots and radio-controlled stuff. Speaking of which, I need to leave pretty soon and make sure my kids are in bed. I've got to play at services tomorrow morning, and it takes an act of God to get the kids up and out on time, even with a full night's sleep."

A miracle occurred.

His face fell. "Oh. You're one o' them religious types? Church and all that stuff?"

A glimmer of hope radiated through me.

"Absolutely. Church every Sunday. And Wednesday. Sometimes Monday. And Thursday."

He pressed his lips together and sighed. "This ain't gonna work out. You're a nice lady, but I ain't into all that religious stuff."

A massive choir started singing "Hallelujah" in the form of Handel in my head.

I should get an Oscar.

I sighed and hung my head a bit. Yeah, I overexaggerated, but I wanted to be thorough. "Well, if you really feel that way, thanks for dinner, and I hope you find someone that suits you better." *One with fur, puppy eyes, and a proclivity for seducing good ol' boy rednecks.*

"Yeah, you too." He pulled out his phone and rapidly tapped at the screen. "Have a good night." What were the odds he was leaving negative feedback on the dating site?

And just like that, my date was done. He was so engrossed in his phone, I wasn't sure if he recognized when I said goodbye and left. So much for country charm and manners.

I parked behind Connor's truck and marveled that the house was still standing. Jacob hadn't built any bombs or rockets, or if he did, Connor had them well hidden from sight. The living room was quiet and—surprise, surprise—neat. Mattie lay passed out on the couch, his little body curled up with a string of drool hanging from his mouth. Jacob was tinkering with something at the breakfast bar. Connor and Sarah were playing a video game. At least, Sarah was. It sounded like she was coaching the man through his first PlayStation experience.

"You have to use the blue button with the slider to the left to make that jump to the next platform."

"Which blue button?"

"The one on the X control. No, the other X control."

"This thing has so many buttons. It's hard to keep track of them all."

"Here comes the boss."

"Yeah, your mother's home."

"No, not that boss. The big one in this level. See the big lion body with the dragon's head and tentacles? That's the boss."

"Holy shiiii—ah—oot!"

"I've heard the word 'shit' before. Mandy says it all the time. Melanie does too when she thinks we're not listening. Aw, man! You just died. We have to start the level over again."

Connor put the controller down. "Not tonight, Sarah. I need to go home and ice my thumbs. Your fingers must be triple-jointed as fast as you move."

"It's practice and good hand/eye coordination."

Government robots! I thought as I moved into the room and slipped off my fashionable torture devices. My feet sang in relief. "Whatever words Mandy or Melanie say don't need to come out of your mouth. Jacob, clear your stuff away. Anyone need showers? Get 'em now, then bed."

"You cuss sometimes too."

I met my daughter's matter-of-fact expression with my silent-mom laser stare. This time it worked. She scurried upstairs with a "G'night, Connor."

I looked back at Jacob and, with a slight shock, saw that he had cleared the bar and neatly put his bits and whatnots in a square toolbox. Perhaps Tom's alien body takeover idea wasn't too far off.

"Who are you, and what have you done with Jacob?"

"Huh?"

"You put your stuff away the first time. It takes my Jacob at least three reminders and one yell to get it done."

"Connor says a good craftsman keeps his work area neat and organized. It's more efficient, and you get more work done."

I pursed my lips and raised my eyebrows as if I contemplated his words. "Gee. Do you think Connor ever *listened to his mother*?"

"He told me she died when he was younger than me. I need a shower."

Damn! Here mouth, meet foot. "Go take a fast one and then bed."

He pounded up the stairs after his sister. Two down, one to go.

I gently shook Mattie's shoulder and used my finger to swipe the string of drool from his mouth. "Come on, Mattie-Boo. Let's get you upstairs in bed."

"Can I have summa chips?"

Stomach first, last, and always.

"Not now. Bedtime."

"How 'bout an ice cream sammich?"

"Nope. We're out, and the store is too far away. Bedtime."

He sighed and groggily staggered toward the stairs. He stopped at the halfway point and tried to sleep on the steps. After a little encouragement, he made it all the way up and lurched toward his shared room. I turned to Connor, who watched the proceedings silently.

"I'm sorry about your mother. I shouldn't have said that."

He shrugged. "Long time ago. I still miss her, but I'm glad I had her for the time I did."

"Thanks for stepping in tonight. It was a bust after all, but at least I can check that one off my list."

"No second date, then?"

I shook my head and lifted the remote to turn off the TV and game system. I was sure I didn't 'shut down' the right way, and I'd get an earful from either Mattie or Sarah on how I didn't 'save' right, but video games were not my thing and, with my busy lifestyle, probably never would be.

"Unless I'm going to grow antennae from the top of my head and turn into a Star Wars cantina character, I can safely say he's not interested. Besides, they say the two biggest deal breakers are politics and religion. Already broke the deal with religion. Never had to get into politics."

"Deal breaker how?

I paused in straightening up the couch cushions. "Tom is a fervent believer in space aliens and seems to be intolerant of anything else. I'm a believer in a higher power, but I'm not set in stone as to what that higher power might be. I'm also not going to judge someone on their beliefs or lack of belief, but I expect the same courtesy. Make sense?"

Connor looked thoughtful. "Yeah, I think so. I'm supposed to be Catholic. Da always said we were, but we never went to Mass. I don't know if that still makes me Catholic."

"Interesting discussion, but that's getting rather deep for a Saturday night. It's still early enough for you to go do something, but I'm wiped from the week. Book and bed sounds really good right about now."

"I'm not much of a go-out person. Once in a while it's nice, but I'm good with home and cable most weekends. Working so many hours during the week has me wiped as well. Good night, Beverly. I'm… ah… sorry about your date."

It was my turn to shrug. "Don't worry about it." I flopped back on the couch and propped my bare feet on the coffee table. My thigh spread was usually very impressive, but the industrial-strength spandex body shaper I wore held everything in check.

"I'm surprised you'd be doing the online dating thing."

I bristled up a bit. "You say that like you're disappointed in me. Melanie signed me up on the Meet-n-Match app, and I'm more or less doing it to appease her. That woman never gives up on an idea. It's easier for me to just go on the dates she finds rather than argue with her."

He shook his head. "No, I'm not disappointed in you or anyone who uses internet dating. I've just never seen the need. You could stand up to her and tell her no."

"Well, when you look like you, you don't need a dating site to find people. Tell Melanie no? That word doesn't exist in her vocabulary."

"Look like me?"

"Yeah, Connor. You're an attractive single man with steady income and a great personality. I should be the surprised one. Surprised you don't have a line of applicants at the door. I bet if you did the Meet-n-Match app, you'd get snapped up in a heartbeat."

He blushed. The man totally blushed.

"I don't really have a lot of time for dating or anything like that right now. I have a list of jobs to do around town that's growing longer every day, and I'm trying to get my business off the ground. Anything else needs to wait."

The little spark in my heart died. For a tiny moment, I thought perhaps… nope, not going there. I wasn't going to be some naïve high schooler who had a crush on her hot neighbor. I was too old for those kinds of games, and I refused to play them.

Who am I kidding? I already have a crush on my neighbor.

"I get it. I wasn't interested in this app until Melanie signed me up. I'll be out of it soon. Until then, I'll let her play matchmaker and be her entertainment for a while. It doesn't hurt me and keeps her happy. Who knows? Maybe I'll actually meet someone."

I heaved myself up with a muted "Oof," and Connor took the hint. "Thanks for stepping in. You're a good man, Connor MacAteer."

"No trouble. Be glad to help again if you need it."

He smiled, still hesitating to leave. I didn't know what he was waiting for, but he finally moved to exit. I stifled the urge to call him back. For what, I didn't know. *God, Bev, get it together!*

"'Night, Bev."

"'Night, Connor."

I entered my room, stripped the bindings from my body, and took the first full breath of the evening. I washed my face quickly, not wanting to wake up to the gumminess of leftover makeup, and slipped into the bedrooms to check on my kids. Sarah lay curled up in her usual position on her side, facing the wall. I imagined she did this for as much personal privacy as she could find in the small shared room. Jacob was under the covers with his e-reader. I let it go, as I knew he would be out like a light soon. Mattie had flipped opposite with his feet on the pillow and his head deep under the covers. I switched the ends of the bed to match, and he muttered, "Cheeseburger," in his sleep.

In my bed, I fired up my own e-reader and opened the book I had started weeks ago but never found time to finish.

A muffled thump caught my attention as the nightly event of noise coming through our shared wall began. I pictured him stripping and getting into bed. I could almost hear his sigh of relief as his workday was over and it was time to rest. There was a sense of comfort in that thought. I didn't know why, but knowing he was that close calmed me.

I clicked off my e-reader, not bothering to read a word, and shut my eyes. Sleep came easily, and I drifted off.

***

Connor leaned back in his bed and stared at the now perfect ceiling. Beverly had a date tonight. An internet setup, but still a date. She wasn't interested in him for anything other than friendship and the occasional house job. When he cleaned his gutters, he did hers too. When he raked up his yard, he did her side as well. She always noticed and said thank you, usually with something she baked or a dinner invitation. That was the total of their relationship; therefore, he didn't have to worry about her or the kids getting too close.

That bothered him. It shouldn't, but it did.

Beverly was one of the hardest-working people he knew, and he admired her for it. She was a complicated woman. Soft, sweet, funny, and smart. Also fierce, determined, loyal, and practical. All that in a beautifully female package. An internet dating site? Men must be blind.

Am I blind? She said I'm attractive.

He thought about it. Could he date his neighbor? Would she be interested? What would the kids think about it?

Sarah had made her feelings known while they played games earlier. Well, she had played; Connor had pressed random buttons in a flurry, trying to keep up.

"I don't like Momma going out to meet strangers."

"She's a big girl. I'm sure she can take care of herself."

Sarah shook her head. "Not that. Momma can take down a grizzly if she needs to. It's just... it's...."

The girl's eyes filled with tears. "Belinda Parker is my friend from school, and her parents got divorced too. Her dad got remarried and has new children. Her mom got remarried and spends more time with her new husband and his kids than she does with Belinda. My daddy is getting married again and doesn't come see us much. What if Momma meets someone and... and...."

That hit Connor deep. "Oh, lassie, I don't think you ever have to worry about your mother doing that to you. You're on the top of her list, now and always. She won't get involved with anyone who will take that away from you."

"Are you sure?"

"I'm positive. Now, let's get back to this game. I'm getting better at it, right?"

Her incredulous look didn't need interpretation. "If you say so."

Connor inhaled through his nose and exhaled through his lips. He liked Beverly, a lot, but the kids needed to come first. Besides, what did he have to offer? No, he needed to stay away. He could be a friend to her and help out once in a while with the house and the kids, but that was all. If she wanted to date random men on the internet, she was allowed to do so. Not his monkey and not his circus.

Don't get involved, boy-o. Not your business.

Then why did he feel so jealous?

Chapter 8

Halloween, the night I dreaded the most out of all the holidays. Weeks of costume preparations, buying the economy-sized bags of candy, decorations, all of this heralding the start of the final big push for the year. From the end of October to the end of December, life always became a flurry of fall school concerts, festivals, book fairs, football playoffs, exams, shopping, decorating, freelance playing gigs, recitals, and whatever else I could cram in a twenty-four-hour period. Vacation was the week between Christmas and New Year's, and I relished that golden recovery time.

Halloween this year landed on a Friday night, and of course there were three school destinations and only one of me. Abby wanted to go to the football game, Sarah and Mattie wanted to go to their school's fall festival, Jacob wanted to be at his school for the book character parade, and all four wanted to go to the church's events. The younger three were to go to the Trunk-or-Treat in the parking lot to pick up as much loot as possible, and Abby was set on going to the youth lock-in after the game. I had attempted to ask

Doug to help, but he answered back "too busy" with some sort of "fall gala" Mandy had arranged. He and the kids were growing further and further apart. They acted like the few visits they actually had with their dad were more of a nuisance obligation.

Sometimes I wondered why I even bothered to care anymore.

I was downstairs loading the dishwasher, and Abby and Sarah were upstairs working on their costumes.

"Mom, I need more hair spray," Abby called out. "Is Phoebe here yet?"

A little knot of pain sparked in my left temple. "Not yet. There should be a full can in the medicine cabinet."

"I used it up already on Sarah's hair."

Seriously? I would need industrial-strength Excedrin before this night was over.

Jacob came tripping down the stairs in his maroon bathrobe, his hair slicked back and a black zigzag on his forehead. "I can't find my wand."

"Breakfast bar where you left it. What's Mattie doing?"

"He's in the backyard makin' his clothes dirty."

That made sense, I supposed. Zombies were dirty, right?

I'd managed to choreograph the night to get everyone where they wanted to be and relatively close to when. Abby's friend Phoebe and her mother were picking Abby up for the game and then heading over to the church for the all-night youth lock-in afterward. The rest of us would go to the fall festival at the elementary school first, then the middle school, and then head over to the church's Trunk-or-Treat.

I might get a small glimpse of Abby as she ignored my presence before the church youth center closed overnight. Ever since she found out Ashton would be there, she had been begging me to let her go. There were lots of parents who would be with them, so I figured it would be safe for the night. The youth leaders asked me about chaperoning, but Abby was adamant I not be there, as I would have to bring the other kids with me. I supposed a mom and three younger siblings in tow would cramp her style and scar her for life. After all events of the evening concluded, I would drag myself and three sugared-up kids home for a B-rated monster movie and pray that they crashed into a candy-induced coma sooner rather than later.

Mattie dashed into the kitchen with a cloud of dust trailing behind him. Connor followed, still in his work clothes. "I found Mattie rolling around in the mud outside. He said he was getting ready for a party. What's going on?"

I flipped an errant lock of hair out of my eyes and firmly closed the dishwasher door. "Halloween. Trick-or-treaters by the hundreds, more sugar consumed in one night than any other of the year, and hopefully no car egging or paper rolling this time. That happened one year, and I had yard cleanup for days."

The astonished expression on Connor's face was priceless. The poor man didn't have a clue.

"Halloween? I forgot that was tonight."

"Hey, Mom, watch my zombie impersonation." Mattie lurched awkwardly around the kitchen and moaned. "Brains. I need brains."

"Yeah, you do need brains." Sarah joined us as the bride of Frankenstein. Abby indeed used an entire can of hair spray to construct the towering monolith on top of her head.

"Is Phoebe here yet?" Abby asked.

"Not yet. Connor, do you have candy to hand out? You can try to keep your lights off and hope they won't bother you."

Connor watched zombie Mattie careen into the breakfast bar and then the back of the couch. "Um, no, I don't have any candy. I've never been trick-or-treating."

Mattie stopped his zombie-ness and gawked at our neighbor. "Never ever?"

"Maybe once when I was really little, but I don't remember much about it."

"Oh my God! I can't believe this! My life is ruined!" Abby's anguished cry reverberated through the house along with the clattering of her Goodwill vintage white go-go boots. "Phoebe just got grounded, so she can't come get me. I group-texted Rachel, Brittany, Pam, Jessica, and Autumn, but none of them have time to give me a ride. I'm so screwed! The pregame show starts in half an hour. What am I going to do? Mom, you have to take me!"

"What's that on your head?" Mattie forgot about his zombie impression and gawked at the lacquered dome on Abby's head. No wonder she needed a second can of hair spray.

"It's called a beehive, doofus. Mom!"

My brain ran through mental gymnastics to figure out how I would get it all done. Two different directions, three schools—bleh, I needed a clone. Preferably one with another car. "If Phoebe can't go, who are you hanging with?"

"The others will be around, Mom, please! I just have to be there!"

"I'm trying, Abby, but I don't see how I can get you there for the pregame. I can take you before kickoff if we hurry, but I want a guarantee you'll be there with your friends and one of their parents."

"But, Mom, that's so unfair!"

"Life is unfair sometimes."

"*I have to be there!*"

The screech that came from her mouth might have shattered wineglasses. It definitely shattered my last nerve as the knot of pain burst into full force and shot through my frontal lobe. I slammed my hands on the counter to get her attention before turning to blast my oldest daughter.

Connor's soft words stopped me. "I can help, Bev."

"You don't have to jump into this mess." I turned my eyes to my crisis-laden daughter and gave her my most pointed mom laser eyes. "My kids need to learn that the world does *not* revolve around them. Especially when they act like selfish little brats!"

Abby huffed but stood down.

Connor smiled, his brilliant white teeth making an appearance in the scruffy beard on his face. "Yeah, that's a good lesson to have, but you don't have to give it tonight when you're stressed and about to blow."

A wise man as well as a handsome one. He was throwing me a lifeline, and I would be foolish not to take it. Should

I trust him to take my kids solo? It wasn't my children I was worried about. He had babysat my kids before, worked with Jacob alone in his woodshop on a mysterious science project, and put his feet under my dinner table more than once. I had no qualms about him being around my kids, but there was a big difference between hanging with them at home and taking them out in public. My kids were a lot to handle, and I had to stock up on patience at times myself. Even if he wasn't interested in me as a woman, his friendship had become something very meaningful, and I didn't want to do anything to lose it. For some people, being around super-active kids equaled trial by fire. So far Connor didn't seem to be one of them; however, he'd not been around a sugared-up, turbo-charged Mattie before.

"Okay then, just remember later you asked for this. Give me your cell number, and I'll call you so you have mine. Sarah and Mattie, you go with Connor to the elementary school. You each have ten dollars to play games and have an hour to do it. Only three pieces of candy while you're there. Three. That's nonnegotiable, so choose wisely. Jacob and Abby, you're with me. We'll go to the high school first, and Abby, I'm serious. If I don't see any of your friends waiting for you at the curb with a parent, you're not getting out of the van. Do not argue, or I'll ground you right now. Jacob, after we drop off Abby, we'll get to the middle school. You'll get about forty-five-ish minutes for your parade and any other activities. After the schools, we meet at the church to set up for Trunk-or-Treat. We'll be the last ones there, but we'll make it before the trick-or-treaters arrive. Abby, you *will* check in with me when you get to the church for the lock-in. Understand?"

All four kids spoke at once.

"Only three? I'll starve!"

"Autumn's mom will be there, I think. I can't be grounded tonight! My life will be over!"

"Mr. Barnard is going as Dumbledore. Maybe I can get a selfie with him."

"Mom, where's your costume?"

Leave it to Sarah to think of details. Inspiration hit me as I put away the dish soap bottle. I pulled one of the gigantic lawn and leaf bags from the pile under the sink, tore a hole in the bottom, and slipped it over my head. "See, I'm a bag lady."

Jacob looked at me in speculation while Mattie scratched his head, not getting the reference. Sarah nodded her approval, the tower on her head swaying with the movement. She looked at Connor in his beard and red plaid shirt.

"I have an idea." She grabbed an unopened roll of paper towels and handed it to the bewildered man. "There. You can be the Brawny guy."

She was right. He did resemble the model featured on the plastic-wrapped roll. Sarah, problem solver and monster bride, at your service.

"All right, people, T-minus three minutes and counting. Zombie and bride to the truck, wizard and go-go dancer to the van. Ready? Break!"

It worked. Color me shocked!

I dropped Abby off with a group of her friends at the gate

and waved to the frazzled mother who was trying to herd the group of excited sixties dancers into the stadium. I gave her a thumbs-up for the effort and drove off to the middle school. I got lucky enough to find a parking space in the lot rather than the street.

"Hey, Mom? Did you know that half the earth's oxygen comes from the ocean? It's from this stuff that floats on the surface called phytoplankton, and it makes oxygen like air plants but in the water. That's why it's important to protect our oceans. Cool, right?"

Since there were four of them and only one of me, private time with each of my kids was hard to do. I relished having that one-on-one with my boy Jacob. He was an amazing kid with so much knowledge of his books and his science interests. I couldn't be prouder of my little egghead.

"That is cool. I guess it is important."

"I'm gonna invent something that can scoop up all the plastic junk in the ocean and turn it into shoes or something else we can use. That way the phytoplankton can make more oxygen and reduce greenhouse gasses. Connor has a *blah-de-blah* that can make a *bliggedy-blah*. All we need now is an enzymatic processor *blah-blah* that breaks down the *bliggety bliggety blah*. Wouldn't that be rad?"

Yup. Proud of my little egghead even though I couldn't understand half of what he said.

While Jacob wandered off to find his favorite robotics teacher, I texted Connor.

Me: **You surviving the zombie apocalypse at the elementary school?**

Connor: **Yes. But next time you limit the amount of candy Mattie can have, you should consider limiting the size too.**

Me: **Don't tell me. Full-size candy bars as carnival prizes?**

Connor: **Bingo.**

Me: **Damn. Happened last year as well. That little booger can kick some serious butt at the ring toss game.**

Connor: **He wants to ride in the truck bed and pretend he's a zombie surfer.**

Me: **Do you have bungee cords?**

Connor: **Yes. ???**

Me: **Just kidding. No, he has to ride in the cab, but you still may have to use the bungees as extra anchors. A seat belt may not hold a sugared-up Mattie.**

Connor: **LOL**

Connor: **Heading out soon. See you at the church.**

I watched as the students lined up for the book parade. Half of Jacob's class was decked out in Hogwarts costumes, and he wasn't the only Harry Potter. I may have been a little biased, but I thought he was the cutest. The parade was one long processional through the school hallway, but the kids had a blast with it, and I took a bunch of pictures. We grabbed two overpriced hotdogs at the concession fundraiser stand and took off to set up for the Trunk-or-Treat.

This was something I loved to do, and the kids enjoyed it as well. It was a last hurrah before the madness of the holidays set in and time became short. The kids and I made a poster board set of big triangle teeth to hang down from the open back of my van. We shaped more red poster board and taped it together to look like a giant tongue that spilled from the back of the van to the ground. My van magically transformed from an old, tired vehicle to a scary dragon waiting to devour anyone who ventured too near.

Connor arrived with Mattie and Sarah as I pulled out the teeth and tape. He had parked in the remote lot and walked with the kids up to the main lot. Cars and other vehicles lined the perimeter and were being decorated in all sorts of creative ways. One car resembled an ice cream stand, another looked like a forest, and another had a scary clown face hanging from the open back hatch. Thank you, Pinterest!

"Mom-I-only-had-two-Snickers-bars-and-one-Three-Musketeers-and-I-won-a-big-frog-too-when-I-played-the-Plinko-game-I-gotta-go-pee!

Mattie dashed by me in hyper sugar speed. I looked at Connor with a raised eyebrow. He shrugged and dipped his head. "Sorry, Bev. I forgot about sodas. He drank a full can of Coke before we got here."

I groaned a bit, but it wasn't Connor's fault. I hadn't warned him about the additional danger of Coca-Cola, Dr. Pepper, or Fanta in any flavor. Mountain Dew was absolutely forbidden in my house for obvious reasons. "It's okay. He'll burn out soon. I hope."

It didn't take long to decorate my van until it was ready to spew out candy goodness to all the trickers who would be parading through the lot for the next several hours. I had two folding camp chairs to sit in and a quilt for the ground.

Four economy-sized bags of candy sat unopened while I dumped the fifth one into a big plastic dollar-store bowl.

Connor put away the tape. "What's next?"

I adjusted my garbage bag. "Nothing for a bit. There's pizza and sandwiches if you want something."

"We had our fill of junk food at the school."

"Toxic red hotdogs?"

Connor's grimace said all I needed to know. "Mattie had two."

The little devil zombie ran up and started jumping up and down. "Mom-can-I-go-with-Bobby-to-the-playground-my-costume-is-wearing-off-and-I'm-hungry."

I handed him a five-dollar bill for the concessions while he babbled, and he took off through the gathering crowd. I saw a handful of other super-carbed-up kids at the playground, their screams of laughter filling the air. I wasn't the only parent looking forward to a hard crash in about an hour.

"Jesus, that kid can eat." Connor winced as he turned in my direction. "Sorry, Bev. I forgot where we were."

I waved a hand, and a tooth fell off the raised hatch of my van. "I'm sure I've said worse. I don't think the idea is that it's just bad to cuss at church. I think it's supposed to be bad to cuss anywhere, but name me someone who isn't guilty of it."

"Jesus?"

"And isn't it a funny thing, we use his name as a cuss word?"

This was from Mike, who came shuffling up to us,

making his rounds. He was wearing a gold tuxedo that I was sure was a Goodwill reject and a fuzzy purple hat with a leopard skin band on his head. He stuck his hand out to Connor in greeting. "Pimp Daddy Mike, at your service. Or just Mike any other time. You sing bass or tenor?"

Confusion hit Connor's face. "Sing?"

"Yup. Choir's always hiring. 'Cept altos. We got enough of them."

"Um… I don't sing."

"You're datin' a key tickler, aren't you? I 'spect she'll have you up front of the choir soon doing solos."

Connor squirmed. His face flamed red when he glanced at me. I could sense his discomfort level rise, and he didn't know how to respond. I stepped in for the rescue.

"We're not dating, Mike. This is my friend and neighbor, Connor MacAteer. He's just along for the ride and helping me with the kids tonight. That's it."

I didn't look back at Connor. I didn't want to see the relief on his face as I defined our nonexistent relationship.

Mike shook his head. "Damn shame. We need more basses. Welp, I'm gonna go find me some widow women to flirt with. See you Sunday morning, key tickler."

The hordes descended. For the next two hours, Connor and I dropped treats into plastic pumpkins, paper bags, and pillowcases. The continuous line of costumed kids paraded by the cars with no breaks in sight. Just when I thought we were done, another group of cars parked and a new surge of goblins and Disney princesses made the rounds. Pimp Daddy Mike manned the outdoor sound system and treated us with repeats of "Monster Mash,", "Thriller," and other Halloween songs.

Mattie came back from his romp on the playground even dirtier than he'd started, if that was possible. He crawled into the van's rear seat and crashed hard. Sarah sat down on the blanket to examine her pile of loot. I wouldn't be surprised if she charted a graph to determine how much of the fun-size chocolate bars, taffy style pieces, hard candy, and lollipops she got. Jacob wandered over to where Mike played DJ and watched as the older man worked the board sliders.

"Thanks for letting me come along, Bev. I haven't had this much fun in a long time."

I looked over at Connor and almost lost my breath. He was smiling so big and happy. This was not a chore at all for him, and he seemed to be relishing every minute of the chaotic night. My anxieties melted away, and I smiled back. "Connor MacAteer, if this is your idea of fun, then either you're crazy or you need to get out a little more."

He just laughed and tossed two Laffy Taffy squares into a tricker's open bag.

Cleanup was easy. Just pull off the paper teeth and toss in the recycling bin. Out of five huge bags of candy, I had about a dozen rejected pieces left. Mattie slept in full REM cycle, and the other two kids both had the unfocused eyes of a post-sugar high. Abby checked in briefly and had gone to the third-floor youth center, hopefully having a great time with her friends. I was in a constant state of worry about my oldest daughter and felt helpless to do anything about it, but for tonight, she was safe.

Connor had taken a load to the recycle bins and was now helping me fold up the blanket and the chairs.

"I'll get my truck and meet you back home."

My stomach thrilled at his use of the word "home."

"Yeah, sure thing."

We caravanned back to the duplex, all three kids in the van with me and fighting to stay awake. I attempted the herculean task of rousing a passed-out Mattie enough to get him in the door, but Connor took care of the problem. He simply lifted my son's dead weight and carried him inside and up the stairs for me. Jacob dragged himself up the stairs to show Connor which one was the boys' room. I led a comatose Sarah into the house and watched as she slowly climbed the steps and disappeared into her own space.

Once he was free from his burden, Connor leaned over the upper banister to look down at me. "I put Mattie on the bed, but he's pretty dirty. Want me to try to get him up and cleaned off?"

I shook my head and motioned for him to come on down. "Nope, it's not that big a deal. Dirt happens, and that's why soap and washing machines exist."

I was still wearing my garbage bag and ready to crash myself. They confiscated the kids' cell phones before the church locked them in for the night, so I couldn't text Abby. I supposed I shouldn't worry, since I knew where she was and who she was with, but worrying about their children was what moms did best, and I was no exception to that rule.

Connor's Brawny man face looked as drawn and tired as mine. I knew he wasn't used to this much bedlam, but he was a real trooper. If he hadn't come through for me tonight, I was sure I would have been in much worse shape.

"Connor, I can't thank you enough for helping. I think I owe you weekly cakes or pies for the next month."

"No trouble at all, Bev. I had a great time. There's a lot of things I didn't get to do as a kid besides trick-or-treating. I didn't play on a sports team or video games, and I've never heard of a church lock-in before tonight. My life has pretty much been work in one form or another. It's really nice to get to be a part of something different. I should be thanking you." His eyes twinkled at me. "Although, if you really want to make me some pies, I won't turn you down."

I laughed and yawned at the same time. "Duly noted. I'm so tired, I could sleep standing up right here. I'm gonna go de-bag myself and fall face-first in my bed."

"I'm right behind you. That is, on my side of the house. Good night, Bev."

Maybe if I'd been more awake, I wouldn't have done what I did next. I stepped in close and hugged my tall neighbor. He stiffened but then hugged me back. It was a long hug. A nice one. I didn't really want to let go. Friends gave friends long hugs, right?

I finally released him and moved back.

"'Night, Connor."

He smiled a little awkwardly and then left. I heard his front door open, then close as I peeled the black plastic off me. Ten minutes later, I climbed in my own bed with my consciousness drifting toward sleep and dreaming of a parade of pies to bake.

* * *

Connor lifted the mask, and the tang of varnish hit his nostrils. The workshop was cold, but he didn't feel the bite of it. After leaving Beverly's place, he trudged to the backyard to spend a little time with his thoughts; working with his hands always helped him focus. Physical exhaustion filled his body but his mind raced.

I have to stop this. I can't get involved. He finished the stain on one table leg and set it aside to dry. He mounted another one between the lathe centers and started the motor. The machine was quiet enough for the sound not to travel to the house and wake the occupants.

You're already involved, his brain argued back.

"Only as a good neighbor. She needed help tonight, and I was there." He dipped the fine brush in the dark color and applied the thick liquid to the spinning wood. His movements were automatic from years of woodworking.

"She's an educated woman. She needs an educated man." The varnish spread along the length of the table leg in a nice even coat. "She couldn't be interested in a man who didn't graduate high school and only by some miracle got his GED."

You're making excuses. What about the kids?

I can't get close to them either, he countered. *I'm just helping out like any decent man would do.*

Who's kidding who? You're already there.

Connor put down the brush and stopped the lathe. Yes, he was already there with the kids. Jacob slipped him a crudely drawn diagram earlier for what he wanted to do as a science project. It was an ambitious task, but one that could be done.

You had fun tonight. Admit it.

Yes, I did.

You miss the big family atmosphere more than you thought, eh?

Maybe.

Maybe you're not cut out to be alone. Maybe you're at your best and happiest when you have people you care about around you. Ones who care about you too.

Connor stared at the finished wood. "I have nothing to offer."

You have more than you know.

Chapter 9

"You got four kids?"

My grip tightened on my phone. I could already tell this phone call was as far as it would go. Melanie's picks were getting more and more desperate, and I wondered for the umpteenth time why I continued to go on her dates. "Yes, I have four kids. One in high school, one in middle school, and two in elementary school."

"That's a lot of kids."

"I suppose it is for some people." *Quell the sarcasm, Bev.*

"And you're a teacher?"

"Yes, it says so on my profile. Just like it says I have four children." *Dammit, at least change the tone of your voice.*

"Singing teacher? That's a real job?"

I gritted my teeth hard enough to remove another layer of enamel. "Yes, it is. As a matter of fact, vocal coaching and choral conducting have been real professions since before the sixteenth century."

"Hmm." The noncommittal grunt said either he didn't

believe me or he didn't care.

It was midafternoon on Thanksgiving Day, and miracle of miracles, Doug actually took the children for the whole weekend. I missed them terribly, but I was looking forward to some pamper time for myself.

"Damn, that's a lot of kids."

How rude will it be if I just hang up on him?

I leaned over the breakfast bar and hit a button on one of Jacob's abandoned contraptions. It rang a brief alarm.

"Oh, listen to that. Someone is at my door. I'd better go. Call me some other time?"

"Uh… yeah, you better get that. I'll talk to you later."

I won't hold my breath.

Silence permeated the house. I could have gone to the beach with Melanie and another teacher. It would have been a blast with three single ladies on the town, shopping the malls on Black Friday, and having some serious female bonding time, but I declined. I just didn't have the money to spare. Christmas was coming, and I got the news from the dentist that Sarah was going to need braces. I had good insurance, but it didn't cover all the cost, and I was still paying for Jacob's. I told Doug about the need, and he hemmed and hawed a bit, asking if the mouth metal was really necessary at her age. I might as well have asked him for a piece of the moon.

The slam of Connor's front door startled me. I had thought about asking him to have Thanksgiving dinner with me, but since the kids weren't there as a buffer, I didn't think it was a good idea. I reminded myself firmly that we were friends. Friends with benefits, though those benefits were helping hands, nothing more. So far, he'd fixed my gutter, kept the yard cleaned up for both of us, and most recently came over to silence the annoying squeak in my clothes dryer. I was sure he didn't mind that one, since the noise was loud enough to bleed through the walls. Every time he helped me, I gave him thanks by cooking dinner or sending him home with a dessert. The man did have a sweet tooth, and he never turned down dessert.

Nevertheless, I could be a good neighbor and at least wish him a nice holiday. I glanced down at my lazy day attire. Paint-stained baggy gray sweats, loose oversized T-shirt, shapeless hoodie, and the fuzzy slippers with JS Bach's head standing up from the toes. *Oh well, he's seen me looking worse. At least I brushed my hair and teeth this morning.*

Connor was locking up when I scooted outside. The wind was cold, but that didn't mean much in North Carolina. That time of year, it was possible to be in winter gear one day and summer shorts the next.

He looked good with his neatly trimmed hair and beard, but then again, he always looked good. Nice jeans, plaid shirt, and a leather bomber jacket. I crossed my arms against the chill and shuffled over to him in my slippers, catching a whiff of his spicy cologne in the process.

"Happy Thanksgiving, Connor. Got a big day planned?" I didn't know why that came out of my mouth, but I was dying to know.

"Happy Thanksgiving, Bev. I'm heading to Bryson City

for dinner and to spend a few days with my sister and her motorcycle club."

I blinked. "Did you say motorcycle club?"

"Yeah, her husband is a member of the Dragon Runners MC, and it's become a big part of Eva's life." He swiped at his phone a few times and pulled up several pictures to show me. I looked down at a shot of a beautiful redhead with the most handsome man I'd ever seen, standing between a pair of large motorcycles. The man's adoration toward his wife was clear in his stance and the way he held her. The next picture was of them and three little girls who were a perfect blend of the two of them. Two of them looked like twins, and the other was a baby. As Connor scrolled through, I saw the man lying on the ground with the girls crawling all over him, pink bow-clad toddlers learning to walk while holding their daddy's hands, the baby curled in the crook of her daddy's arm, and so many others. Happy family. Happy times.

One picture caught my eye of Connor smiling up at a camera lens and holding a drooling baby in a cone-shaped pink party hat. "My eldest niece on her first birthday. I came to the Lair for the party. Eva grabbed my phone and took this pic. I call her Jessie-bear, and she calls me Uncana." The pride in his voice was unmistakable.

I handed him back his phone. "Beautiful family. What's a lair?"

"That's the nickname of the private clubhouse the MC owns. It's more like a fancy lodge resort than a clubhouse. The old family business, Irish Pub Builders, did a rebuild job for them some years ago, and Eva met Stud while we were there. Those two are about as mismatched as you can get, but they still managed to fall in love."

Connor smiled down at his phone as he closed the photo app. "God has a real sense of humor. Stud was a big ladies' man before he met my sister. Now he's married and the father of three beautiful little girls, who are sure to grow up into strong women like their mother. He's got his hands full for sure."

I had no words. My heart leaked a little at the thought of a man I'd never met looking so totally devoted to his family. My eyes moistened a bit. I'd had that once, or at least I'd thought I did. I had hundreds of digital pics of my once-upon-a-time family that I spent hours arranging into albums and slideshows that ran across my computer screen in show mode. Doug used to tease me about the time I spent making those albums of family memories, and now those pics were all I had left of that part of our lives.

"What are your plans today? I don't hear the kids."

I dashed away any maudlin thoughts and answered with as much cheer as I could dredge up. "I have the rare opportunity to have the house to myself. Do you hear that?" I cocked my head to the side.

He tilted his head and gave me a puzzled look. "I don't hear anything."

"Yes, isn't it niiiiiice?" I closed my eyes tight as if relishing the taste of the word. "I need me time, and this is the perfect opportunity to get it."

Instead of laughing, he looked at me with concern. "I don't

like the thought of you spending the day alone. Do you want to come with me? I'll call Eva and she'll make room for you, or if that's too much, I'll drive you back here tonight and leave to go back there in the morning."

The kindness of his offer pierced my heart, but I didn't dare take him up on it. Seeing him around his family would be more than I could stand, and the PSI would drastically increase for my crush on him. "Aw, that's so sweet, but I'm set on having my day here."

"Are you sure that's what you want?"

No, it's not what I want. I can't have what I want.

"Are you kidding? I'm going to soak in a tub of hot water until I prune up. Then watch a bunch of movies that are not kid related. *Uninterrupted!* I'm very sure. Go. Have a good time, and eat lots of turkey." I waved him off with an exaggerated grin. For a minute or two, I thought he was going to say he changed his mind and would stay home to keep me company. I didn't know if I could keep myself closed up if he did that. I held my breath until he got in his truck and finally pulled out of the driveway.

I gathered my bath supplies and started the water. Maybe it was the look in Connor's eyes. Maybe it was the man I spoke with earlier who was not happy about my having four kids. Maybe it was remembering the words from my first disaster date where Mr. Hot Body had pronounced me fatter than the women he normally dated. Regardless of the reason, I did something I hadn't done in forever.

I stripped and looked at my naked body.

I wore a size sixteen to accommodate my thick legs

and rounded hips, but my waist nipped in, giving me a true hourglass shape. After breastfeeding four babies, my boobs were big and soft, not as perky as they used to be but not drooping to my knees either. I ran my hands over my pooched stomach. There were silvery stretch marks from my pregnancies, and the skin wasn't tight. It jiggled when I walked, and there was no way I would ever sport a six-pack on my abdomen, but was it really necessary to have a hard body at my age? I raised my arms and looked at the slight hang. Not quite the waving grandma bingo arms yet, but with all the piano work, performing and conducting, the arm fat wasn't terrible. My under chin was still pretty tight, probably from all the facial exercise I got lecturing and singing. My bikini days were definitely over, but that didn't mean I was out to pasture, right?

I looked at my hair, hanging thick and long. It might be simply styled, but it was always clean and groomed. Paying for fake nails or their upkeep wasn't in my budget, and besides, I had to keep them short and clean for my piano work. Spas were also out of the question, but I regularly shaved my legs and underarms and kept a nightly moisturizer to fight off wrinkles as long as I could. All in all, I wasn't bad. I wasn't bad at all. I was a large woman and likely would always be a large woman, but I was in great health, I had four beautiful children, and I worked hard and did the best I could with what life had handed me. Maybe it was time for me to work on my own attitude and outlook. If a man could only find value in my body mass index, well, there were worse things in life than being single.

I had just settled back into the hot water, my glass of wine on the closed toilet seat along with my Kindle, when my cell phone rang. I thought it was Melanie calling me, but Doug's name came up on the screen. Dread hit the pit of my belly. There was only one reason he would be calling me. He changed his mind and wanted me to come get the kids.

"Hi, Bevvie. It's Doug."

"I got that from the caller ID." Damn, I sounded surly. Maybe I was. My super soak had just been interrupted, after all.

"I hate to do this to you, but…."

"But what?"

"Well, you see… Mandy, she… well…."

"Just spit it out, Doug."

"Mandy got us a cabin at the Lake Lure resort, and we were going to head up there and pick up the Thanksgiving meal from Ingle's on the way, but I looked up the address and it's only got one bedroom. The boys are okay with sleeping on the floor, but Abby and Sarah are having a fit about it."

I would be too. A precooked grocery store Thanksgiving meal? The southern woman in me cringed. Yes, I cut corners in the kitchen out of time necessity, but there were some dinners that had to be homemade, and Thanksgiving dinner was one of them. It was a law. The kids were crowded enough in their bunk beds here, but camping out on the floor in one big pile for the next three nights? The edge of the phone cut into my hand as it tightened. I'd bet a dollar to a donut that Mandy deliberately booked the smaller cabin just so the girls would freak and want to come home.

"The boys said if the girls go home, they want to go as well."

I splashed out of the tub and dried off one-handed. "So you're bringing them home."

"Well, I guess I could make a side trip and bring them to your place before Dee-Dee and I head out."

Dee-Dee? Again? I threw up a little. "Are you going to have dinner before you bring them home?"

"Dinner?"

I said a quick prayer for patience and pulled on a clean pair of blue leggings with green stripes down the sides. "Yes, you said you ordered a premade meal from Ingle's. Are you going to eat that dinner before you bring them home?"

He missed the sarcasm in my carefully repeated question.

"We can't. The Ingle's we ordered from is the one closest to the cabin. It's too far to go there, get the food, and come back here just for us to drive back again."

"Give me an hour, and then bring them home."

"Um… do you think you could—"

"No, I don't." I shut my phone before he attempted to talk me into coming to get them.

Standing before my open pantry door, I looked at the meager contents for inspiration. I hadn't gone grocery shopping since the kids weren't supposed to be with me. No turkey in the freezer. No stuffing. No cranberry sauce. No pumpkin pie. When I spotted the box of lasagna noodles, the light bulb clicked on. I had half an onion, two cans of tomato sauce, and a quartet of those little cottage cheese mini cups. The freezer held ground beef and a bag of mozzarella cheese, and my cabinet had dried oregano and basil in it. Did I have salad makings? Yes I did. Not a lot, but I could stretch it for five. Dessert? Betty Crocker brownie mix to the rescue.

It was only a half hour later before Doug pulled up to the duplex with the kids. Not that big a deal, I supposed, since I was just sliding the lasagna into the oven next to the pan of brownies. Still, it would've been nice if he would've waited the hour I asked for. I wrestled my anger into a box, locked it, and plastered a big smile on my face.

"Hello, my little darlings! Did you miss me?"

Abby ignored me and ran straight to her bedroom. The echoes from her stomping feet reverberated through the ceiling above my head. Jacob and Mattie gave me a muted "Hi, Mom" and plopped down on the couch to play a game. I glanced through the open door to see the taillights of Doug's newest car, a tricked-out SUV. He hadn't bothered to walk them to the door.

Sarah was the only one who joined me in the kitchen. She sat at the breakfast bar, her face solemn and even more serious than usual.

"Something on your mind, sweetheart?"

"Does Dad still love us?"

Mack trucks hit lighter than those words. I had to set the knife down where I'd been cutting up cucumber slices so I wouldn't slip and open a vein by accident. "Of course he still loves you, baby. You'll always be his little girl."

"We don't see him that much anymore, and when we

do, we just go to his house and sit around watching movies and playing games by ourselves. He and Mandy go out to parties and stuff and leave us alone. Last time we were there, he ordered pizzas, and then he and Mandy went to dinner somewhere fancy and stayed out all night. I think he loves her more than he loves us. More than he loves me."

Sarah's voice was breaking, and my own throat closed up. I stepped over to my youngest daughter and pulled her into my arms, holding her tight and wishing I could take away the pain in her young heart. The anger welled up in me, breaking out of that box. The molten burn of it sat behind my ribs, trying to burst through. I struggled against the urge to let it out. There was no way I could've reined it back in.

"I know it's rough, Sarah-boo. It's hard to understand, and I'm not sure I can explain everything, but your father does love you, I promise. He loves Mandy, but in a different way, and that won't take away his love for you."

The words were acid on my tongue, but I had to keep it from showing. My daughter was more important than my rage.

"I don't think so, Mom." Jacob came over and burrowed into my arms next to his sister. "He didn't ask me about my science project at all."

God in heaven, I was going to lose it. I had no words to make this right. What was I supposed to say to my hurting children when their other parent had all but abandoned them?

Mattie flipped over the back of the couch and beaned his

head on the corner. He popped up and rubbed the red spot. "Ouch. Are we having dinner soon? I'm hungry."

Mattie's statement helped me get the control I needed. It was still there bubbling away, but I could keep it inside for now. Screaming into my pillow would come later.

"As a matter of fact, we are. Not exactly traditional, though. Instead of a Thanksgiving turkey, we're having a beautiful Thanksgiving lasagna. Should be ready soon. Sarah, call Abby down here to help. Jacob, get the sandwich bread out and I'll improvise garlic toast. Mattie, can you set the table without breaking any dishes or yourself?"

My little imp grinned at me. "No promises, Mom."

Abby came down from brooding in her room. Her red eyes told me she had been crying by herself. I pulled her in and kissed her forehead. "Love you, Abby-pie."

She pulled away and rolled her eyes. "Yeah, whatever."

Yup. Definitely gonna be some pillow screaming tonight.

We sat down, and I put the big oblong dish in the middle of the breakfast bar with a flourish. "Ta-da! No turkeys were harmed in the making of this fabulous Thanksgiving meal."

"Is Connor coming over?" Sarah reached for a piece of buttered garlic toast.

"No, sweetheart. He left earlier to see his sister and her family today."

"Wheyr do dey liv? Ar dey kwose?"

I dipped out salad onto my plate. "Mattie, don't talk with your mouth full. They're not too far away, just in Bryson City. Apparently they're members of a motorcycle club."

Jacob jumped out of his chair. "Like the Dragon Runners?"

I blinked at my young scientist. "How do you know about the Dragon Runners?"

"Connor told us about them once. He has a motorcycle in his woodshop, and he said he likes to ride with them sometimes." My logical little Sarah was back. At least for now.

Jacob added to the conversation by waving a piece of bread in the air. "Bryson City is where the train is. We went there once for the Thomas the Tank Engine day."

I remembered that day. Doug had bowed out at the last minute, saying something about work. That wasn't too long before I got blindsided by the separation papers. Apparently the kids did too, as the mood dropped.

"Ah wike Condor. Ee's dice." Mattie's stuffed mouth changed the subject perfectly.

Abby scrunched her nose at her younger brother. "Jeez, brat! Say it, don't spray it!"

Sarah copied her older sister. "That's so gross! Mom, make him stop. Why are you smiling?"

I didn't stop the belly laugh from coming out. Yeah, my day of self-indulgence didn't happen, but I really didn't care. Life limited my time with my kids. Someday they would grow up and make their own way in the world. I'd have plenty of time for long bath soaks then. "I'm just glad all y'all are here. You know, I miss you like crazy when you're not around."

Abby gave me her most sincere look. "Mom, you are so weird."

Mattie swallowed the masticated mass in his mouth.

"I'm glad we're home too. This is the bestest Thanksgiving lasagna ever."

"Thank you, Mattie-boo. We'll have the bestest, most fantastical brownies that have ever come from a box for dessert, and later the bestest, most fantastical game of Harry Potter Clue the world as ever seen."

Jacob scooped said fantastical lasagna into his mouth. "I second what Abby said. Mom, you're weird."

Love my little snots!

* * *

Connor tipped the bottle back and swallowed the last of the liquid. It was his third; however, since he was spending the weekend in Bryson City and wasn't driving anywhere, he could afford to have a few beers.

The Lair was lit up both outside and inside. The cavernous main room was full of people. Husbands, wives, kids, and a few singles scattered around, sitting on the many couches, playing video games, or just talking. Music played in the background, and the place was awash with noise.

Connor knew most of them from the job several years ago. There were new faces amongst the old, and every one of them reflected the joy of the season. He'd toyed with the idea of prospecting and joining the MC at one time but decided the occasional visit and bike ride were enough for him.

"You want another one, big brother?" Eva came up to

him with her youngest daughter on her hip. The twins were sitting on the floor in a corner with their father. Stud was learning the intricacies of the sticker books Connor brought the two girls. So far, he had three stars and one heart stuck to his cheek.

"I'm good, little sister. Work much these days?"

Eva hefted the drooling bundle to the other side. "I take on a short remodel gig when I can. Most of my time is spent chasing after my little hellions."

"Still sewing?"

She smiled as the baby squirmed. "Yeah, but not as many lounge pants or lap quilts. I've been making little girl smocks, aprons, and dresses. Mostly for this bunch, but I'm still selling a few at the craft store. Don't ever let anyone tell you kids are easy. They are not. I don't know how single parents handle it without help."

Connor's thoughts went straight to Beverly, and he wondered if she was enjoying the break from the kids. He was still uncomfortable about her being alone on a holiday and wished she would have come with him. Eva would have peppered him with questions, and Stud would have shaken his hand, but he could survive their scrutiny.

"How 'bout the custom furniture? Any big orders yet?"

"A few. I made some bistro tables and chairs for a local businessman. A couple of his friends want their own set now. I'm still working local jobsites and doing some handyman work. Keeping me busy."

"Bro, you need a life." Stud came over, peeling the stickers from his face. The two girls were now sitting in a big group with a number of the other children in front of a huge TV, watching a Disney princess movie about a woman who froze stuff with her hands. "Seeing any one special?"

"Nah, too busy. I don't need that headache right now."

Stud wadded up the sticky paper into a ball and stuffed it in the pocket of his jeans. "I used to think single was the only way to be. Now, I can't imagine a life without Eva and the girls in it. It took a serious gamble on my part, and man, did it ever pay off. I have more love in my life now than I've ever had, and I wouldn't trade it for anything. I hope you find that someday, bro."

The image of Beverly popped in Connor's head again. What was she doing now? Still in the tub? *Shite, gotta stop thinking about her, man.*

"LET IT GOOOOOO! LET IT GOOOOO!"

A sudden chorus of children's voices singing loud and off pitch filled the air. Connor smirked at the timing.

"All right, lower the volume, kids. Food's up." Betsey, the matriarch and unofficial grandmother to everyone's kids, made her announcement with authority, and a scramble of bodies jumped up from the floor. "Line up like you do in school. Lord have mercy, children, I promise there is plenty of food. No one goes hungry in this house."

Adults served plates and settled the young ones at several card tables set up for them. It didn't matter whose kid was whose, everyone in the club took care of all of them.

Eva smiled at Connor. "Come on, *A ghrá.* You don't want to insult Betsey by not stuffing yourself sick today."

Connor leaned in and kissed his sister on the temple. "Be

right there." He pulled his phone from his back pocket and typed a quick text to Beverly.

Connor: You doing ok? Not too pruned up?

Beverly: Great. The kids came home, so no marinating in the bathtub for me.

Connor: ???

Beverly: Don't ask. Long story. Enjoying your Thanksgiving?

Connor: Yes. Getting ready to eat now.

Beverly: Great. Have some turkey for us. I had to adapt and make a lasagna. Mattie says hi.

Connor: Tell him I said hi back. I'm sorry you didn't get your alone time.

Beverly: I'm okay with it. I'd rather the kids come home than be somewhere they don't want to be. Tub soaking can wait.

Connor fingered the screen for a minute, not sure of what to type back. A whirlwind of thoughts and emotions filled his head. Most of all he missed that he wasn't there.

Beverly: Not that I want to miss baths. Showers are good too. ☺

Connor: ☺

Beverly: Sarah is yelling for me to take my turn at Harry Potter Clue. I better run. Be safe and enjoy the rest of your weekend.

Connor: You too. Glad you're okay.

The three little dots bounced around a few times, then went still. Connor glanced up at a burst of laughter and spotted Blue and Psalm, another husband and wife in the club. Blue picked up a square of something chocolaty and teased it against Psalm's lips. Every time she tried to bite it, he pulled it away. After the third time, she picked up a similar square, but instead of playing back, she smashed it firmly into Blue's nose, smearing his face with chocolate.

Betsey handed him a towelette packet. "Serves you right for being a smartass."

Stud laughed and pointed. Eva smacked him on the shoulder and handed him the baby. He winced and rubbed the spot before taking the child. Connor watched as Stud pulled Eva to him and kissed her like no one else was there.

He was happy to see Eva, his nieces, and her extended biker family, but the depth of his disappointment in missing the makeshift Thanksgiving meal surprised him. He visualized a picture of the homey scene. Mattie stuffing his face, Jacob chattering about his latest science experiment, Sarah debating the current news, and Abby ignoring everyone with a teenage snit. He couldn't be two places at once, but he wished he could.

"It took a serious gamble on my part, and man, did it ever pay off."

Stud's words echoed through his brain. He slipped the phone into his back pocket and moved to join the food line. Maybe it was time to roll the dice.

Chapter 10

It was bound to happen sooner or later. This was pick-your-virus month, and eventually, one of my kids would catch something. Of course if one got it, the others did too. I was only slightly immune. After so many years of exposure to hundreds of kiddie cooties, it took something pretty big to put me in a sick bed. Even if I managed to avoid the teeming pool of germs brought home on a daily basis, I still had the problem of being only one person. If Abby got sick, she was usually okay on her own to stay home. Jacob was a maybe. Mattie or Sarah, definitely not.

This time it was Sarah who started the flu train in my house. She managed to wait until the weekend to go full-blown viral; unfortunately, she chose the weekend I was taking my chorus to the winter choral festival. Abby was staying with Phoebe, and Jacob was staying with his friend Andrew. I only had my youngest two to handle while on this day trip. I tried to switch weekends with Doug, but he never answered my texts or voice mails. None of our regular sitters were available, so I had no choice but to load my two youngest with me and drag them along. The bus left at 8:00 a.m. on Saturday to go to Winston-Salem and would get back around ten at night. Long day, but a good one for my wonderful, hard-working chorus students.

It happened shortly after the bus pulled onto the interstate.

"Mom, I don't feel so good."

Sarah's pale face and whine started a mild panic in my gut. I put my hand on her forehead. Years of motherhood practice told me she had a fever. Low grade, but still a fever.

"How's your stomach?"

"It's all twisted."

Oh shit. "Are you going to throw up?"

"I don't know. I might."

She leaned against me, and I could feel the heat from her small body soak into mine. I pulled up my backpack and purse from the floorboard and starting digging around in the contents. With four kids of my own and thirty more going crazy with excitement behind me, I carried a backpack of every kind of pharmaceutical need you could think of, from Band-Aids to diabetic glucose tablets. My purse held more personal stuff, and I hoped I had children's Tylenol with me. A bottle of the cherry-flavored liquid was hiding at the bottom. Sarah took a shot direct from the bottle since the little plastic medicine cup held the dried-up remnants of whoever was sick last. The expiration date hadn't passed yet, so it should still be good.

"What's wrong with Sarah?"

"She doesn't feel good, Mattie."

"Oh. She said she didn't feel good last night either."

I turned to my youngest child, who was attempting a handstand in the bus's center aisle. "Put your little butt in the seat and keep it there. What do you mean, she didn't feel good last night? She didn't say anything to me."

He plopped down on the bench and proceeded to bounce up and down. "You were talking to Abby about her attitude. Sarah said she didn't feel good and went to bed."

My eyelid began to twitch. Yes, I had been talking with Abby—or rather talking to her as she stonewalled me. Lately, she had taken argumentative teenager to new levels. If I said the sky was blue, she would argue it was magenta. If I asked her to straighten her room, she made it messier. If I told her to babysit her siblings so I could go to the grocery store in peace, she huffed and puffed that I was taking advantage of her. Trying to reason with her was like trying to reason with a toaster. Her side of the conversation was a combination of eye rolls, huffy sighs, and a lot of "whatevers." I had long sleepless nights of worry that something bad was around the corner for my oldest daughter. Guilt flooded my head that I didn't see my youngest daughter was sick.

I flipped open my cell phone and hit Melanie's number.

"You have reached the voice mail of the fabulous Melanie Meiser. You know what to do!"

"Melanie, I'm on a bus with thirty kids and a sick Sarah. Any way you can help me out? Please call me back ASAP."

I clicked off and tried Doug's number.

"This is Doug. Leave me a message."

I gripped the phone as the tic in my eyelid increased. "Hi, Doug, this is Beverly. I'm on a chorus trip to Winston-

Salem, and Sarah's not feeling well. I need to know if you can come get her. Please call me back."

I then tried Beatrice, another teacher friend. The school required so many parent chaperones on school trips to go with the students and travel on the bus. Usually one or two parents would drive, but this trip everyone decided to ride in the bus. I had other adults, but no one to drive Sarah back to Asheville, and so far no one to stay with her.

Sarah groaned and put her arms across her stomach while I scrolled through my contacts. There had to be someone available.

Call Connor.

I discarded that thought the moment I had it. He left that morning at the same time we did, wearing work clothes and heavy boots. He told me in a brief conversation that right after he got back from Thanksgiving, the job crew had gone into overtime, as the deadline for the site completion had moved up.

"It's a right pain in the arse, but the money is good. When this job is done, we'll celebrate."

I didn't know what he meant by that, and I wasn't sure I wanted to.

Every day this week, he'd left early and come home late. Only as a last resort would I dial his number.

I tried Doug again and got his voice mail again.

"Mom" was the single-word warning I got. I had a plastic grocery bag out in record time, just before Sarah heaved into it.

"Ewww, gross! I'm gonna barf too," Mattie contributed.

The smell of kid vomit was pretty nasty, and my own stomach cramped a bit, but I was the mom and the adult in charge. I unearthed another plastic sack and double bagged the mess. I gave Sarah a piece of gum to chew just as my phone rang.

"Damn, Bevvie, what happened? How's Sarah?" It was Melanie.

"Just threw up. I think she's got the bug everyone's been passing around the schools this year."

"Did you get the flu shot for the kids?"

"Yes, but you know it's hit or miss some years. Definitely a miss this time. Are you around today?"

"I'm in Nashville for the math teacher summit weekend. God, I'm so sorry, Bev. Have you tried Bea?"

"Voice mail."

"How 'bout Jessica White's mom?"

"Here with me chaperoning."

"Damn, Bev. I'm guessing you already tried the troll?"

I knew she meant Doug. "I called his number twice already. Voice mail."

"Miss Silicone Boobs?"

My eyelid rapid fired.

"You really think the future stepmother of my children will take the time out of her busy day of mani-pedis to come take care of a sick kid?"

"Point taken. What about your gorgeous neighbor?

"I can't ask him to take care of my sick kid. Besides, he left for work this morning. Told me overtime hours for all."

"Shit, Bev, what are you going to do?"

Good question. What could I do? "I'll keep trying to get a hold of Doug. Thanks anyway, Mellie. I'll call you later."

"Good luck, sweetie, and give Sarah-boo a hug for me."

I clicked off. The bus driver handed me an industrial-strength barf bag over his left shoulder. "Try this instead of the grocery sacks. I get one or two sickies every week this time of year, so I keep me a good supply of 'em at all times."

I thanked him and triple bagged the mess. Sarah groaned again and lay down across my lap as best she could. Mattie started bouncing in time with my eyelid. I dialed Doug again and left another message.

Connor. Should I call Connor?

The bus dropped us off outside of the college music building where the festival was taking place. I made the executive decision that we would sing during our time slot in a few hours and leave immediately to go back to Asheville. It would disappoint my students to not wait for the evaluation results, but unless Doug called me back, I had to get Sarah back home as fast as possible. The other parents were sympathetic to my plight, as all of them knew what it was like to have a sick child.

My chorus students filed off the bus and lined up on the city sidewalk. Mattie got off and started turning cartwheels.

"Mattie!" My snap made three of my bass singers jump.

"Sorry, Mom." He changed from cartwheels to skipping in circles around a huddled group of sopranos.

Does Xanax come in an IV drip?

Sarah leaned heavily against my side. I put an arm around

her as I gave instructions to my students and parents. We went to the warm-up area, which was the school's orchestra room. Sarah slumped to the floor. Mattie skipped over to a set of covered timpani and tried to bang on them.

"Mattie, settle down. Now."

He paused and wandered around the room, sticking his fingers through the open bars of the instrument lockers, trying to touch the cellos and basses inside.

"Mom, I'm gonna be sick again."

This time I wasn't so lucky with getting a bag out in time, and Sarah left the rest of her stomach contents in a Rubbermaid trash can. One of the chaperones ran to find out if building maintenance was around while another took the can outside. I gave Sarah another swig of the Tylenol and prayed it would work. Feelings of complete helplessness threatened to overwhelm me. My little girl was sick, we were miles from home, and there was nothing I could do about it.

My students didn't argue when I made the announcement that we would sing our slotted times and leave. The sight of Sarah curled up on the floor next to me probably had a hand in that. I checked my phone for any callbacks and dialed Doug one more time. Voice mail.

"Mom, I'm stuck." Mattie's arm was elbow deep in a grated locker door.

"Good. You'll stay put for a bit."

"Mom!"

I counted to twenty and moved to rescue my youngest child. "Mattie, I know it's a tough day, and you really didn't want to be here, but I couldn't find a babysitter for the whole day. I need you to be still and stay out of trouble, especially now that your sister is sick. Can you do that for me?"

He screwed up his face. "I'll try."

My eyelid started up again.

I went back to stand in front of the chorus and take them through their warm-up routine. My movements were automatic, but my mind was on the sniffing bundle at my feet. Sarah might be an adult in a child's body, but when she was sick, she turned into every other kid who felt bad. She should have been in bed at home with fresh Tylenol, lots of fluids, and nothing to do but rest. I glanced at my watch. Our time slot began in thirty or so minutes. The full chorus had fifteen minutes to perform, another half hour wait until sight-reading evals, and then an hour before small chamber groups started. I had three on the schedule at various times, and unless the judges started running behind, we had at least four or more hours of being there. Tears of frustration threatened to fall, but I managed to suck them up and keep going.

We were in the cathedral-like foyer outside of the stage area when I lost it. Sarah and Mattie were supposed to hang with one of the parent chaperones while the chorus performed. I lined my students up and got ready to process when I heard a loud bang behind me. I turned to see Mattie halfway up some scaffolding that was pushed to the side. He had knocked over a box, and several tools had fallen to the floor. Sarah was sitting against the wall, her head back and eyes closed. The parent who volunteered to watch them during the performance was nowhere to be found.

Last nerve. Last straw. I blasted my youngest son. "Matthew Edward Archer, get your fanny down from there NOW!" My chorus students froze, and I was sure the judges heard my yell through the thick walls of the recital hall. I could see Mattie's lower lip quiver from where I stood, and it didn't take a genius to figure out a meltdown was on the way. His and mine.

"Yo, key tickler. What's wrong?"

Mike Hodges sauntered up with a younger female version of himself. "This is my daughter, Mary. She and her husband live over in Clemmons, and I came to see my granddaughters do their thing at this caterwaulin' party. What's going on? Your youngin in trouble again?"

I sniffed back the emotion that tried to find its way into my voice. "Hi, Mike. I couldn't get a sitter today, so I have Mattie and Sarah with me. Sarah's sick, and Mattie's bored."

The older man pursed his lips. "Hmmm… got that flu bug, right? Nasty one this year. How much longer you got to stay here?"

"At least another four hours. Could be longer."

Mike pursed his lips and whistled. "I'm sure you done called your people to see if you got anyone. I tell you what. We're heading back to Mary's house for a spell. We don't have to be here again until five thirty. How 'bout we take Sarah and Mattie back to her house? Sarah can rest in the guest bed, and Mattie can get his ya-yas out in the backyard with the dogs. We'll bring 'em both back before you leave to go home."

God liked me. He really did for this lifeline to be dropped in my lap out of nowhere. I didn't know Mary, and handing my kids off to a strange woman wasn't something I'd willingly do, but I knew Mike. He cared about my kids, and I could trust him.

"What do you think, Sarah?" I asked of my daughter. The Tylenol had finally kicked in and her forehead was cooler, but she was still one sick little girl. Her nod was sleepy, and I expected she would conk out very soon.

I looked at Mike. "You sure you want to take on Mattie? You already know he's a handful."

My favorite bass singer grinned at me. "I ain't worried 'bout me. Mary's got three big German shepherds that love to play Frisbee. We'll get that little booger tired out quick."

Another request for a dog was on the horizon, but at the moment, this was my best option.

Kevin, one of my prize students, ambled over and plucked Mattie from the pseudo monkey bars. He was a huge African American kid whose voice was so deep I called him a contrabass. The football coaches wanted his six-foot frame on the playing field; however, Kevin's plans were to major in music and teach someday himself. I think my teaching inspired that in him.

Mary took my kids with her just as the proctor called our school name to the stage. My students started their entrance, and I took one last look at the retreating backs of my kids, Mike, and Mary. Mattie was jumping up and down by Mike's side, and Sarah was leaning on Mary. Multiple emotions swelled up in my gut, and sorting them was impossible.

Get it together, Bev. You have a job to do, and a lot of people are counting on you. Suck it up and get it together. The kids are in good hands.

I sucked it up. At least most of it. My eyes were wet when I made my bow of acknowledgment and lifted my baton. All the bright faces of my students shone back at me in focused expectation. Kevin blew a single note on a pitch pipe at my cue. Then I brought the baton down. I only half conducted them, as my sick little girl occupied most of my mind.

My wonderful students seemed to realize I was not in a good spot. We'd prepared and rehearsed like crazy for this moment. They knew the music backward and forward and took over, working together as one cohesive unit. Oh my God, how they sang! One of the songs was an a cappella piece in Latin, and their enunciations were perfect. Cutoffs were even and precise, no one dropped a cue, and their dynamics were flawless. They were magnificent, and when the last notes came, Kevin dropped down to a low D that reverberated in my chest. I stopped trying to hold it back and let the rivers drop from my eyes.

That was why I was a teacher. Moments like that, when the hard work of my students came together in such beauty it brought us close enough to touch heaven. They knew I was on my last nerve, and they made the magic happen. I wasn't the only one feeling it, as I saw two of the judges wipe their eyes.

Needless to say we received a superior rating, which was

the third highest score of the day overall.

We got through sight reading and chamber groups. No one wanted to enter the solos or duets, and I hadn't pushed anyone to try. Mike and Mary brought back my kids just as my last group performed. Sarah had some color back in her face. Mary had taken very good care of her. "Campbell's chicken noodle soup, crackers, and Gatorade. Best remedies for flu on this earth," she informed me with a wink.

Mattie was tired but gabby with excitement about his afternoon with the dogs. "And then Elvis jumped the fence to get the Frisbee and Mike called him back over, but he couldn't figure out how to jump back in, and Mike had to go open the gate, and then Mya tried to run out…"

His head slumped over against the bus window as his power bar finally reached zero. Kevin loaded him in the van for me once we got to the school building. I texted Abby and Jacob to check on them. I got an immediate response from Jacob about the cool microscope his friend had and could he have one for Christmas. I got nothing from Abby. Three texts later, after I threatened to show up at Phoebe's house in the next ten minutes, she finally sent me one back in all caps: **I'M FINE!!!**

Once all the chorus students had left or been picked up, my day was finished, and I could go home to collapse. Later. I still had stuff to do.

I called Beatrice and that time got her instead of voice mail. She agreed to come sit for me in the morning. Sarah would stay home while I played the church service. Mattie would still go with me. Jacob and Abby would meet us there, and I'd bring everyone back home in the afternoon.

I roused a groggy Mattie, and he made his way up to his room. Sarah took another shot of Tylenol and went to bed herself. I walked out on the front porch to make the dreaded phone call to the kids' dad. Doug never called me back to see about Sarah, nor had he texted. Yet I still thought he should know about his daughter's illness. I flipped open my phone and dialed, expecting to get voice mail again. I was surprised when he answered.

"Jesus, Bev, what the hell is it now?"

I blinked at his tone as he panted loudly in my ear. "Did you get my messages about Sarah?"

"Yeah, she's sick. What am I supposed to do about it? Drive all the way to Winston-Salem to get her? You're out of your mind."

I heard a light female giggle in the background. "Hurry up, Dougie! You need to finish what you started, baby."

Dammit, they were fucking. It was Saturday night, and they were fucking. A shard of icy pain hit my heart, and I lost my breath. It should not have made any difference to me what Doug and Mandy did, but the up-and-down roller coaster of the day had taken its toll on me.

"I thought you'd want to know she's feeling better." Damn, why was my voice so small and pathetic sounding? Where was my biting, sarcastic self?

"Great, I'm glad she's feeling better."

The phone died in my hand.

No, it didn't die. He hung up on me. The father of my children hung up on me because he had "better" things to do than worry about them. Like sticking his dick into his blonde toy.

Any joy I'd experienced from my students' beauty was gone. The relief from Mike showing up to save the day was gone. Replacing all the good stuff was worry about Sarah, guilt at having lost my temper at Mattie, unease about Abby's recent behavior, and to top it all off, humiliation that I called when my ex-husband was fucking his girlfriend. Underneath all of it was a raging frustration that had constantly bubbled in my veins this past year.

"Bev, you okay?"

I turned and saw an equally exhausted Connor make his way over to me on the porch. He was covered in construction detritus, and his face was streaked with black. Apparently, he had just gotten home from his own long, hard day and was exhausted himself.

I should have said yes, thanked him for asking, and then gone to bed. I should have swallowed the ball of anger that had lodged in my throat. I should have simply walked away.

Instead, I spewed venom. "No, I am not okay. I'm sick to death of other people's shit!"

He stepped back and his eyebrows came together. "Jesus, Mary, and Joseph, what the hell is wrong with you?"

Too much was in me to hold back anymore. I went nuclear. "I've had the total day from hell, and I am completely out of shits to give. Sarah got sick, and I had no choice but to make her finish the day when she should have been home in bed. Abby is so far in her own head, I can't find her. I completely lost it with Mattie today and almost made him cry. My piece-of-shit ex can't be bothered to help with his children because he might be *inconvenienced*. Everything concerning them is dumped on me, and I need three of me to keep up. The school administration is talking about another budget cut, one that affects my insurance rates. I have no more hours I can work, I'm working as hard as I can, and still I'm in a perpetual state of being flat-ass, busted broke! I'm fucking sick of it!"

Connor shook his head in confusion. "Sarah's sick?"

"Yeah, and the timing was just perfect. She started throwing up on the bus, and everyone I called to come get her wasn't available. Melanie had a real excuse 'cause she was a couple hours out of town in the opposite direction. Doug was too busy doing other shit, like fucking his pretty blonde trophy. The only saving grace of the day was that Mike from the church showed up when I lost it on Mattie. He's the only reason I got through the day with any sanity. My students did a fantastic job and should have been there for the ceremony after the festival to get their awards, but I had to cut their trip short, because no one could be bothered to give enough of a shit to help me. I had to let my kids *and* my students suffer today, and I had no say in the matter."

"Bev, you're not making any sense."

"I don't give a fuck!"

He stood up straight, his shoulders going back. "You need to calm down, Bev. You didn't call me for help."

I should have recognized the stance as a warning that I was going too far. I didn't. The dam burst in me, and I let the acid flow.

"Don't tell me what I *need* to do. I know what I need. I need a fucking break. You were working overtime like you've been doing all week. No time for me or my kids, so why should I waste my time calling you? Like you'd really drop everything and come get a sick child who's not yours to begin with."

He reeled back as if I'd struck him a blow. "Now I really think you need to calm down."

"I still don't give a fuck! You're my neighbor, not my fucking boss. Not my boyfriend. You're not my kids' father. You have no say in this shit, and you can't fix it."

I knew I had gone too far the moment the words left my mouth. Connor got angry. I'd only seen patience and kindness from the quiet man who lived next door to me. This was a big change, and it was enough to break me out of my uncontrolled tirade.

"Fine. You're right I have nae say. I also don't need this shite in me life either. I've spent four decades on this earth taking care of other people and getting shite on aboot it. I'm done! I'm sick of being the good guy, the one who fixes plumbing and gutters and getting my arse reamed for it. Your kids see me more often than that peckerless *gobshite* of a father they have. I didna seek them out, nor you. We're neighbors, and I've beena bloody good one. Babysitting and science projects and bloody fall festivals. I've finally broken free of one life-sucking family, and the last thing I want to get involved in is another one."

The fight leaked out of me as I took the verbal blows. I started it, but he finished it. He tromped across the porch to his front door and pulled out his keys. I tried to bring my sense of outrage back, but it was gone. Replaced by painful regret.

He opened his door and looked back at me with both anger and disappointment in his eyes. "You know damn weel I would have dropped everything to come get Sarah."

With that parting shot, he stomped in his house. The sharp snap of the door closing sounded like a punctuation mark. I lifted my hands to my face and found them shaking. *Fuck me, what have I done?* A single sob escaped my mouth before I could stifle it.

Mattie was out cold on top of his bedcover. He'd only put on his pajama top and made it halfway with the bottoms before conking out completely. I took the blanket from Jacob's bed and covered him up. Sarah was asleep as well. I placed a hand on her forehead. She was warm, but the fever was gone. I let my fingers stroke over her pretty blonde hair. She got her looks and hair from Doug and her feisty attitude from me. *God, I love my children.* They were worth everything.

I did my nightly routine robotically. I still had stuff to prepare for tomorrow morning's work, but at the moment, I didn't care. When I was finally in my safe place, I pressed my pillow to my face and let it go. I cried into the polyester and cotton until I was empty. It took a while. I'd heard that a good cry released endorphins or some other hormone in your brain and that was what made you feel better. My cry? Not.

Time was linear and always moved forward. This was

just another bump in a long road. A big one, but still a bump.

I survived a gut-wrenching divorce. I can survive this too. Next time I see Connor, I need to put on my big girl panties and apologize. We may not be friends anymore, but we could still get along as neighbors. At least, I hoped so.

My head was stuffy, and my eyes puffed out from my pillow therapy. I let them close and hoped they were normal by tomorrow morning.

* * *

Connor pulled down a bottle of Jameson whiskey and a shot glass from his kitchen cabinet. "Bloody feckin' hell," he muttered as he put the glass back, unscrewed the cap, and took a swig directly from the bottle. The burn lit up his throat as he swallowed. His back spasmed as he tilted the bottle up and took a second drink, reminding him he was not a young man anymore. The day had been filled with miscommunication from the site foreman, which turned into more time on the clock to complete the framing deadline. By the time this work week ended, Connor had logged in just under one hundred hours of labor. The time-and-a-half pay was great for his bank account but not so great for his body and mind.

When he'd worked with his father in the family business, overtime pay was forbidden. If extra contractors had to be hired, Fergus expected his sons to take up the slack to avoid paying out time-and-a-half wages. Usually, it was Connor who did the time. Today had been a bitter reminder of those days.

"Connor, did you get the supplies ordered for the Jamestown Inn job?"

"What Jamestown Inn job?"

"The one we start next week."

"When did that get booked?"

"I told you about it last month!"

"No you didn't. It's not on the calendar schedule."

"Yes I did."

"We need to delay, then. Everyone is working sixteen-hour days to get this job done, and we're running behind. I'll need to get some independent contractors to have a hope of finishing in time."

"Jesus, Mary, and Joseph, boy! We don't have the budget for that! You and your brothers will just have to work harder."

"There's only twenty-four hours in a day, Da. We can't work 'round the clock. Tired men are not safe men."

"Pah, you lot are too soft. Find a way to fix it, Connor."

"Fix it, Connor."

"Fix it, Connor!"

"FIX IT, CONNOR!"

He cried out and slammed the cabinet closed, knocking one of the hinges off. Fuck, how many times had he heard those three words over and over again during the last years he worked for the family business? He cared deeply about his family, but the weight of their responsibility had nearly brought him to his knees and driven him mad. His father blamed him for the dissolution of the company and rarely spoke to him. Maybe that was why he had some affinity for the kids next door.

Beverly. Goddamn Beverly. She looked devastated when he saw her on the front porch. As tired as he was, he wanted nothing more than to take her in his arms and hold her close. He wanted to find out whatever it was that put that expression on her face and take it away. Instead, she exploded. Her words about Sarah being sick alarmed him, as he had dealt with that when Eva was a child. But after that, the jumble that fell from her mouth drove spikes into his heart. Memories flooded his brain of the times his father screamed at him for not working hard enough, and when he drove himself to the brink of exhaustion, Fergus expected more. Da was never satisfied, never grateful, never gave the slightest nod of approval or accolade for a job well done.

"No time for me or my kids, so why should I waste my time calling you?"

Did she really feel that way?

"Like you'd really drop everything and come get a sick child who's not yours to begin with."

Christ, that hurt. That really hurt.

He took three more pulls from the bottle before putting it on the counter. The alcohol hit his empty stomach and went straight to his head. Any residual energy he had left drained away as he made his way up the stairs. He stripped and flopped on his bed, not bothering to brush his teeth. A muffled sound behind his head caught his attention. Beverly was crying. He'd heard it before, but this time it was more intense and raw.

Fix it, Connor.

"No. Not this time."

Chapter 11

Christmas was my most favorite time of the year. I loved the music, the decorations, putting up the tree with all the kids' handmade ornaments, the snow, shopping for presents, and wrapping everything in pretty paper. Every year, I swore to scale back, and every year, I always went a little overboard.

The church was full of happy chaos in preparation. It was Christmas Eve, and the evening service would be full of pageantry for the season. The choir would be singing several anthems, the youth group had prepared some skits, and the kids had their manger scene. All my kids were involved. Abby had several speaking parts, Sarah would be in the kids' choir, Jacob was running the lights and sound with Mike, and Mattie was Christmas tree number five. I got recruited to sing a solo while the handheld candles were lit. I loved it!

The church had become much more than just a place of worship. My little family became a part of a bigger family, one that didn't judge or look down on me for being a divorced woman. The support my kids had from their friends and the other adults in their lives probably didn't make up for an absent father, but it came close. Abby was a solid part of the youth group, and even though I was sure her fascination with Ashton was part of her drive to be there, she still seemed to find a place for herself. Jacob had fallen in love with the tech board, mics, and other sound equipment, and the people who ran that committee loved having him work alongside them. Sarah mostly stuck with me in the music department and sang in the young kids' choir. She really did have a nice voice and was starting to use it more and more. Mattie? He fit in wherever he went. That kid never met a stranger.

"Mom, I need the programs." Jacob ran up to me while I was finishing Mattie's green makeup tree face.

"Out in the foyer."

"I didn't see them."

"Check the podium on the left."

"Oh. Okay." He headed off in that direction.

"How's my face? Do I look like a Christmas tree?"

I smiled at the green grinning face looking up from his decorated cardboard triangle. "Yes, Mattie-boo, you are the best Christmas tree ever."

"Coolio!"

He wandered off to join the other four trees, all of them awkwardly sandwiched between the cutout costume and bumping into each other.

There was about ten minutes left before the service started. Sarah finished handing out candles to the massive amount of people pouring through the doors, then came to sit with me at the piano bench and leaned in to my body.

"Dad's not coming tonight."

Shot to the heart.

"I don't know, sweetie. I told him about it, but I didn't hear one way or the other. Maybe he'll show up."

"I'm singing a solo. It's not a big one. Just a couple lines, but it's my first one."

Sarah had been getting more and more depressed over the lack of time with her father. She had always been a daddy's girl, and lately, that was getting harder for her to handle. He'd never called her when she was sick, and knowing my smart little Sarah, she noticed.

"I'm sure he's running a bit late."

Sarah shook her head. "He's on a cruise in Bermuda with Mandy for Christmas and New Year's."

Shit. Doug didn't say a word to me about those holiday plans. I had no idea he would be out of the country for the holidays. I asked a few weeks ago about when he was going to see the children, and he said he would get back to me when he could. In all the hullabaloo of the past week, I hadn't called to remind him about it and made the assumption he would see them sometime between the two holidays. I could tell my back was tightening up, but now was not the time.

"Well, there's a whole church stuffed full of people to hear you sing, and Jacob is up in the tech room filming. We can get a copy and show your dad when he gets back. Melanie is coming tonight too, and when we're done, all of us will go home and open one present apiece before Santa comes."

She gave me her look. "Santa's not real, Mom. Even Mattie knows it's you who puts out the presents."

I sniffed and put my nose in the air. "Santa will always be real in my household, and besides that, it's the perfect excuse to have cookies and milk at midnight. Now, I have to get the prelude going. Are you sticking with me or sitting with the kids' choir?"

"Kids' choir."

"Best get to it, then."

She hopped down from the bench, and my eyes followed her to the group of kids sitting on the third row. How could Doug miss another… *nope, I can't think about it now. I have a job to do and it's Christmas. I'm not about to let him spoil it.*

I took a cleansing breath, held it, and let it out slowly. Showtime.

The church had a fantastic music ministry. I accompanied the children's groups as well as the adult choir. When Sarah got up to sing her two solo lines, I saw her face light up with a big smile. My heart clenched, thinking her father showed up after all to make her night, but when I risked a glance over to where she was waving, I didn't see Doug. I saw Connor. He smiled and gave Sarah a little wave back. I hadn't talked to him since the night I had my meltdown a few weeks ago. Jacob was still in his good graces and had been in the workshop, and I was forever grateful that Connor was not a vindictive man. He could have refused to help my son after the shit I spewed at him. Sarah made a special point to invite him to services to hear her sing. I was glad he didn't take his anger at me out on my children.

His hair had been recently cut, and he was wearing khaki trousers, a dress shirt, and a tie. This was the first time I'd seen him in something other than jeans or work clothes. He looked really good.

Next to him was a pretty blonde woman. I almost missed my cue as a stab of pain hit my gut.

Stop it, Bev. That ship has not only sailed, it was never in the harbor to begin with. Even if it was, you put an anchor through the hull and set it on fire.

The service progressed as smooth as silk. The choir sounded great, the lights and sound system worked perfectly, Abby didn't stutter or stumble when she spoke, and Sarah's solo was beautiful, if I did say so myself. Mattie danced around with the other Christmas trees, completely entertaining the people in the congregation. When it came time for me, I got up to sing during the lighting of the candles.

Don't look, don't look, don't look, I chanted to myself. *I'm a professional and need to be on task here.*

The organist started the classic carol "O Holy Night." I closed my eyes so it was just me and the music and let the rich flowing notes wash over me. I opened my mouth and let it pour. I filled my voice with all the emotions in me and let it ring throughout the rafters of the church. As the tiny candle flame passed from person to person, I sang my hurt. I sang my loneliness. I sang my heart. At the end, my voice soared, and I could feel the warmth of the sea of candlelight shining back on me. It was brilliant.

My throat closed up at the final notes of the song, and the congregation erupted in applause. I finally braved a glance at Connor. His eyes met mine as his hands clapped together, and he smiled at me. I smiled back. An ache bloomed in my heart.

After the service, I played several carols as the people exited. My kids came running up to me.

"Mom, Mike says I ran the lights like a pro."

"The candles were so pretty."

"I didn't miss any of my words."

"I'm hungry."

I laughed at the green face shining up at me from between the two triangles. "We'll go home and get some food in a bit."

"Beverly?" Connor suddenly appeared, and I couldn't breathe.

"Mom, Connor came!"

"Did you hear me sing?"

"I was an awesome tree, right?"

Connor looked down at my clamoring kids. "The most awesome tree I've ever seen. Sarah, your solo was fantastic. All of you were great." He looked right at me. "All of you."

I swear if he'd touched me right then, I would've shattered. *Shit, Bev, get it together!*

"Bevvie! That was sooooo good! Damn—I mean darn, girlfriend. I knew you had a nice set of pipes, but holy sh… ah… sugar that was great."

Thank God Melanie showed up and broke the spell. "We're still on for Christmas at your place, right? I got a car full of presents for your hooligans that are dying to be opened, and we have to do it tonight!"

I mentally shook myself. The euphoria of the performance had worn off, and I was back in my normal mom mode, slipping into that persona easily.

"My house is always open for presents. Give me twenty minutes to get this bunch home and we'll do the hot chocolate and Santa thing."

"Deal." Melanie turned to Connor. "You coming over too?"

"I can't tonight. This is Camille, and we have a party to get to."

Camille smiled and raised her chin like she was coming down from her high throne to join the masses. "Connor's told me so much about you. You have a nice voice, Belinda."

"It's Beverly, and thank you."

Connor didn't notice the glare his companion gave me. "Mind if I come by tomorrow? Give the kids their presents?"

"Yeah, that'd be fine, Connor. We'll be home."

"Oh no, Connor, we'll be at my parents' house all day, and it will be very late before we get back." Camille's trill was polite but grating. She clung to Connor's arm like she was afraid he would leave her alone with the throng of kids surrounding us.

Melanie jumped in. "Too bad. We have our own party going, don't we? It's a pajama day of food, games, presents, and binging on all the classic Christmas movies."

Even Abby showed some excitement.

"Merry Christmas, and enjoy your evening. Connor, we

really have to get going."

He looked at the woman hanging from his arm, smiled, and nodded at her. "I'll come by sometime next week. Merry Christmas, everyone."

He turned to go.

"Connor?" I stopped him in a small voice, and he turned back, meeting my eyes. "I'm sorry."

Two words. That was all I said. I'd been rehearsing a long, heartfelt apology speech for days, and all I had in me was those two little words.

He nodded and his face relaxed. "Me too."

He left with Camille, off to something fabulous, I was sure.

I stayed mostly silent. My smartass-ness just wasn't there. Melanie took over and hustled the kids to the van. I drove home on autopilot while the kids picked over each nuance of the evening.

"Did you hear my high notes? I nailed them all."

"Mike said I did a great job with the soundboard. Even when he tried to mute the altos and I wouldn't let him."

"Lots of people said they liked my tree dance. Mom, you did really good too."

"Thanks, Mattie-boo. Almost home. Who's ready for hot chocolate?"

A chorus of "me" rattled the windows as I pulled into the driveway. Connor's truck was there, but his lights were out. I guessed he had ridden with Camille in her car to the party, 'cause there was no way he could have beaten me home that quick. Melanie pulled up and parked on the street. Five minutes later, I was nuking mugs of water and opening envelopes of Swiss Miss hot chocolate mix with mini marshmallows. The girls had gone upstairs to change clothes. Mattie and Jacob were next to the tree sorting packages into individual piles.

"So, what's the deal with Connor?" Melanie leaned against the counter and picked up a spoon. "I thought we were making progress."

"We weren't making anything. Connor is a friend. That's it." *At least, I hope he still is.*

She stirred the powder into the hot water. "There's more there if you'd just look, Bevvie. He's always over here, fixing something, hangs out with the kids, eats with your family, and he even came to church to see you tonight."

"Correction. He told me he gets discounts from the landlord for fixing stuff around the duplex. The kids go bother him more than he comes and bothers us. And the church thing? Did you not see the swanky piece he was with? He came to see the kids, not me."

"Of course he came to see you."

"No he didn't."

"Yes he did."

"Mellie, I promise you, he didn't. We had a sort of fight a while back, and we haven't spoken much since. You remember the show choir's field trip when Sarah got sick? I had the day from absolute hell and took it out on him. I need to find time to apologize to him for real instead of two lame words."

She dropped the spoon into the next cup with a splash.

"Jesus, Bev, send the man a text already."

I shook my head. "Nope. Some things you have to do in person. Breaking up is one. Apologizing is another." I picked up four cups in two hands, easily carrying them from years of practice.

Melanie grabbed the other two. "You broke up with him?"

"How can I break up with someone I'm not dating? We had a fight. One I started, and I need to make an apology."

"But don't you miss—"

"You can't miss what you never had. Please, Mellie, drop it. He's out with another woman and spending time with her family this holiday. I'm spending time with mine and hoping the kids don't feel the sting of their father's absence too much."

Melanie's face darkened, but she nodded in agreement. "Okay, Bev. I'll table myself for tonight, but I'm not gonna cry if Doug gets his ass chewed up by a shark."

I grinned at her quiet hiss. Whatever happened in this life, I knew I had my BFF at my back. "All right, kiddie-winkies, who's up for presents?"

In ten minutes or less, my small living room was awash in colored paper and ribbons as the kids tore into their stuff from Melanie. The rest I made them wait to open Christmas morning. Abby loved her new makeup kit with all the different eyeshadow colors. Sarah wanted to start the friendship bracelet kit she got. Jacob perused all the different slides in his microscope set, and Mattie screamed in excitement over the video game he'd wanted. Other smaller, more practical gifts came from me, like colored pencils, drawing paper, socks and underwear, and sweaters. Doug would give them gift cards or money. Eventually. I hoped.

Sarah put a DVD in, and we started watching the movie *Elf*. The kids settled on the sofa with Melanie and me. Abby didn't bother watching at all; she excused herself to go to her room and play with her new makeup. A big plate of cookies and gingerbread men was slowly demolished.

After the excitement of the gifts, one by one we started crashing. Mattie was out cold by the end of the opening credits, and both Jacob and Sarah were staring blankly at Will Ferrell's antics. I hustled them off to bed and roused Mattie enough to crawl upstairs. He still had some green on his face, but I let it go. Melanie made it through half the movie before she gave a big cow yawn and made her excuses to leave.

The house was quiet with the kids tucked in, the lights off, the noise gone. Me? I was lonely as hell. Being by myself during the holiday had finally gotten to me. I changed clothes, washed and moisturized, brushed, and did as much as I could to waste time before I had to climb into an empty bed. I placed my hand on the shared wall between Connor and me. Silence was all that came from his side. I sniffed a few times and let the tears flow down my cheeks. It was safe for me to do that now. I didn't have to explain or justify my feelings to anyone. I let the congealed pain in my heart drain out as I quietly cried into my pillow.

If Connor came home, I didn't hear him.

Chapter 12

I sucked in a breath and forced the spandex over my thighs, hips, and stomach in one go. Past experience told me that I had one shot at getting a body shaper in place before it rolled up in a painful tire around my waist. The unforgiving elastic snapped under my breasts, and I prepared to not take a full breath for the next few hours.

New Year's Eve and I had a date. A nice one. Melanie found one last gasp for me on Meet-n-Match and gave him my contact information. I read his profile when she sent it to me, and I have to say, I was rather impressed. He was a lawyer at a well-known firm, specializing in constitutional law, and he was up for a partnership. He played tennis and golf and coached several youth club teams. The picture he posted showed a tall man with a slim but athletic build, styled dark hair, and blue eyes, wearing a suit and tie. He was handsome, professional, probably articulate, and totally out of my league.

But he was also nice, and dammit, I was lonely.

He was taking me to a swanky restaurant and then to a

New Year's Eve bash at a fancy resort hotel. His text came a few nights ago.

Joe: **Hello, Beverly. I'm Joe from Meet-n-Match. How are you this evening?**

Me: **I'm fine. Hope you are as well.**

Joe: **Yes, I'm well. Our team has been working on one case for months, and this morning, we won. Great start for the new year. I saw on your profile you teach chorus and freelance as a piano accompanist. You must be incredibly talented. I love working with students. I bet you do too.**

Me: **Thank you. I see you're a lawyer and do some charity work with kids.**

Joe: **Yes, however, I don't consider it charity. It's a privilege to coach and help children that may not get the chance to play otherwise. Some people say golf and tennis are games for rich people. I think games are for everyone.**

Hmmmm. Good answer.

Joe: **Do your kids play any sports?**

Me: **My youngest son played soccer at his school this past fall. He wants to join a summer league. My other kids are not sports-minded.**

Joe: **It takes a strong person to handle so much. Four children, a full-time career, and freelancing? Must be hard to find time for yourself.**

As I read those words, a tingle in my sinuses started. Yes, it was hard. Very hard. Doug called the children Christmas morning and spoke to them for all of ten minutes. No presents and no promises of anything. The vacation week from Christmas to New Year's was my time to regroup and recharge for the second semester. So far, I was still burned out. Emotionally, spiritually, and physically burned out.

Joe: **I know this is out of the blue and probably too soon, but are you free?**

Me: **I'm not free, but I'm not expensive either.**

Joe: **LOL You crack me up! I meant for New Year's Eve. Do you have plans?**

Me: **I'm flying to New York to party like a college kid and freeze my ass off while watching the ball drop. If you turn on the TV, I'll be the one waving at the camera.**

Joe: **LMAO**

Me: **Seriously, I'm probably going to stay home with the kids, eat junk food, and watch the ball drop on TV.**

Joe: **How about I offer you an alternative?**

Me: **???**

Joe: **I'd love to take you to dinner at the Omni and then the New Year's gala. Music, dancing, and fine wine. I know it's a little much for a first date, but I'm betting it's been a while since someone treated you to a nice night out with your kind of schedule. I could use one myself. I've not had a break from work in quite a while. I promise no pressure. Just a nice time with good wine and good conversation. Interested?**

Me: **I'm not sure I can get a sitter.**

Joe: **What about your oldest girl? Fifteen right?**

Me: **Last time I let her watch the younger ones for an evening, I came home to a ceiling fan on the floor and an**

explosion of every ingredient I had in my kitchen.

I remembered that night well. I had gone to a movie with Melanie and came home to find Abby had spent the last two and a half hours texting her friends and doing something called a "selfie train," while Jacob tried to replicate some bread experiment he found on the internet and Mattie played Tarzan. Sarah watched and took pictures.

Joe: **:-D**

Joe: **No chance, then? I'd really like to see you and get to know you better.**

I had hesitated. I was still mixed up about Connor. He and Jacob were still working on his mysterious science project, and Sarah had sat on the front porch watching and talking while he shoveled snow from the driveway. The interaction between us had regressed back to the hi and bye waves from when we first met. Our one visit this past week had been for him to bring over some presents he bought for the kids. He gave Abby and Sarah gift cards to their favorite clothing store, a chemistry set for Jacob, and a copy of Dance Dance Revolution for Mattie.

He had smiled when he handed the video game to my youngest. "Here ya' go, lad. Maybe this will burn off some of that extra energy."

What did he give me? A hundred-dollar gift card to Target. Not exactly something that screamed romantic interest, but the practicality of the gift meant more to me than some plastic or glass object I had to dust.

What did I give him? Much less than he gave me. I got him a school hoodie with the printed mascot on the front and baked him a Christmas coffee cake ring. Lame, I know, but it was what I had and what I could afford. When I handed him the sweet treat, I took a big breath and dialed up my courage. "I owe you an apology for jumping at you like I did. That day really sucked big-time. I wasn't in a good mood, and I took it out on you. I didn't mean a word I said. I know you're there for my kids, and I'm more grateful than I can ever say that you're in their lives." *Mine too.* "I'm really sorry." *Sorrier than I can find words to express.* "Can you forgive me someday?" *I miss you so much.*

As an apology, it was lacking a lot, but he smiled at me in acceptance. "I understand, and I'm sorry too. I shouldn't have said what I said. I think both of us were in bad places. Let's put it away and forget about it. Deal?"

His green eyes looked into mine, and I held my breath. God in heaven, he was beautiful! He seemed to relax and stuck out his hand. I took it and repeated, "Deal."

I stared at Joe's invitation and thought about Connor's face when I took his hand and shook it. At Halloween, he was happy. Thrilled to be with me and my family, having a great time, and his smiling face showed it. The night I went off on him, he looked hurt, betrayed. I should know what that feels like, as it was done to me. My apology garnered forgiveness, but the friendship between Connor and me changed. Fuck me, I did it. I owned it. I had to live with it and move on from it.

Joe: **You still there?**

Me: **Yes, I'm here. I'm thinking. Abby might try again if I promise her a trip to the mall. I can ask my friend**

Melanie if she's free. I expect she already has plans.

Joe: **It would mean a lot to me if you can make arrangements. If you need to hire a sitter, I'll be glad to help pay for that. I'm not trying to be pushy or impress you with how much money I have. I just want you to know I can help and I'm glad to do it.**

I read those words several times and made my decision.

Me: **You don't have to pay for anything. I'll figure something out. I'll text Melanie and see what she's doing. If not, I'll try Abby again.**

As luck would have it, Melanie had broken up with Gabe, or Ian, or whomever she was seeing at that moment and jumped at the chance to hang with the kids and let me go out for a night of adult company.

I was wearing my bargain basement little black dress and Bach-head slippers when Melanie arrived.

"Yass, girlfriend! You look fantastic. You *are* going to change footwear, though, right?"

"Of course I am. I'm gonna wear my work sneakers in case we go dancing at his ritzy club."

She sat on my bed and started rummaging through her suitcase of a purse. "You know, I don't know whether to take you seriously or not. I think you'd wear those sneakers in a heartbeat if you thought you could get away with it. That's why I brought you these. I use them all the time."

She handed me a pair of oblong cushions that resembled jelly. "Put them in your heels and your feet will last longer."

I fingered the mushy inserts. "Are you sure about this? These things feel like they'll topple me over."

"Just try the damn things, Bevvie."

I slipped them into my black heels, put them on, and stood up. The gel squished around but surprisingly felt kinda good. "I can live with this. Thanks, Mellie."

"You can thank me by letting me do your hair and makeup."

I held up one hand. "Oh, no. I'm still out of hair spray from Halloween, and my makeup is minimal utility from CVS, not the Sephora counter. Last time I let you mess with my face, I ended up with fake lashes that wouldn't come off. It felt like caterpillars were crawling on my eyelids."

She huffed at me. "I'm not gonna go overboard. I've got hot curlers and some Mary Kay samples in here that will work for your skin tone. I promise nothing elaborate, just a little extra frosting." Her eyes begged me to give in. "Please, Bevvie, let me do this for you."

I gave in with the caveat that if I didn't like it, I could go wash my face and redo it myself.

When she was done I had to admit she did do a nice job and was subtler than I'd ever seen her do for herself. She highlighted my cheekbones with a little gold shimmer with a light contouring blush, which somehow made my eyes pop. No false lashes, but she did use some heavy-duty mascara that didn't clump up like it did when I applied it. My hair turned out long and wavy, and instead of letting it hang freely, she produced a rhinestone barrette and clipped the dark mass high on the back of my head to fall down my back. I looked in the mirror and almost didn't recognize myself. I looked… pretty.

"You have a great neckline, Bevvie. Here is the only finishing touch you need."

She produced a pair of glittering chandelier earrings that threw off iridescent sparkles. I knew they were rhinestones; Melanie bought high-quality costume jewelry. These were expensive as hell.

"I can't wear those. What if I lose one?"

She shrugged. "I've had them for years. Not many occasions to wear them, and besides, they don't have real good memories from the last time I wore them. Maybe you'll have better luck."

I wanted to ask about those memories, but the doorbell rang. My stomach suddenly knotted. "Joe's here." I was going on a real date.

Shit, I'm going on a real date!

I might have hyperventilated except I couldn't take too many deep breaths in the spandex around my middle.

Melanie took my hand and looked into my panicked eyes. "Calm down, Bevvie. Joe wouldn't be here if he wasn't interested. I stalked him on Facebook, and his page is full of pics of the kids he coaches. There was one of him accepting an award and a few of him sipping wine at a vineyard. I know I said it before, but this guy is the real deal. Just relax and be yourself. You give so much to everyone around you and forget yourself in the mix. It's high time you get your slice of life's happiness, girlfriend. Take it with both hands and run with it."

Tears built up in my eyes at her words.

She dropped my hands and shrugged. "If things don't

work out, at least you might get laid."

I couldn't help but burst out laughing. Leave it to my BFF for a real pep talk.

"Mom, someone's at the door."

Sarah's monotone yell came up the steps. I grabbed my long coat and gloves from the bed and made my way carefully down the stairs. The gel moved weirdly between my toes, but Melanie was right—my feet were pain free. Sarah glared at me from the bottom with her arms crossed. She didn't like me going out at all and didn't hesitate to show it. Mattie and Jacob were oblivious to the goings-on in the room, both of them working the video game controllers. Abby stayed in her room and didn't bother to come out, even when Melanie arrived.

Joe stood just inside the door in a dark suit and tie with neatly styled hair. His handsome face broke into a big smile when he saw me. He had a bouquet of roses in his hand, and his eyes glowed as he scanned me head to toe. I felt like a teenager on prom night, and his admiration seemed genuine.

"Beverly, you look amazing. I'm honored and happy you're coming out with me tonight."

He bent in to kiss my cheek and handed me the roses. Forget prom night. I had a serious case of first-date jitters. I sent up a quick prayer that my breath was fresh and I wouldn't spill anything on my dress at dinner.

"I have reservations for us at the Vue, the restaurant in the hotel. Some of my colleagues from the firm will be there, but I got a table just for us. I hope that's okay?"

"Yes, that's fine." My voice came out a bit breathy, but I put that down to the spandex.

Melanie clapped her hands. "All right, kids. Check both ways before you cross the street, and no set curfew. Have a great time. Now scoot!"

Joe's low laugh reached my ears as he lifted my hand and placed it in the crook of his elbow. My stomach clenched even harder as his fingers threaded through mine.

"'Night, kids. Behave yourselves. 'Night, Mellie, and thanks for everything."

She winked as she closed the door. I heard her call out, "All right, kiddie-winkies, who's up for pizza and Jenga?"

I stared at the ground, concentrating on every stiff step I took to make sure I didn't trip or catch my heel in something. Joe drove a low-slung Audi sports car that I was sure cost more than what I earned in a year. Probably two. He opened the door for me, and somehow I managed to maneuver into the seat without flumping or falling down. Damn, even the interior smelled high class.

He got in on his side as I was fastening my seat belt. "Mind if I get this out of the way now?"

I looked up at his question. He reached his hand to my neck and drew me closer to him over the middle console. Then he kissed me.

Oh. My. God. He *kissed* me!

I should have jerked back, told him off for being so forward, and exited the car without falling out of it.

I didn't.

His lips moved over mine, gentle and soft. He slanted his

head, fitting his mouth against mine and taking us deeper. A zing ran all the way to my toes. Heat flushed through my body, and my breasts suddenly grew heavy. The kiss continued on and on, Joe taking his slow, sweet time. His fingers stroked under my chin and rested against the pulse in my neck that I was sure gave away my racing heart. When he finally ended it and pulled away, I could only imagine what I looked like. Flushed, perhaps some pupil dilation, and definitely breathing hard.

"There. Now it won't be so awkward later when I kiss you at midnight."

He smiled and winked at me before he settled back in his seat, fastened his own seat belt, and started the car.

For once in my life, I had no words. Nothing. I sat in a luxury sports car with a handsome professional man who had just touched me in a way I hadn't been touched in a long time. I couldn't even call up a memory of feeling this way when Doug and I shared intimate moments. I was sure there were some, but at the moment, my brain only thought about the buzz in my middle and how much I looked forward to midnight.

The Omni was a high-end resort hotel that had a beautiful view of the surrounding mountains and overlooked its own private golf course. I played piano at a wedding there once in the grand ballroom and remembered the majesty of the place. From the stone façade, the classic furnishings, the carved fountains, to the spas and pools, it was the epitome of opulence. One night there in a regular room would be the equivalent of a month's grocery bill. One night in one of their fanciest rooms would cost me an entire month's salary.

Joe drove up in the circular driveway, leaving the purring engine running as he jogged around the front to open my door. He offered his hand, perfectly willing to help me out of the car. Better than him see me heave my body upward solo. I teetered on my heels but remained upright. He nodded to the waiting valet and moved my hand to the crook of his elbow again.

"Ready?"

Absolutely not. This is way over the top for me. I do not belong here. I'm in over my head. What the hell was I thinking? I blinked and covered my crazy running thoughts with a big smile and a confident "Whenever you are."

The Vue had a five-star rating. I was sure if I looked it up, it would have four or five dollar signs next to it, indicating it was also super expensive. The tables were decked out in fine china and crystal, and a gazillion forks and other cutlery surrounded the shiny plates. Maybe not a gazillion, but a lot more than I knew what they were used for. I was afraid to sit in the dark wood chair, both because of how pricey everything looked and how my dress would ride up my spandex-wrapped thighs. My body shaper crept down a bit. God help me if I had to get up and pee; the thing had a snap crotch that was awkward as hell to open and then refasten.

Joe helped me into my chair and sat in his own across from me. After making a wine request to the hovering waiter, he took my hands in his, making me put my elbows on the table and lean forward a bit. His eyes glowed in the mellow light of the short candle in the middle, and his thumbs circled gently over my knuckles. The ambiance of the dining room was old-world lavish and intimately romantic, especially with the spectacular view of the setting sun over the mountains. It was so beautiful, and I so didn't belong.

"Beverly, are you okay?"

I looked at Joe, his handsome face showing concern. Since we left my ratty little duplex, he had done nothing but treat me like a queen. Even the kiss we shared in the car was more giving on his part than mine. *Get over yourself, Bev.*

"I'm fine. I'm just not used to this level of lavishness. I guess I'm just a little nervous."

"I get that. I'm a little nervous too."

I gave him my teacher look. "Why would *you* be nervous?"

He dropped his eyes to our clasped hands. "I finally got matched up with this fantastic woman, and I haven't been able to get her off my mind. Even on the internet, first impressions last the longest, and my first impression was she's gorgeous, talented, strong-willed, and I'm really attracted to her. When I asked her out, I was sweating bullets, because she might refuse and she might say yes. She did say yes, and I knew I had to go all out. The best restaurant, the best wine, the whole nine yards. I'm anxious because I want her to be pleased with me."

It surprised me that he had been so worried. He appeared to be calm and in control, and his masterful kiss earlier wasn't uneasy in the least. I kicked up a corner of my mouth.

"If you need to hear it, I'm very pleased."

He smiled back at me and seemed to relax. He kept a hold of my hands, only releasing one when the waiter presented and uncorked the chosen bottle of wine. Joe tasted the sample and nodded his approval. The rest of dinner was full of questions and conversation. I found out Joe had three older sisters and was originally from Connecticut. Never married, but had come close once before he moved to North Carolina.

"I couldn't be what she needed, and she couldn't be what I needed. The breakup got pretty ugly, which is another reason I took this job here in Asheville. I needed the peace of these mountains to heal from that."

"I can relate. When Doug left, I was shell-shocked at first. I thought we were happy and in the marriage together, raising our kids, building our home. I was wrong. Somewhere along the way, he got unhappy. I couldn't make him happy anymore, and by the time he schemed his money and left, I'm not sure there was any happy worth saving. He found a new happy with another woman, and here we are now." I shrugged. "I won't lie and say that it doesn't sting. It still does, but I've gotten okay with it. My problem now is how he treats the kids. But you know, I can't change that, and one day, he may look back and regret what he lost when he threw away his family."

Joe's eyes stared into mine. "You're beautiful."

My heart fluttered. This man was into me. Really into me, and it felt so damn good. I was riding on cloud nine when the steaks arrived and still floating when I spotted

Doug and Mandy being seated a few tables over from us. She wore a creamy winter white and gold bandage dress, and her strappy heels were higher and spikier than the ones I wore. Doug wore a shiny suit that I bet had a fancy designer name attached to it. *I guess he lied about the cruise to Sarah.* Anger briefly flashed through me that he would be that callous to his kids, but truthfully, nothing surprised me about that man anymore.

I visualized getting up, walking over to their table, and giving Doug a piece of my mind, but with my luck, I'd trip and fall over. I could see my dress riding up and exposing the cloth cage holding me together. Instead, I took a sip of wine and settled myself.

Stop it, Bev. You're on a date with a really great guy. The food and wine are fantastic, and Joe is really, really nice. Take a breath and relax like Melanie said. You got this.

I hazarded another glance at their table. Mandy might have looked like a runway model, but her mouth curled down in a frown. It appeared she was mad at something, and from the hand gestures she made, that something was Doug. His jacket hung open, revealing his soft belly pooch, and his hair looked unkempt for a change with two pieces sticking out next to his ear. His demeanor was placating as he tried to use words to soothe his angry fiancée, but she wasn't having it. She crossed her arms and turned away from him in a major showy snit.

I stifled a laugh.

"Something funny?" Joe cut into his excellent steak and lifted a brow at me.

A huge smile broke out on my face, and I had to share. "See that couple over there? That's my ex-husband and the woman he's now engaged to. Looks like they're having a lover's spat."

Joe looked over and his eyes widened in surprise. "*That's* your ex? His fiancée? Jesus, I've seen that guy around. I thought the girl was his daughter."

I laughed out loud and didn't try to suppress it. Out of the corner of my eye, I saw Doug look over at our table. He didn't recognize me at first but then did a double take, and I knew he saw me. Really saw me. It was at that moment Joe took my hand and raised it to his lips, kissing the back of it.

"I'm glad you're here with me and not him."

This was a picture-perfect romance novel, and I was right in the middle. It was amazing what a little confidence boost could do. I preened a little.

Dinner was delicious, and if I used the wrong fork or something, I didn't care. Joe never said a word of criticism about anything I did or didn't do. He was solicitous the entire time, smiling and winking at me, paying attention to whatever I said and adding to the conversation himself.

I was having a blast. Maybe it was the wine. Maybe it was the way Joe treated me. Maybe it was seeing Doug not so happy with his new life. Whatever it was, I wished I could bottle and sell it. My kids could go to Ivy League colleges with the profit I'd make.

Joe escorted me to the ballroom, where a band had set up and was playing tunes from the 80s and 90s. There was no pain in my feet thanks to Melanie's magic jelly thingies.

Hmm… it was probably the wine. We had polished off two bottles at dinner, and it went to my head.

"Are you pleased?" Joe asked once we got to the ballroom.

"Very much. Thank you so much for asking me to this. I'm having a great time, and I appreciate everything you're doing for me."

He kissed my hand again at my compliment. "Would you like to dance or find a table and sit?"

I grinned. "Dance."

I hadn't been dancing in years that didn't involve moving around the living room with my kids. It was freeing in a way to move with the steady rhythm of the drums. The bass vibrated heavily in my chest as the spinning lights flashed across the wooden floor. I had tried to talk Doug into ballroom lessons with a Groupon I found, but he wanted nothing to do with it. I bet Joe would have done it. He was a good dancer.

I was out of breath when the music slowed and the band started playing a love ballad. I thought about sitting down when Joe took me in his arms and pressed me close. I laid my head on his shoulder as we swayed back and forth. His body flexed and slid against mine, and his hands stroked up and down my back.

I vaguely noticed Doug and Mandy were also in the ballroom now, sitting at a table at the edge of the dance floor. Her arms crossed her body, her pinched face turned away from him in annoyance. Clearly she was still in the midst of her snit, if her aloofness was any indication.

Doug had a huge tumbler of something alcoholic and was gulping it down like soda. He shot one glance at me before he drained the glass, then got up to weave his way to the bar. His movements were unsteady, and I imagined he would be staggering by the time midnight came around. It was a little shocking to me that I didn't care. His sobriety or lack thereof was not my problem. I sighed and snuggled into Joe's shoulder, and he lightly kissed my temple. I could really get used to this.

Two bottles of wine at dinner and another one at the gala meant that eventually I had to break the seal and go pee. The bathrooms were just as decked out as the ballroom. I took a few minutes to text Melanie, and she texted back that the kids were fine, the house was still standing, and Mattie was winning at Jenga. I sent back a smiley face and left to take care of business. The spacious stalls helped as I pulled up my skirt and contorted myself into a pretzel to open the crotch of the shaper. I heard someone else come in the bathroom while I finished up and twisted to refasten myself. I tugged down my skirt and left the stall, running into none other than Mandy. My heart rate jumped, and I moved a few sinks down to wash my hands.

"I know why you're here." Her tone was acidic and spiteful.

"Really? Is it that obvious?" My tone was sarcastic. She missed it.

"Of course. You're all dressed up tryin' to get Doug to pay attention to you again. He's been watchin' you all night. But it won't work. That escort you're payin' looks real good and puts on a nice show, but that's all it is. A big *fat* show."

I knew what she was implying, but I was in too good a mood for her bite to get to me. I dried my hands with one of the linen towels put out for that purpose, then turned and faced her directly, raising my chin. Her forehead wrinkled with her precision-sculpted eyebrows meeting in the middle. For the first time since I met her, I thought she looked ugly. "Yep, you caught me. I guess I must give up on my old, broken-down, forty-year-old ex and let you have him. Just my luck, I have to deal with the gorgeous hunk of a lawyer I'm out with tonight." I gave an exaggerated sigh. "You got one thing wrong, though. I don't have to pay someone to like me." My eyes drifted down her perfect size six body. "With money or anything else."

Her jaw dropped. I smirked and left her in the bathroom before she could respond. Joe was in a conversation with another couple, and I started toward him when a hand on my shoulder stopped me. I turned to see Doug leaning heavily against a table.

"Bevvie." He burped, and the fumes hit my nostrils. *Ugh.*

"Doug."

His vision wandered before both eyes focused back on me. "Wh-where ar' da kidz?"

Damn, I'd never seen him this drunk. A little buzzed once in a while but not this staggering, stinking mess. "They're at home with Melanie, playing board games and eating pizza."

"Arn yoo suppoz' to be home with 'em?"

"I'm home with them every night of the week."

He blinked as if he didn't understand my answer. "How com' yoo 'er here?"

I looked at my ex. Really studied him. His skin was loose and slightly gray. He wasn't in the best of shape during our marriage; however, he had put on some weight, which made his appearance pudgier than he was a year ago. Flecks of dandruff decorated the shoulders of his fancy suit. I knew he had dry scalp issues in the winter, and I used to buy him medicated coal tar shampoos to help keep the problem under control. Apparently, he wasn't using that shampoo anymore. I tried to see the attractive man I once loved and vowed to stay with forever. He wasn't there.

"I'm here because I have a life and I plan on living it." I turned on my heel, not bothering to hear whatever he had to say next, and made my way to Joe. He welcomed me with an arm around my waist, pulling me close to his side.

"Beverly, this is Paul and Rachel Gilhead. Paul is getting ready to retire from the firm."

I shook each of their hands. "Nice to meet you."

I listened with half an ear as the two men chatted about some big case coming up and let my eyes drift around the room. This was what rich looked like, the world Doug wanted more than his family. Was it really worth it?

My thoughts drifted to Conner. Sarah told me that morning that he had left to go spend New Year's Eve with his sister and her family in Bryson City. Connor wouldn't fit in here any more than I did. I bet he wouldn't abandon his family either. God, I missed him!

Joe's arm tightened around my waist, and my attention

came back to him.

"Can I get you anything?"

A shot of tequila wouldn't be out of line, would it? "I can handle another glass of wine. You have great taste, so I'll let you choose for me."

He kissed my temple, then flagged down a waiter and ordered another full bottle. If I kept this up, I'd be just as drunk as Doug.

"I don't really want another whole bottle. Just a glass would be fine."

Joe's face dropped. "I'm sorry. I hope I didn't displease you."

He sounded kinda funny saying those words. I grinned at him and gave him a playful punch on the shoulder. "Just don't let it happen again."

He grinned back. "Yes, ma'am."

We drank and danced some more, and I tried to put Connor out of my mind. There was an ache in my heart not unlike grieving. I could finally admit to myself that, yes, I had wanted to be with my neighbor, and I would get over it, eventually. I survived a divorce I wasn't expecting; I could survive this. I may always have that little bit of heartache whenever I saw him mowing the lawn or fixing the gutters, or when he took time to hang with my kids, but I would keep it to myself and just take whatever friendship he still had in him for me.

Joe, on the other hand, was an unknown. This was moving faster than I expected it should, but he was treating me like gold, saying all the right words, doing all the right things, and, by all indications, was genuinely interested in me. Was he really out of my league?

Waiters circulated with glasses of champagne. The ball was dropping in a few minutes, and the countdown had begun. The past year had been one big emotional struggle. The sudden separation, the move to the duplex and the severe downsizing, lawyers, divorce papers, custody, and the never-ending battle regarding the effects of all this crap on the children. Maybe it was time. Maybe this was a chance for a little personal happiness. Maybe I needed to open up and find something good.

Joe handed me a glass of the bubbling liquid and took one for himself. "Here's to a new year and a new beginning of something special."

He seemed so genuine. *Can this be real?* Maybe I needed to take a hint from the Disney movie *Frozen* and just "let it go."

I closed my eyes and mentally kissed my crush on Connor goodbye.

A disturbance to my left caught my attention, and my eyes popped open to see Doug stumble over a chair. Mandy was standing over him, her arms crossed and her face flushed. I bet this was in the top ten embarrassing moments in her life, but I didn't really feel much sympathy for her.

Joe's gentle touch on my arm brought me back to facing him.

"I'm sorry you had to see that, but I'm not sorry you're here with me tonight."

The front man for the band started the final countdown

and the crowd shouted with him.

"Ten. Nine. Eight. Seven."

Joe put his arms around me and pulled me in close.

"Six. Five. Four. Three. Two."

He leaned in and kissed me for the second time that night. His lips formed perfectly to mine, coaxing and gentle, and, if I had enough word choices, worshipful.

Elsa's voice rang in my head, and I did it. I let it go.

Chapter 13

"For all that is holy in the world, Abby, get a move on!"

I didn't try to hear her reply back. She had doubled her prep time in the bathroom, and we'd had the makeup and clothes argument daily since life resumed after the holidays. The other three kids sat at the bar, downing microwave breakfast burritos as they were getting boots and coats on.

"Mom, where's my blue folder?"

"I need to brush my teeth."

"Can I have another burrito?"

The Omni had turned into a fond memory. Reality had set in, and I was back to normal as the harried mother of four who couldn't seem to find enough time for a haircut. Gone was the woman with the glittering chandelier earrings and fancy dress, and back were my normal teacher clothes, ponytail, and minimal cosmetics when I had the chance.

"Abby! Now!" My blood pressure was ready to go through the roof.

Doug had called once in the last two weeks and had already called off taking the kids this weekend. I kept his early cruise return to myself. No need to hurt my children when they already noticed Dad's holiday absence.

It was Wednesday, and not only did I still have the church gig, but the kids had a lot of activities there too. They'd made so many friends and so many connections at the church that they liked going as often as we did. Mattie had dropped soccer and joined up with the church's little league sponsored team. Sarah signed up for Girl Scouts and was making a lot of friends. Even Abby was motivated to go, though I was sure Ashton had more to do with it than an actual worship experience.

The regular pianist decided his archeological dig was a long-term job and emailed the church to resign the position permanently. Mike was pleased as punch to offer me the gig on a full-time contract. That meant a year-round obligation, but the money was too good to turn down, and I could give up my other piecemeal freelance work.

"Great to have you, key tickler. Now, 'bout them altos." He'd slapped the contract down on the piano last week and handed me a pen. God, I loved that man!

The Meet-n-Match trial had finally expired, and Melanie had dropped the app from her phone. It was a good thing, because I had no time and zero interest. Any extra time I might have for me was sucked up by practice, running the kids to their various places, trying desperately to keep up with the housework, and somehow working in private time with all of them. I felt I was running a marathon and losing.

Joe had called or texted every day with a pretty phrase

or thought and asked for another date whenever my load lightened.

Joe: **Getting ready for court this morning and thought of you. Having a good day, beautiful?**

Me: **We're on the great shoe safari. Mattie has two feet and only one sneaker. I need an APB put out on a blue and white left Puma, boys size 4.**

Joe: **LMAO, you're so funny! I hope you have time for me soon. Good luck with finding the shoe.**

Me: **Thanks. I'm about to enter the jungle of the boys' room. If you don't hear from me later, send a rescue party.**

Joe: **You're adorable.**

At first, I found his constant compliments to be charming and nice, and he understood that my schedule was too tight at the moment. His patience was endless, and I liked that about him. A lot.

Now, the continuous praise was getting a bit annoying, as it seemed contrived and over the top.

Abby finally came downstairs in a fitted, long-sleeved crop top that showed a strip of flesh right above her denim leggings and boots.

"Abby, go change. You realize that's a dress code violation, and you'll get called out for it."

She stuck her nose in the air. "The administration should be more worried about what curriculum is being taught than what I'm wearing."

"While I applaud your efforts and your reasoning, I don't have time to argue with you. Go change."

"It's not a fair system."

"Life is not fair. Go change."

"It's repressive toward women."

"You're right, but it's also too cold out there for a crop top."

"Dress code is a violation of my rights."

That's it. I'm done.

I rounded on her and slammed down my bag of sheet music on the counter. "Fine. You wanna wear that top and freeze? You go right ahead. Once we leave this house, I *will not* bring you home, and the guidance department *will* make you wear one of those humongous nasty gray sweatshirts all day."

She looked furiously at me for a moment, then turned and ran back upstairs. "Five minutes!"

"Two minutes, or I'm leaving you here and you can take an unexcused absence!"

I hadn't heard anything from Connor's apartment, even though we were making a hellacious racket, with the kids pounding up and down the stairs as they remembered this notebook or that folder they needed.

My phone dinged, and I looked down at the text.

Joe: **I hope your day is shaping up to be a great one. Miss you and want to see you soon.**

I couldn't describe the absurdity of that idea.

Abby came back downstairs in a longer pink sweater that hung off one shoulder enough to display a purple bra strap.

I was pretty sure my face was turning the same shade.

We were ten minutes late when I finally got my

squabbling herd into the van.

"Abby, did you get the burrito I put on the counter for you?"

"No, I need to lose some weight."

"You do not need to lose weight, and even if you did, skipping breakfast is not the way to do it."

"Mom, you just don't get it."

I was ready to blow, and of course, now was not the time. When I turned the key in the ignition, the engine made one click and died.

"No," I told the red dial that said my battery was low. "No, no, no, no, NO!" I pounded the steering wheel as if that would miraculously start the van. I sucked in a huge breath and held it so I wouldn't burst into tears or start cussing so much a sailor would blush. *Pull it back, Bev. Pull it back.*

"If the car won't start, does that mean we won't have to go to school today?"

I looked at Sarah in the rearview mirror as I jerked out my phone. "I still have to go to work." I'd think about what this repair was going to cost me later.

I texted Melanie first. She was already at school and stepping into an early morning meeting with the principal.

"I'll tell the front office what's going on and come get you as soon as I can."

I tried Joe next. He gushed about how happy he was to hear from me but was due in court in a few minutes and didn't have the option of leaving.

I even called Doug out of desperation. Voice mail. Not surprised.

I sighed and pulled up the Uber app just as I saw Connor coming out of his side. He was dressed warmly in a jacket, hat, and leather gloves.

"Look, there's Connor." Sarah wiped at the condensation steaming up the window and waved wildly. "Maybe he can fix it."

"Yeah, Connor can fix anything."

I looked back at Jacob. "Connor fixed a lot of stuff for us already. He doesn't have to fix this too. I'm getting an Uber for us, so sit tight. If you need something to do, write out your tardy excuses and I'll sign them when we get to your schools."

"But Connor's right here, Mom. Just ask him." Mattie had already undone his seat belt and was now in a handstand between the seats.

"Get your feet off the ceiling and sit down. I'm not asking Connor."

"But he's nice."

"Yes, he's very nice. I'm still not asking him."

Sarah stopped waving. "Are you still mad at him?"

"No." *Damn, my Sarah is observant.*

"Then why not ask him?"

"I'm… I'm…."

Connor tapped on my window. I sighed and turned to face him. He looked distorted through the frost coating the glass. I tried to roll down the window, but it wouldn't budge. *Why me? Seriously, why me?* I stepped out of the van and stood in front of my neighbor. *Dammit, why did he have to look so good?* The theme song from *Frozen* started playing in my head. Was it possible to choke a cartoon character?

Snow was starting to fall in big white flakes, and I wrapped my arms around myself to keep warm in the piercing mountain cold. "Good morning, Connor."

"Mornin', Beverly."

Beverly. Not Bev or Bevvie. It was hard to hear. I swallowed that hurt down and cleared my throat of the lump that had formed.

"Something wrong?"

"Yeah, mind if I ask you to jump me?"

He blinked sharply at my words, his eyes wide and his face slackened. "Pardon?"

I replayed my last sentence. *Oh shit!* "No… I mean, yes… but not me… I… my van…."

I flushed so hard from embarrassment, I was no longer cold. Hell, I probably threw off enough heat to make a hot spring right there in the front yard.

Connor threw back his head and let out the biggest belly laugh I'd ever heard from him. He didn't stop. Mirth bubbled up in my lungs after a moment, and I joined him. We laughed so hard, we started tearing up and gasping for breath. I had to lean against the van or lose my balance. I was sure the kids were watching us, shaking their heads and wondering if they would ever understand adult behavior someday.

Connor gulped for air and wiped at his streaming eyes. "Oh, Christ, I needed that."

I drew in painfully frigid breaths. "I did too. It's been a hellish morning. Forget the morning, it's been a hellish year so far."

"Yeah, it has." He was back under control, and so was I.

"This may be a weird question to ask, but I'm going to do it, anyway. Are we still friends? I… um… I really miss you." *If only you knew how much.*

He looked into my eyes. His were full of sincere promise. "Always, Bev. Always."

I was Bev again. That meant more to me than anything. Hmm… almost anything.

"Well, then, friend, I don't suppose you have jumper cables I can borrow?"

"Yeah, I got a set. Pop the hood and I'll get them set up."

"I can take care of it if you'll let me use your truck for a hot minute."

His eyebrow rose again. "Do you know how to set jumper cables?"

I bit my lip. "Um… I can ask if Google does."

He huffed a laugh. "Get in your van, Bev. I got this."

Jacob hopped out of the van to watch Connor clamp the doohickeys to the thingies sticking up on the battery. "Red to this one and black to this one, understand, Jake?"

Jake? When did my kid become Jake?

"Okay, Bev, your turn."

The van started up, and he let the engine run for a few minutes to make sure it would stay that way. He turned to me as the kids scrambled back into the van. "Your battery probably needs replacing. I have to go to the parts store anyway, so I'll pick one up for you and put it in tonight." His eyes sparkled, and he grinned. "Call me if you need me to jump you again."

"You're never going to let me live that one down, are you?"

"I doubt it."

"Even if I make you my world-famous deluxe pecan pie?"

He laughed and his eyes sparkled. "Maybe."

Thank you, God, I have my Connor back!

I had nothing else to say, and he didn't either. The sound of the running engines filled the silence between us as steam poured out of both tailpipes. The snow was coming down thicker now.

Connor disengaged the cables and started coiling them up. He wasn't looking at me when he spoke again. "I meant to tell you, you looked beautiful New Year's. Really beautiful. Sarah sent me a text and a picture before you left the house. Is it serious between you and that guy you were with?"

"I don't know yet. He seems to be interested in me, but I'm not sure I'm there yet. I'll probably see him again when I have a free night. Probably next New Year's, the way my life is going." My words were light, but my heart wasn't feeling it. "How 'bout you and Camille? You've been out a couple times now and already met the parents. How's that going?"

He shrugged as he opened the toolbox on the back of his truck and threw in the neatly bound cables. "I don't know either. She's nice but a little pushy sometimes."

That little heart stab was back. *Jeez, Bev, you gotta get*

over yourself!

"Okay, well, we'll have to swap stories later, but right now we are so late. I need to get these kids… hey, where do you think all y'all are going?"

All four kids had exited the van and were trudging back to our side.

"Just got a text alert. School's closed for the day. Buses are turning back, and no one is allowed on campus. Anyone already there has to leave and go home."

I looked back at Connor, my eyes widening and my face going slack this time. He bit his lip and tried hard to contain it. It didn't work.

I wondered how many calories I'd burned from laughing so hard.

* * *

Connor put his hands in front of the wood stove to warm them up. He'd installed the square metal box in the shop for heat when he needed it. The jobsite shutdown for the day because of the snow, so he ended up spending the time with his own work. The custom bistro tables he made for the Beer Kettle had led to six more orders from similar shops. He had three dozen tables to make and two sets with matching stools. One person asked him to refinish an antique chifforobe, but that would have to be a spring job. Mid-January's weather was too cold for varnishing.

He pulled out a handful of mahogany scraps and chucked

them on his mini-lathe. He spun down a dozen blanks and center drilled them for brass tubes. Making pens was hobby work and just something to occupy his time and brain. He and Beverly were back where they were a few months ago. At least he hoped they were. He had a long talk with his sister last week, and for once in a long time, he opened up.

"I can't believe I lost it, Eva. I lost my temper and yelled at a woman."

"From what you told me, she started it."

"Yeah, she was having a real bad day."

"So did you."

"That's no excuse."

He heard Eva sigh. "Maybe not in your mind now, but at that time, both of you were stressed out and loaded. Both of you made a mistake, and both of you talked it out, right?"

"Yeah."

"So what's the problem?"

He gripped the phone, trying to find the right words. "Eva, this woman is… I… Jesus, Mary, and Joseph, little sister, I liked her. I really liked her. I didna want to get involved with a woman just yet, but hell, she's the first person I think aboot when I wake and the last one I think aboot when I sleep. I wonder about what she's doing during the day, if she's havin' a good one or a bad one, and what I can do tae make it a bit better. She worries me some, because she spends so much of her time workin' for so many others. She needs time for herself. I wanted to give that to her. Now it's too late."

"Shit, Connor, you got it bad if your Irish is showing that much. Why is it too late?"

"She's got a new man."

"So? You mentioned you've met this Camille woman. If you're seeing someone, and she's seeing someone, what's the problem?"

"I don't know."

"I bet I do, big brother. You still like her, don't you? You have a stronger connection with her than this Camille, and that's tearing you up. That's why it hurt so damn much when you two argued."

"Yeah."

"Do you love her?"

Connor stayed silent for a moment. Did he love Beverly? God help him, he did, but he couldn't say it out loud. That would make it real, and his heart already ached with the lost chance of being with her. "It doesn't matter now, Eva."

"It might. I think you ought to man up and tell her how you feel. She may feel the same way and you don't know it."

Connor shook his head and chuffed. "Christ, you're a stubborn woman."

He could imagine her smiling on the other end of the call. "That's right, mo rún. When it comes to my favorite brother, I want him to be as happy as I am. I've heard you talk proudly about the kids and about the talented, hardworking, smart Beverly until I want to puke. You need to cut Camille loose and go after the woman you really want."

"What if you're wrong, Eva?"

He finished gluing the tubes in the blanks. Snow was still falling softly outside, and he could see the lights in Beverly's side of the house glowing. He pictured her in her favorite school hoodie and yoga pants, playing a board game with the kids or doing some chore around the kitchen. Could he admit to her he had feelings? Was that the right way to go, or should he just live with it and count this as the one that got away?

Pecan pie, he thought as he put away his tools. There was more work he could do, but his mind wasn't on it. He closed the shop and went to his side. He had beer and food in the fridge and a subscription to Netflix. Binge-watching something and getting away from life for a few hours sounded like a good idea.

I jerked awake when my phone rang, and I glanced at my clock. No one called me at eleven o'clock at night unless there was a problem. The last time I got a call this late, it was Melanie who was dealing with the joys of a kidney stone and needed to go to the hospital, the pain was so bad. Before that, I'd had to take Doug to the emergency room late one night during our initial separation. He had chest pains that turned out to be bad indigestion. It seemed whenever there was a crisis, my number was on speed dial.

I flipped open my phone. The number was local, but I didn't recognize it.

"Who is this, and what's wrong?"

"Mom?"

I wasn't expecting my daughter to answer. Loud head-banging music blared in the background, and kids' voices were yelling, laughing, and having a good time. School had been closed Wednesday, Thursday, and Friday, which meant all five of us ended up housebound for three days. When Abby asked to go to a sleepover at Phoebe's place, I jumped at the chance to get at least one of them out for a while. From the sounds I heard on the phone, she was somewhere else.

"Please don't be mad." Her wavering voice sounded like she was on the verge of tears.

"I make no promises for later. What's wrong?"

"I… Ashton… um… we…."

My stomach plummeted at the boy's name. "Abigail Marie Archer, where are you?"

"I'm at Ashton's house. There's a party and… and it's getting… um… kinda wild."

I was up and grabbed the closest pants-like clothing near me, a pair of stretchy leggings. "Wild how?"

"Well, there was a lot of beer at first. You know? From Ashton's dad's work? He owns the craft beer place on Third and Main? Anyway, he got a keg of something, and that's gone now."

An entire keg of beer? Visions of the drunken parties in every 80s teen movie ever made danced in my head. I balanced the phone on my shoulder as I tried to wrestle the Disney princess leggings over one thigh. *Damn!* These were Sarah's. I jerked them off and snagged another pair. That time I got my housework yoga pants with the big rip in the side. Good enough.

"When the beer ran out, they started drinking out of the liquor cabinet. Ashton broke the door off 'cause his dad keeps it locked."

I pulled the phone away from my head long enough to jerk on a T-shirt that read 'singers have great pipes' across the top of it along with my faded school hoodie. I put it back to my ear and caught the words "… lots of people just showed up."

I gripped the phone so tight my knuckles turned white.

"They're not from our school. I think they might be from the college. I don't know any of them. They brought a lot of… um… well… there's a lot of w-w-weed. I can't find Ashton anywhere, and I l-lost my ph-phone."

I could tell the meltdown was imminent.

"Abby, what is Ashton's address? Are you in a safe place? Can you meet me outside?"

"I'm… I'm… I'm hiding in his parents' bedroom. I have the door locked, and I'm on the house phone. There was this guy who was looking at me… like a lot. Just staring."

I jammed my feet into my nasty yard sneakers without bothering to put on socks.

"Abby, address?"

"Momma, I'm scared!"

"I'm on my way. Can you get outside?"

"I can't! That creeper might be waiting for me in the hallway."

"Abby, I still need the address."

"I can't text it from a house phone."

Another stress wrinkle formed between my eyebrows.

"You can tell it to me with words."

"I don't remember all of it. Only the street name."

"I'm sure I can figure it out. Probably the one with a lot of cars and a loud party happening."

"Oh, yeah."

As she rattled off the street name, I recognized a rather affluent area of the city. The same one where Doug lived now. "It's gonna take me at least twenty minutes or more to get there. Call me back at that time."

"Okay, Momma. Please hurry."

I knew she wasn't just scared, she was terrified. She hadn't called me "Momma" in years. I tried to call Doug's cell twice to see if he could get to our daughter faster. Both times it went to voice mail. I hated to leave my other kids alone, but it couldn't be helped. I woke up a groggy Jacob and told him I had to go get Abby. He nodded and flopped back asleep, probably not comprehending much. I thought about calling Joe, but this would not be the way I'd want him to officially meet the kids. We had our New Year's Eve date, his daily texts, and several phone calls but so far hadn't been able to plan another get-together. I tried Doug again and was so caught up in getting to my van that I didn't see Connor on the porch until I ran into him. Literally.

I landed on my ass in a big pile of snow that Mattie had tried to turn into a snowman yesterday. My phone flew from my hand, still stating for me to leave a message.

"Jesus, are you okay?"

I looked up at him and wished I could melt through the cracks in the cement. He was dressed up in his nice khaki pants, a collared dress shirt, and a brown leather bomber jacket. Damn, he looked hot. Clearly, Connor had been out somewhere and had just come home. Camille stood next to him, appearing in her finest as well. Here I was sprawled out on the ground in the sloppiest of my sloppy clothes. I hadn't even bothered to comb my hair in my haste to get to my daughter. Could this night get any worse?

"Um… yeah, I'm good. Sorry for running into you like that. I'm kinda in a hurry."

He glanced at his watch. "It's after eleven. What's wrong?"

He reached a hand down to help me up as he parroted my earlier words.

"Abby's at a party, and I need to go get her."

His eyebrows went north far enough to reach the pole.

"Abby's what?"

"At a party. She's supposed to be at her friend's for a sleepover but apparently decided to go to this party instead. She says the place is getting out of hand. She's in over her head, and I need to get to her."

He jerked his chin to my closed door. "What about the other kids?"

"I woke Jacob and let him know I'm leaving for a bit. The door's locked. They should be fine, but I really need to go."

Connor turned to his date. "Would you mind staying with the kids until Bev and I get back?"

She blinked at him. The dirty looks she gave me said she was not happy about this turn of events.

I shook out the snow that had gotten to my skin through the big tear in my pants. "Thanks, Connor, but you don't need to come with me. I can get Abby just fine. I don't want to spoil your evening."

"Is Abby in trouble?"

"Oh, yes, Abby is definitely in trouble. Trouble enough that she's grounded for the rest of high school. I need to go, Connor."

My joking tone didn't help lighten the tense mood.

"Please, Camille. I'll be back as soon as I can." Even though he said please, I could hear the underlying order. Even if Connor and I had cooled our friendship, I knew he cared about my kids, and if she wanted any kind of chance with him, she would need to help out now.

"Of course. I hope everything is okay."

I wondered how much that gritted smile cost her.

Connor unlocked my door, and Camille raised her eyebrow that he had a key to my place but didn't say anything. He ushered me to his truck, and we both got in.

"Where are we going?"

"Briar Cliff Road in the Forrest area development. Ashton Fordham's place. I don't know the number, but I'm betting the party noise will give it away."

Connor looked over at me. "That's William Fordham's son."

"Yup. That's him. How did you know?"

He started the truck. "I did some work for him recently at his store, the Beer Kettle. He mentioned he'd be out of town this week on business and wanted me to start a new project in his home basement. I've met Ashton."

The tone of his voice and the tightening of his hand on the steering wheel told me he wasn't too impressed with the teenager.

When we got to the address, it looked exactly like the

party scene from the movie *Sixteen Candles.* Cars were jammed in anywhere they could fit on the slushy lawn and in the circular driveway. The house blazed with lights while loud music blared away. A few people wandered around outside with red plastic cups or glass beer bottles. Most of the partygoers were stuffed in the building and visible through the windows. I recognized several of my students. Abby had not called me back yet, and I was gearing up to storm the beaches when Connor put his hand on my arm.

"Stay here."

"Connor, you don't—"

"Beverly, there are a hundred or more drunk people in there, and some of them aren't teenagers. I'm betting they're bigger and meaner when a mom shows up to a private party to rescue her daughter. I don't need to worry about your safety too. You stay here and I'll get her."

I could argue, but the faster Abby got out of there, the faster I could hug her close. I could yell at her faster too. "She's hiding in the master bedroom."

I watched as Connor entered the house like he was on his way through the gates of hell. I bit at my thumbnail as I sat in his truck, feeling the winter air start to leak in. I looked at my phone: 11:36 p.m. My imagination started running amok. A lot could have happened in the twenty minutes since I spoke to my daughter. I stared at the door Connor had entered just a minute ago. It seemed like a year. My phone read 11:40 p.m. when he emerged with Abby wrapped in his jacket. Those were the longest four minutes of my life.

My nose tingled with a potential crying jag, and I pulled

my stern mom face to keep it at bay. Abby got in the vehicle's extended back seat, and I turned to lay into her. The sight of her tearstained face had me rethinking the stern-mom thing and going back to relieved mom.

"Are you okay, sweetheart?"

"Yeah."

That was it. One syllable. Dead, numb voice.

Connor got in the truck and started it. Heat poured through the vents, and I absently put my hands up to the warm air. He swiped open his phone.

"Bill? Connor MacAteer here. I hate waking you up like this, but you need to know what's going on at your house right now. I'm in your driveway, looking at what's left of your lawn and watching a bunch of kids tear up the rest of your house. Big party going on… Real big… Ashton? Yeah, he's in there… No, I'm not going back in… I have two women in the car with me and I'd rather not say… Yeah, there's damage… A lot… Okay… Okay… Talk to you next week, and good luck."

He hung up and backed out of the driveway.

I took another look at my eldest daughter and was barely able to recognize my girl. Her face, though streaked, had artful makeup applied, and she looked much older than her fifteen years. There was such a shattered and zombie look to her, panic rose in my throat. *My God! Did someone touch my little girl?*

Connor's free hand came across to grasp mine as if he was reading my mind. "She's fine, Bev. Just shaken up. She got an eyeful of stuff she shouldn't be seeing at her age. Let her process tonight and deal tomorrow, yeah?"

I forced down the boulder choking me and nodded. The rest of the ride was silent. We reached our house right after midnight and Camille stood in the doorway as we exited the truck. As we entered the house, I glanced up the stairs to check if the other kids had been disturbed at all. Thankfully, nothing moved.

"Abby, why don't you go on in and go to bed? Your mom will be there soon."

Abby broke out a sob and ran to me. She flung her arms around me. "I'm s-s-so s-s-sorry, momma!"

My throat clogged, and I swallowed to clear it. I had been "Mom" for years, and that name was usually accompanied by a huff or an eye roll. "You're home and safe, sweetheart. You do as Connor says and go to bed. We'll talk some tomorrow."

She nodded wetly against my shoulder and turned to stumble into the house on someone's borrowed high-heeled boots.

Connor came up behind me and placed a hand on my shoulder. The comfort in the weight of that small touch nearly broke me.

"Thank you so much for helping me tonight." My lower lip started to tremble. *Dammit! Not yet!* "I'll go get your jacket."

"Bev, look at me."

I turned and looked into his kind, concerned face. Concerned for me. This man dropped everything in a hot minute to help me and my child. He was the kind of man I wished my ex had been. Even when I blasted him, he was still there for me.

"Are you okay?"

Dammit! There goes my control. "Shit, Connor. That was my baby girl in that mess of a house tonight."

I let out one sob, and Connor folded me into his strong arms. "It's okay, Bev, we got her. We got her before anything happened."

It was wrong, but I did it anyway. I took that moment for myself and reveled in the sensation of Connor holding me. The crisp scent of his cologne, his firm hold, the strength of his hard body—I soaked it up like a sponge and filed it away in the "best of my memories" folder. This would never be mine, but God, how I wanted it!

"Everything okay?"

Camille had come out on the porch, and I stopped in my tracks. A cold shower couldn't have awakened me faster. "Yeah, everything is good now, though my daughter might not think so tomorrow when we're having our come-to-Jesus meeting. Thanks for hanging out while Abby learned a lesson in teenage delinquency."

Camille's laugh was about as genuine as the dollar-store earrings Doug bought me as an anniversary gift a few years ago. "I was glad to do it."

Uh-huh. I bet you were.

Cut it out, Bev. Stop with the jealousy shit!

"I need to get in and nail the window shut in Abby's room before she gets any more bright ideas. I'll leave you two alone and, uh, enjoy your evening."

I turned away and walked to my door, dragging my feet every step and trying not to listen to their conversation, but it wasn't exactly being kept private.

Connor sighed. "Camille, it's been a long day, and I'm really tired. How 'bout we call it a night and I'll call you tomorrow, yeah?"

"What? Why? You said you wanted to talk to me about something."

Oooo! She sounded pissed! I wondered how tasteless it would be to skip a little on the way to my door.

"Yeah, I did, but I'm beat, and I don't think I can do it now. My day started around five this morning, and it's well after midnight. Text me when you get home so I know you're safe. I can stay awake that long."

"Are you breaking up with me?"

I didn't hear his answer as I entered my house. Abby was waiting for me in the living room. I heard an anguished "Momma" before a flying fifteen-year-old body collided with mine. She sobbed on my shoulder, and my own sinuses filled. For a long while, I held my child and thanked whoever was looking out for her that she was safe in my arms.

"Can you talk to me now, or should I just ground you for the rest of your natural-born life?"

"Can we negotiate a little?"

"That depends on how much snot you just smeared on me."

She chuckled, which was my goal. My Abby was in that rough void between kid and adult, and getting her to talk to me was almost impossible. She had been keeping secrets.

Big ones. The best way to get her to open up was to simply sit and listen, so that was what I did. The floodgates burst open, and I found out more than I really wanted to know.

Abby sniffled and wiped at her puffy, black-smeared eyes. "I'm sorry I lied to you about being at Phoebe's house. I just really wanted to go to this party. I thought Ashton invited me special, and I had to be there. I *had* to. If I didn't show up, Carla Maples would be with him, and on Monday, she would be his girl instead of me."

His girl? The Ashton I knew from the school had a bunch of girls who followed him around. I also knew Abby had a major crush on him, but I hadn't known she had joined his harem fan club.

"Anyway, I got there, and she was around him, like a lot, all night. She's a senior like him, and she was drinking beer like everyone else. He was paying a lot of attention to her, and I thought I would look older if I drank some too."

She wrinkled her nose. "That stuff is sooo nasty! He said it was his father's best, but it tasted so bad!"

I nodded in agreement but stayed silent.

Abby sniffed and wiped again. I handed her a tissue from a box on the coffee table. "Anyway, I kept the cup with me so it looked like I was still drinking."

Hmm… not a bad idea. My girl is smart.

"OMG, Mom. There were so many people, and they just kept coming in! There were a lot from school but lots of older people I didn't recognize. Men, not boys. They got mad when the keg ran out, and that's when Ashton broke into his dad's liquor cabinet. One of the men started following me around, asking me if I wanted to take a shot. I got scared and ran upstairs to get away from him and went into one of the bedrooms. Ashton, Carla, and a couple of other seniors were in his room, and they were… they had….”

I bit my lip to keep my face blank while inside I was raging.

She honked into the tissue and reached out for another one. “I don't know what it was, but they were snorting something. I've seen actors do that in movies but never in real life. Carla's face turned red, and she said it burned. None of them saw me when I ran to hide in his parents' room. No one was in there yet, so I locked the door and hid behind the bed and thought I would just stay there until everyone had gone or passed out and sneak away, but then someone tried to get in the room and started banging on the door and cursing real loud. I thought it might have been that guy who was following me around, and I got scared. I used the landline to call you. I didn't want anyone to see me and think I was too much of a baby to be there, but I didn't know what else to do. I stayed behind the bed, crying the whole time, until I heard Connor calling for me. I was sooo glad to see him, Momma!”

My performance was Academy Award worthy. I sat there breathing normally, or at least faking it, while my heart raced and my head cycled through fear, anger, and relief over and over again. “Grounded for the next month. School events might be negotiated, but curfews are not, and if you blow it, all bets are *off*. If you need study time, your friends can come here.”

Just like that, my teenager switched gears. She flounced out of my arms and flipped her hands through her hair, tears drying up instantly as she morphed into dramatic mode. "Mom! You can't be serious! A whole month!"

"I can make it two. Or three. You lied to me, Abby. Trusting you is going to be hard, and I'm willing to give you a chance to earn it back. Listen to my words and get them on your brain. You. Have. To. Earn. It. Back."

She deflated a bit. "What do I say to my friends? I'll be so embarrassed!"

"Make me the bad guy."

"Huh?"

I sighed and explained. "Make me the bad guy. You can huff and puff about what a mean ol' mom you have and how she won't let you go anywhere or do anything. I'm suppressing your freedom and controlling your life, and you're so angry about it. It's all right to blame it all on me. I have a thick skin and can take it."

"You'd be okay with that?"

"Sure. Let me show you." I put the back of my hand against my forehead, made a tragic face, and spoke in my best valley girl voice. "OMG, my mom is so, like, mean! I'm so grounded over the party! She never lets me go, like, anywhere. And, like, when I do, she makes me, like, call her every hour, and like, she's a freakin' control freak, and like, I have to stay home and never go anywhere, and she, like, makes me stay locked in my room like it was a prison and only feeds me stale bread and water from the toilet, and like—"

"OMG, mom, stop!" Abby was laughing even though she was trying to act cool and aloof.

"I'm serious about the grounding, Ab. You could've really gotten hurt and possibly in a way that is permanent. Tomorrow, you need to thank Connor for his help. Right now, it's late and it's been a rough night. We'll deal with anything else tomorrow, or rather later today."

Cue teenage sigh. "Okay. Mom, I really am sorry."

"I know, sweetheart."

Abby dragged herself upstairs. I heard her shuffle around a bit, and then I turned away when the bathroom door closed softly.

A light tap on my door caught my attention. Connor's date had left, and he was standing outside, concern written all over his face. I stepped out to join him and the cold air bit into my skin.

"Abby okay?"

Emotion rose in my throat, and I couldn't swallow it this time. It should have been Abby's father who went to rescue her. It should have been her father to help lecture and ground her. It should have been her father to worry about her well-being. It should have been her father who mowed the lawn, fixed the sagging gutters, helped Jacob with his inventions, and sat at my dinner table on Sunday afternoons.

Shit, Bev, keep it together. Don't lose it now! I was sure I just cut new half-moon nail scars in my palms with how hard I gripped my fists.

"Yes, she's good. Not happy about the grounding, but she'll get over it. I'm guessing Ashton may experience more than a grounding?"

Connor sighed and jammed a hand over his face. "Probably. Bill is pissed at his son, and I expect there's gonna be a reckoning when he gets home tomorrow. He just called me for more details and decided to cut his trip short. There's no way that kid can clean up that much damage in that little time. I told him about the drugs. He asked me not to call the police. Maybe I should've, but I thought it best to give Bill a chance to set Ashton straight first."

"You sound like you have some experience."

He lightly snorted. "My two youngest brothers ended up in the drunk tank more than once for picking bar fights. Da always left them there to marinate, and I had to go bail them out in the morning 'cause he wouldn't. I think if he would have tightened up his parenting skills earlier in their lives, they wouldn't have gotten into so many scrapes as adults. Best if Abby learns those lessons now rather than at a time she won't have her mom at her back."

"I hope you're right and Abby learned something tonight. I'm sorry for ruining your date. It was nice that your… girlfriend stepped in."

He shrugged, and I could see his fatigue. "We met when I built a kiosk at the mall for her before Christmas. She sells special makeup and shampoos and stuff. Pretty expensive. I never thought I would see a hand lotion that costs seventy dollars a bottle."

I choked a little. *Seventy dollars for hand lotion? What does it have in it? Gold?* "I can't remember the last time I stayed up so late it was a new day. I'm ready to fall asleep standing here."

Connor stifled a yawn. "Me neither. I'm heading up. I'm glad Abby is okay."

For a long moment, we just looked at each other. A need to step in to him again surged through my body. I was sure if I did, he would open his arms in welcome. His slightly parted lips looked full and warm. What would he do if I kissed him? Would he run and never speak to me again, or would he kiss me back?

"'Night, Bev." His voice was husky, and I had to force myself to stay put.

"'Night, Connor." My feet managed to break free and carry me through my door. Connor waited for me to get inside, and I heard his screen click shut. I leaned back on the wood panel and resisted the desire to pound my head against it. Too many feels, too many emotions. I noticed he didn't acknowledge Camille's status in his life, but he also didn't deny it either.

Put it away, Bev. It's not yours, and it's not going to be. You'll get over it and survive.

At the moment, I wasn't so sure.

Chapter 15

I stomped up the steps to the front porch of the house, holding my coat closed, as I'd managed to rip off a button in my hasty exit from Joe's condo. We finally managed to find time for a second date in mid-February just after Valentine's Day. Doug had taken the kids for the night and planned to bring them to the science fair at the school tomorrow morning. This was the first visit he'd had since Christmas, and it was only for Friday night, as he and Mandy had tickets to some Broadway show tour coming through town on Saturday. I had promised Joe that at the next opportunity, we would get together for dinner and a movie at his place. Bad move.

Dammit, why does this shit always happen to me?

"Here now, Bev. What's the matter?"

I jumped a bit at Connor's voice coming from the far corner of the porch. He was sitting on the fabulous bench and side table he made, a bottle of water and an open bottle of whiskey at his elbow. He was holding a chunky glass filled with ice and amber liquid.

"Hi, Connor. Nothing's wrong. Everything is just peachy. Life is great."

He sipped at the drink. "From the tone of your voice, it sounds like anything but great. Thought you went to see that Joe guy tonight."

"Yeah. Dinner was great, but that's about it."

He refilled the glass and held it out toward me. "Looks like you need this as much as I do."

I hesitated for a moment and then, with a huff, plopped my ass down on the bench next to him. It was cold enough to still have a smattering of snow on the ground. A bite in the air predicted more was on the way. I had no idea what Connor was doing outside drinking in the dark by himself.

I practically snatched the glass from his hand and shot back a healthy swallow. Fire scorched down my throat, and I choked but didn't release the glass back to him. I tossed the rest back as my eyes teared up and more heat filled my gut.

"Easy, lass! Sip it with a little respect." Connor chuckled as he finally got the glass back. I coughed and panted from the harsh burn.

"Damn, now I remember why I drink wine. Jeez, that's strong!"

Connor grunted at my statement as he filled the glass again for himself and added a tiny bit of water. This was not his usual behavior.

I cleared my throat. "Didn't you have a date with Camille?"

He took a swig, and I watched as he swirled the remainder

in the glass. "I did. Not anymore."

Oh my! I couldn't tell if he was hurt, angry, or depressed. Probably all three. Melanie dealt with her breakups by going out on the town and finding a replacement as soon as possible. Apparently, Connor dealt with his by staying at home and getting rip-roaring drunk. I was debating between the two methods for myself. "Care to share what happened, or is that private?"

He handed me the glass, and I took another sip of fire. It wasn't so bad now, and the burn was fading into a nice glow. Maybe he had it right.

"Maybe you can tell me. She wanted to take me shopping for new clothes 'cause she doesn't like the ones I have. She doesn't like my truck. Asked me to shave my beard 'cause it doesn't look professional. Doesn't like me working manual labor 'cause it's dirty. It seems like she doesn't really like that much about me."

I drained the last of the whiskey and handed the glass back to him. He refilled it and started emptying it again.

"I work construction and in a woodshop. I need a workin' truck, not a bunch of business shit to wear, an' I've had me beard ever since I was old enough to grow one."

He swallowed half the glass's contents and handed it to me so I got the other half.

"She comes from money. Lots of it. Her parents own a chain of furniture stores."

I eyed the whiskey bottle. We had a way to go before it was empty.

"Camille was nice an' all fired up to be with me, an' I

liked it. I liked that I had a pretty woman interested in me. It was good. Never had a real girlfriend. Spent me whole life working every day, takin' care of the family business, takin' care of me family, an' didna have time for meeting a lot of women. Even when I did, we never stayed in one place long enough ta' make it stick."

The alcohol had really done a number on him. His speech slurred only slightly, but his Irish accent was getting thick. Maybe it was time to slow down a bit. I held the glass, thinking he wouldn't top it off if I didn't hand it back.

"She was talking tonight 'bout me quitting the work crew, selling me own business, and moving with her to Hickory. Her daddy's bought her a storefront there for her seventy-dollar lotion and her twenty-dollar soap. Christ in a handbasket, she had me life planned oot and I had nae say in it."

He reached for the glass and tugged it out of my grip. I stifled a burp, but it came out anyway.

"Long story short, I told her I didna want to sell my business, didna want a bunch of clothes I can't wear to me jobsite, didna want to move again, and didna want to shave me beard. I didna lose me temper and yell at her. Thas nae how you treat a lady. She yelled at me, though. She got in a right snit aboot it and drove off. I doon't think she'll be back."

He poured again but only swirled the potent alcohol around the glass. "I didna want to hurt her feelin's, but I've been thinkin' aboot breakin' it off with her for a wee bit. There's nae enough between us to make a real go of it.

Especially when nothin' I have is good enough. It's for the best."

I watched the glass as the edge of the liquor moved round and round. It was mesmerizing. "I know all about that shit. I'm sorry it didn't work out, but if she's wrong for you, you're better off without her. I think you're perfect the way you are. You work really hard, and you care a lot about the people in your life. If I haven't said it before, I'll say it now. I love the way you treat my kids. They've eaten shit for a couple years, and I can't tell you how nice it is to have a solid role model in their lives to show them what men are supposed to be like."

He smiled into the glass. "Oh, my beautiful Beverly, you ha' no idea what that means to me."

He put the full glass down on the table and turned to face me directly. "What happened that's got you so lathered up? I thought this was a man you liked pretty well. You told me you were thinkin' aboot when to bring in the kids for a 'get ta know ya' thing."

"Well, that's not going to happen in this lifetime or ever," I managed to croak. I was starting to feel the effect of the whiskey pretty heavily. I'd always been a lightweight when it came to alcohol. Melanie made fun of me at one of the faculty parties when I got seriously buzzed off one glass of wine. To be fair, it was on an empty stomach. "Let's just say he showed me his true colors, and that was more than I could deal with."

Connor's mood changed instantly, his voice getting tight and angry-sounding. "What happened, Beverly? Did he try to hurt ya?"

I burst out in laughter. Damn, the whiskey was really getting to me now. That shit was strong! "Not hardly. You need to reverse that statement."

He blinked at me and shook his head. "You need to explain that, *bhean ólta*."

"Bean what?"

"It means drunk lady."

"I ain't drunk. Oops, I'm not supposed to say ain't. Maybe just a little tipsy now. Never could hold my liquor."

"Talk to me, Beverly."

"Can I have another drink?"

"No, you can't. If you have another one, it will be hard to carry ya into your bed."

Ooooh! Pretty please? "Are you saying I'm fat?"

He blinked again, his bleary eyes looking at me with surprise on his face.

"How the hell didja come up with tha'?"

"You said it would be hard to carry me to my bed. Ergo, I'm fat."

"Christ on a bicycle!" He closed his eyes and dropped his head back. "You're not fat. Ya have the body of a real woman, and yoo're sexy as hell. Please tell me what happened."

"I don't want to. It's embarrassing."

"For him or you?"

"Both."

"Well, he's not here, and I'm not going to rat ya to Melanie. Talk to me."

"No."

"Did he try something?"

"Um…."

"Did *you*?"

"Hell no!"

"Then what hap—"

"He turned *Fifty Shades* on me!" I spat out, tired of arguing.

Connor jumped up from the bench and swayed a bit. "Son of a bitch, you said he didna hurt ya! I'll kill him!"

It looked like Connor was ready to run out and tear Joe a new asshole. I got up and grabbed him by his upper arms, both to stop him from leaving and to keep myself upright. My head was spinning around, and I was sure I would fall over.

"No, no, Connor, you got it backward. First of all, if couples like that sort of thing, it's okay for them. Just not me. I don't have anything against people who like that lifestyle. I've read the books, and to tell you the truth, I've been curious about it, but not like what he wanted. He didn't want to spank me. He wanted *me* to spank *him*."

Connor's rage diffused. "He wanted wha'?"

The confused expression on his face was priceless!

"He has pictures all over his apartment of female bodybuilders. He likes big muscles and big, tough, aggressive women. We had dinner, and it was nice. Then he went into his bathroom and came out in… uh…."

"Came out in what?"

"I can't…."

"Can't what, Beverly? What happened?"

"It's so embarrassing!"

"Nae for you. Tell me what happened."

"No."

"Tell me."

"I doan' wanna."

"Tell me anyway."

"Connor!" The whiskey was bringing out the whiny in me.

His arms came up and broke my grip only to seize my shoulders and stare into my face. His eyes were piercing into mine, and I found myself frozen.

"Tell me." I felt the low growl in my belly.

"He went to the bathroom and came out crawling on the floor, wearing a diaper and some sort of strappy leather harness. It was hard to understand him with a horse bit in his mouth when he said he was ready for me to whip and mount him. He asked if I was pleased, but all I could think about was how ridiculous he looked. If that was supposed to please me and get me turned on, then as my kids say, 'big epic fail.' That's just a little extreme for a second date, don'cha think?"

Connor blinked several times. "He didna touch you?"

I sighed. "Nope. I just got my purse and left. I didn't even help him with the dishes."

The alcohol was putting me in a maudlin mood. "Dating is hard enough when you're younger, but I suppose it's what I should expect now. I'm an overweight, middle-aged woman with four kids, and I play the piano for a living."

Connor's grip tightened on my shoulders. "What's tha' supposed to mean?"

"I'm sure you haven't missed the line of men at my front door looking to be with me or even just date me. I don't bring a lot to the table, and most of what I do bring is baggage. My kids aren't a burden to me, but single men aren't looking to take on a ready-made family."

I tipped my head back and looked at the peeling paint on the porch ceiling. "I might as well get it settled that I'm gonna be an old, fat woman who lives by herself with a bunch of cats. I need to get some cats."

That move was a mistake, as my head spun. I closed my eyes and nearly pitched backward. I would have fallen if not for Connor's hold.

"You don't have a fucking clue, do you?"

Connor dropping an F-bomb had me snapping upright, my eyes popping open and focusing on him as my head swam. "Huh?"

His face was angry, his jaw clenching and those gorgeous eyes of his flashing fire. He growled deep in his throat as he jerked me forward and slammed his mouth down on mine. Lightning exploded in my belly as he slid a hand to the back of my head, deepening the kiss, his tongue demanding entry. I opened my lips to him and he dove in, taking complete control while I hung there and let him.

Connor was kissing me. Oh. My. God. *Connor's kissing me!*

It was magnificent. He tasted faintly of whiskey and all man. Where Joe's kiss had been slow and sweet, it didn't hold a candle to the rough power of Connor's. Whatever buzz I had disappeared, and the lightning bolt that had run through me started a slow smolder in my gut. My nipples tightened so much I could feel them against my bra. Connor kept kissing me and kissing me, demanding that I recognize him as a man and not just a friend. I clutched his shoulders and kissed him back with everything I had in me.

When he finally ended it, both of us were breathing hard, panting in each other's faces. My knees had gone to Jell-O, and I would have collapsed if not for his arms holding me in place. I was tight against his hard body and was feeling the outline of his erection at my stomach. Just knowing his excitement sent more shock through my system. This was my quiet neighbor Connor. My friend. The man I could safely perv after, and yet he'd just kissed the ever-lovin' bejeezus out of me. What the hell was going on? Dare I think he might feel the same way I did? His actions sure backed it up.

"Now do you get it, Bev?" His words wafted across my lips, and I wanted nothing more than for him to kiss me again. "Watchin' you with all those *gobshites* was hard. All I wanted, and all I want now, is to be the man at your side."

I didn't answer him. I, always with the quick witty comebacks and smartass mouth, had nothing. I just stared. Tears pricked the back of my eyes, and I was startled by the sudden urge to cry. I tried to call up my mantra of *Get it together, Bev*, but that voice was silent. Instead, I heard Melanie's words in my head. *"It's high time you get your slice of life's happiness, girlfriend. Take it with both hands and run with it."*

Connor released me to put some space between us but not enough to let me go completely. He raised a hand to stroke over my cheek to my neck. I nearly lost it from that touch on my hypersensitive skin. "The Jameson has been working on both of us tonight, but I know this for sure. You said you're done with that bloody app, and I'm done with waiting. Camille threw a lot o' shite at me, and she got a few things right. I'd rather spend my time workin' with Jake, buildin' something. I'd rather be playing a game with Sarah and gettin' me arse whupped at it while watchin' Mattie tumblin' over the couch. I'd rather be rescuin' Abby from a bad place than dating a woman who doesn't like me beard an' clothes. And I'd rather be with me lovely neighbor, a woman sae fine and sae good, it makes me heart pound out of me chest just to see her going to work in the morning. I may be a wee bit drunk, but I'm completely clear on this. I love being with you, and I want more of it. I've wanted it for a long time, and by the way you just kissed me, I think you feel the same way."

I was buzzed, turned on, and stunned by Connor's admission. I never dreamed he had these feelings for me. He didn't use the L-word, but he came damn close. I sensed this was a big moment, a turning point, and once I made my choice, either walking away or letting him in, there was no turning back.

He kept talking. "If you don't care for me in that way, it's okay. We can say it was the Jameson working on us and just be friends. If you do have feelings, I hope you can find it in you to take a chance with me. What do you want, Bev?"

"I have cellulite on my ass."

Yup, that was what came out of my mouth.

"And a stomach pooch I'll never get rid of. And stretch marks. And saddle bags that won't ever go away. I'm overweight. I keep thinking I'll lose weight someday, but I just don't have the time to… I'm not…."

"Bev, take it easy, luv. Do you really think I care about that? You have curves like a real woman should. You're soft and round from bringing four lives into this world, and it's beautiful. So incredibly beautiful. You work hard at what matters most, taking care of your family and your students, not worrying about fingernails chipping or your toenail polish matching your shoes. You have an incredible talent. You're smart. You're fun to be around. And you care so much. Christ almighty, Bev, how you care for the people around you."

He tipped my chin back with his fingers and looked down into my eyes. "I'm in awe of you."

Heart. Melt.

"I've watched you for months. Did you know me bed is just on the other side of your wall? I've laid with me head next to yours, wishing I could be with you. Didna think I'd ever get the chance, but now I've got it, and I'm really scared I'm gonna fumble and mess it up. I want to get this right so you'll let me stay. You're worth the risk, and I'm the luckiest man in the world right now because you're with me. You are with me, aren't you, love?"

I had no words. And I was glad I didn't, because any

I could think of were inadequate to what I was feeling. Connor's fingers stroked my chin, and he lowered his mouth to mine.

"It's high time you get your slice of life's happiness, girlfriend. Take it with both hands and run with it."

I made up my mind, in my head and heart. I folded my arms around his body and took a giant leap. "Will you spend the night with me?"

My whispered words had him hesitating against my lips. "It's a big step, Bev. Are you ready for this? If you're not, we don't have to do anything. I can just hold you all night if that's what you want."

Should I pinch myself? I must be dreaming. This is my fantasy come to life. "What I want is for you to take me upstairs."

His smile brushed across my mouth as he pressed in for another deep kiss.

Going up the steps to my cubbyhole bedroom gave me time to think, and my brain started second-guessing my heart.

Is this too soon? How well do I know him?

He's been in your life for the past seven months. I'd say you know him pretty well.

How will the kids react?

They've known him for the past seven months too.

What if he doesn't like me naked after all?

He's seen you hot, sweaty, and dirty. He's seen you in school clothes. He's seen you dressed up. He's seen you sloppy as hell. He's still here, and he wants to be here.

I wonder if he's watching my ass while I'm climbing these stairs?

Probably. It is *a fine ass, after all.*

We reached my bedroom, and I saw Connor glance at the spartan furnishings. My bed, chest of drawers, and a small nightstand were all I had in there, and in truth, that was all that would fit. I was sure there were dust bunnies lurking in the corners, as my room was on the bottom of the list for house cleaning days. Since no one ever came into this room on a regular basis but me, I didn't need to have it spit polished for visitors.

He reached for the table lamp, and the click echoed in the room. His hands slid down my shoulders and over my back, leaving a warm trail as they descended to cup my round bottom. He pulled me closer into his hips, and his hard cock ground into my stomach.

Oh my!

I toed off my simple wedge shoes and lost an inch of height. It didn't faze Connor as he leaned in and kissed me with a thoroughness that rekindled the fire in my belly. My hands brushed over his shoulders, and I marveled at the hard feel of them.

The moment of truth came sooner than I thought when he reached for the hem of my long, loose tunic. He pulled it over my head, and I held my breath in mild panic as he took his first real look at me. Plain beige front-hook bra, no spandex cami to hold back the rolls, this was just me. I trembled, not from the temperature in the room but from anticipation, waiting for his face to show shock or disdain.

His fingers traced the straps of my bra. "May I? It's okay if you've changed your mind."

My chest hurt. I almost didn't recognize my whispering voice. "Do you want me?"

His eyes darkened. "More than I can find words to say."

He pulled at the clasp between my breasts, trying to figure out how it opened. "I didna think these things came with combination locks."

I couldn't help the laugh that came out. The tension broke, and his mouth curled up on one side. I slid the clasp open, and he spread the cups wide. My nipples puckered in the cooler air as his warm hands cupped the large, soft mounds. His thumbs circled the tight peaks, sending sparks straight to my clit.

"Perfect."

Oh, how I needed to hear that!

He reached behind his neck and pulled his Henley off, mussing his hair in several directions as he did. I'd seen his naked chest before when he was mowing the lawn. He was a work of art when watching from a distance. Up close I could see some scars from past injuries, a dark mole near his left nipple, and a scattering of gray hairs on his chest. I didn't consider these tiny imperfections a problem. Truthfully, they enhanced his male beauty, and my mouth watered with the urge to put it to his skin.

"Perfect," I echoed back to him. A long breath released from his mouth. He must have had some trepidations too. The thought surprised me that he would feel as vulnerable and nervous as I did. That bolstered my own courage, and I went for broke.

I hooked my fingers into my leggings and attempted to bend over and strip them off in one movement, panties and all. The clumsy move almost landed me on my ass. Connor looked a lot more elegant as he shucked his jeans and briefs. His stiff cock bobbed between his thighs, and a drop of fluid winked from the dark purplish head. My sex pulsed as I thought of how it would feel when that beautiful shaft slid inside of me.

Like the handsome prince in my favorite fantasy, he scooped me up to set me on the bed. All two hundred pounds of me, and it didn't faze him in the least. He came down over me, and I welcomed him with open arms. His mouth met mine. The taste, the texture of his tongue as it played with mine, I reveled in every bit of it. His hands roamed my body, tracing the curves and valleys. If he was fumbling, he was doing a damn good job. His head lowered, and he drew a nipple into his mouth. *Oh, yes!* I arched as he gently sucked and stroked. The thrill of being touched was heady, and I was getting drunk on it. He seemed to take delight in my gasps and cries of pleasure. The buzz in my middle grew, almost painful as time stretched out. He was in no hurry.

"Beautiful," he murmured. I had a moment of panic when he moved lower and kissed at my soft belly just below my navel. "Absolutely perfect" were the words he spoke against my flesh as he moved lower. I separated my legs at his touch, and he settled between them. Cool air moved over my exposed sex, and every nerve in my body was vibrating with anticipation. Doug seldom bothered to go down on me, saying it just wasn't his thing. My hands clutched the sheets as I lay there, open and vulnerable. The heat from his breath washed over me, and I shivered.

Then his mouth came down on me, and my world reduced to this point of contact. Connor seemed to relish it and explored every fold with a thoroughness that had me quaking. Icy thrills shot through me, centered at my core. My hands twisted the bedclothes as he sucked and teased my clit. Tension built in me. Tension and frustration. My orgasm hovered just out of reach, and just as I was about there, he stopped or switched strokes, letting me down and building me back up again. Over and over again, he tantalized, stroked, caressed, and flicked until I was one big bundle of need.

"Oh my God, Connor. Quit teasing me!" My body arched, looking for release. He finally gave it, latching on to that uber-sensitive bundle of nerves and drawing on it hard.

I screamed. Yes, I actually screamed, and the sudden burst of pleasure kept going and going. I'd had orgasms with Doug, not every time but a few. I'd also enjoyed self-induced ones, but they were mild in comparison to what I experienced now. My eyes watered with emotion as Connor lifted up and gazed at me with his beautiful green eyes.

Light glanced off the sheen of his lips as he whispered, "Okay, luv?"

I smiled. "I'm more okay than I've been in a long time."

He reached for the condom he'd placed on the nightstand

earlier and tore open the crinkled packet with his teeth.

"Are you ready for this, Bev? Stop me if you're not, but I'll not budge in letting you know I'm aching to be inside you right now."

I'm aching for you to be inside me too. "Absolutely, yes."

He wasted no time in sheathing himself. I watched as he rolled the latex over his hard flesh. The sight brought a new arousal to my sex. I had just come. Hard. Harder than I could ever remember, and now I was ready to go again. Twice in one night? Was that possible outside of my fantasy romance novels?

He settled between my legs again, and I felt the hard tip of his cock press into me. I was dripping wet, but he was a big man, and it had been a long time. He rocked back and forth, pushing in a little deeper every time. My channel enveloped him, opening and taking more with each push. It was a tight fit, and I was fully aware of every hard inch. His arms were tight with strain as he hovered over me, and I stroked my fingers over his knotted muscles. Tension radiated from him, but he still held back, slowly working himself inside until he was fully seated. Holy shit, he was huge! I was fuller than I had ever been, and I zeroed in solely on that hard length finally joining us together. His cock flexed deep inside me, and I jumped from the thrill that coursed through my middle. I heard his low groan in my ear. "Jesus, Mary, and Joseph."

He began to pull and push, savoring each stroke like he was tasting a fine wine. I lifted my hips and looked down between our bodies where we were joined. I watched the flex of his stomach muscles as he slid out and thrust back in, each movement sending frissons of pleasure through me. This was Connor inside me, making love to me. I ran my hands over his strong back and buttocks, feeling them tense and relax as he kept a steady rhythm. It wasn't fair for me to compare him to Doug, but I couldn't help it. Doug sometimes treated our sex life as a race to the finish line. For a while, it was another task to check off on Saturday nights. Then it was twice a month, if even that often. Toward the end of our marriage, we hadn't been having sex at all. Connor acted like I was giving him the honor of a lifetime, and he was going to treasure every moment.

Gone was any buzz from the whiskey, and every cell in my being had one focus—Connor, the magic he was working. He lowered himself so his chest hair brushed against my supersensitive nipples. The angle of his cock stroked a spot inside me, and my body reacted. My stomach spasmed, and I gasped.

"Good?"

"Yes, very. Do it again."

He did it again. And again. And again.

I writhed under him, whimpering and twisting, wanting relief for the ache he created and yet not wanting it to end. My body lost control, and a scream burst from me as I crested over. He groaned as my channel contracted around him. He buried himself as far as he could reach, and his cock pulsed as he shot hard into the latex sheath. He relaxed his arms and came down on top of me. It felt good to carry his weight and to hear his panting breath in my ear. His cock had softened some but was still deep inside me.

It hit me then. I was in my house, in my bed, and Connor MacAteer had just come inside me. Maybe I should have felt guilty, self-conscious, scared, or something like that, but I felt none of those emotions. I felt satisfied. Good. Comfortable. Loved.

This was right. *We* were right.

Connor kissed my cheek and propped himself back up. His hand came to stroke my cheek as he regarded my face. He frowned when he saw the wet coursing from my eyes. "Jesus, Bev, did I hurt you?"

I shook my head. I hadn't realized I was crying. "No, I just… I'm so full, I sprung a leak."

He reached down and tasted my tears with his tongue. "Happy tears, *a mhuirnín?*

I had no idea what that meant, but it sounded nice. "Absolutely."

"Good. Means we can do this again soon." He kissed me lightly and slid out. I felt empty without him inside me, and I pulled the covers up as I watched him walk to the bathroom, presumably to take care of the condom. His fine beefy ass was high, tight, and perfectly sculpted atop tree trunk thighs dusted with dark hair. I'd had the two most mind-blowing intense orgasms I'd ever had in my life, and I was getting turned on just watching Connor's butt move.

For the brief minute he was in the bathroom, I pondered what to do next. I assumed he would spend the night. Should I hunt for my underwear and put it back on? Should I put on something sexy, one of my old T-shirts I normally wore to bed, or sleep naked?

He came back into the room while I was thinking, and I got an eyeful of his male beauty hanging between his legs. Even sated, it was impressive. He pulled the covers back off me and took any doubts away by sliding in next to me and spooning me from behind. His hands stroked over my side, waist, and hip before settling across my soft belly.

His voice rumbled in my ear. "This changed things between us, Bev. You're mine now, and I don't want to give you up. We have something special here. Something that can grow. No more blind dating app, yeah?"

"It was on Melanie's phone and already expired. I'm done with it."

"You nervous about there being an us instead of a you and me?"

I thought about it. "Maybe a little. I don't know what's going to happen tomorrow or the next day, but I can tell you that I'm not scared to try. This is real, isn't it?"

He growled and his cock twitched against my bare ass. "As real as it gets, *a mhuirnín*."

His hand came up to cradle my breast, and his thumb rasped over the tip. I jumped at the contact. His lips were warm as they kissed the back of my neck.

I found out what his idea of "do this again soon" meant. Deliciously so.

Chapter 16

Before the sun winked over the horizon, Connor drew my nipple into his mouth and sucked me awake. He had done this twice during the night and made love to me both times. I lay back with my eyes closed and reveled in the heat of his mouth on my flesh. He was out of condoms after the first round, but they weren't necessary. I'd had my tubes tied after Mattie, and since I had my suspicions about Doug's fidelity, I'd done the tests to make sure he didn't leave me with any nasty surprises. Connor never had sex with Camille and had a clean bill of health at his last checkup. Feeling his hard cock slide into me without any barriers between us brought a deeper intimacy.

"Mornin', luv. You too sore for this?"

"Not at all. I do have morning breath, though."

He kissed me and opened his lips on mine. "Mmm, me too."

The level of comfort between us boggled my mind. It was as if we had been together for years instead of last night. Zero to one hundred and sixty in twenty-four hours. Melanie would appreciate the numbers. I imagined she would be happy as hell that we got together at all and concerned for the speed we were going. I supposed I should have been worried too. I wasn't. Connor and I were so right for each other that I had to wonder why we waited so long to see it.

He slipped inside me, fitting like a glove, and found that perfect angle. I moaned underneath his flexing hips. He chuckled and pressed farther. "I love when you make that sound, Bev. I don't think I'll ever get tired of it."

I agreed with him. When I climaxed, he took my cry into his mouth and gave me back his own sound of satisfaction. Another first in my life, morning sex. Could this day get any better?

"I'm gonna head back to my place and shower. I'll come back after, and we'll make our plans for the day, yeah?"

"You're talking about the science fair today, right?"

"Yeah. I want us to go together and meet the kids. You said Doug would drop them off. It would be a good way to gauge how they feel about me being in their lives as more than a neighbor. What do you think?"

I smiled. "I think we have a plan."

The middle school science fair was the ultimate event of the year, not just for the students but for the parents and the community. It was held on a Saturday with food booths, games, and a book fair in the library. Demonstrations of the various projects went on all day, and the prizes were awarded later that afternoon. There were prizes like a chemistry kit, a year's subscription to *Science Weekly*, and a complimentary membership to the local science museum. The big one was a scholarship to next summer's science camp, and I pictured Jacob drooling over that one.

I got out of the shower and stood in front of my closet, debating on how far to go today. How much makeup to put on, my usual utility-daily light or more like adult-evening-date heavy? Should I break out the hot rollers and curl my hair or just ponytail it like usual? Would it seem like I was trying too hard? I finally picked out a pair of leggings and a fitted tunic that actually flattered my robust figure and vowed once again to give up carbs. When Connor knocked on the door, my heart pounded and a zing of lightning struck my sex.

Stop it, Bev! You're an adult, not a moony-eyed high school teenager. He did look good, although the memory of the night before might have had something to do with my reaction. Nice jeans, buttoned-up plaid shirt, and his bomber jacket made him appear relaxed. He leaned in, and I could smell the light masculine scent of his aftershave.

Down, hormones! Down!

My brain almost won that battle until he kissed me with the same thoroughness as that morning. I tasted toothpaste. My nerves channeled another lightning strike, and a silent *squeee!* went through my head.

He smiled and reached up to stroke a single finger just under my chin. "Take you to breakfast before we go?"

"There will be bagels and donuts at the school, but I wouldn't say no to a drive-thru coffee."

He nodded and turned to the door, at the same time threading his fingers through mine. "I'm thinking we should take your van, because the kids are coming home after the fair, right?"

"Yes. I expect Abby will ask again if she can go to the mall, and I'll have to tell her no because she's still grounded. Sarah will stay in her room with her nose in whatever books she gets at the book sale today. Mattie will be wild, and Jacob is a crapshoot depending on what happens at the science fair. You sure you're ready for this?"

His smile remained. "Not a problem."

He palmed my keys and led the way to my van. Apparently he was planning on driving. He seemed so calm and sure of himself. I should have been quaking like a Chihuahua, but I was cool.

Connor opened my door for me, and I climbed in. Once he was in his seat and belted, he looked at the console and frowned. "We need to make a quick side trip before hitting Starbucks." *Gah!* I had forgotten about the almost empty gas tank. I had the habit of pushing it until I absolutely had to fill up. So far, I hadn't run out; however, I'd come close many times.

Connor pulled up to the closest Quality Mart. I pulled out my wallet to get my debit card, but he was already out of the car. He pulled the pump and swiped his own card.

Connor just bought me a tank of gas.

Holy shit, Connor just bought me a tank of gas!

Out of all the flower deliveries, roses at the door, chocolates in big heart boxes, sparkling jewelry, and all those other little trinkets men bought for women, nothing meant more to me than that tank of gas. If there was any doubt in my mind about Connor's feelings toward me, eighteen gallons erased it.

Cars were parked in any available space, legal or not, and it didn't thrill me to see the faculty lot was full too. We had to park down a side street and walk several blocks. Connor tossed our empty coffee cups into a nearby trash can and tucked my hand in his as we made our way to the school. The air was bitter cold, but the wind wasn't blowing, so our noses weren't too red by the time we got to the school gym. It was packed with row upon row of every kind of science thing you could imagine. Spinning things, frozen things, things that spewed liquid, things that changed color, and somewhere there was a thing that Connor had helped Jacob build back in his woodshop.

I spotted Melanie with her latest beau and waved. Her mouth formed a perfect red "O" when she saw my plus one and spotted our linked hands. I knew she would be chill at least for today, but come Monday morning, I expected her version of the Spanish Inquisition.

"Hey, Bevvie. Looking good there, Connor. Big day for Jacob."

I smiled. "Yep. I can't wait to see what he made."

"You don't know?"

"I wasn't allowed in the male-bonding ritual over power tools and whatchadoodles. They kept their secret cult building ceremonies back in the woodshop."

Connor grinned at my words and nudged me with his elbow.

"Well, you're in for a real treat. His display is the big one on the end of the second aisle."

We made our way through the crowd, getting waylaid here and there by a number of my high school students with younger siblings and their parents. Connor stayed patiently by my side. He was polite and shook hands with everyone, being the casual, easy person I knew him to be. At some point, he slipped his other hand back into mine and kept it that way. My brain pulled up a list of heart attack symptoms as the organ in my chest doubled in speed. *Jeez, Bev. You're turning into a sex maniac.*

"There it is, Bev." He pointed to a rather large floor display with a big blue ribbon on it.

It was my mouth's turn to gape.

Jacob and Connor had made a solar-powered robotic Archimedes screw. His quest had been on how to get water to areas that didn't have the natural resource. The ancient method of plumbing was turning slowly, drawing water from a bucket and emptying it into a trough at the other end. PVC pipe formed the screw, and it turned by a belt attached to a motor run by a solar-charged battery. Jacob's idea was like one of those giant, long oil pipelines, but instead of oil, it would be water that would flow, and the desert sun's energy would keep the screw turning in perpetuity. The display was the model for a much larger project, and it looked fantastic with detailed pictures, data on the energy used, time and water evaporation statistics, and probability for success. It was a well-thought-out and very thorough project, and best of all, it worked!

I resisted the urge to do the proud mama happy dance,

and turned to Connor. "First prize. My little egghead won first prize. Oh my God, thank you for all your work. I knew you two were spending a lot of time on this, but I had no idea it was this much."

He shook his head. "I was just grunt labor. This was all Jacob's idea and his design. I only cut and helped him put the pieces together. He did all the research for it. We got most of the materials and pipe as scrap from some jobs I've worked the last few months and rigged up the motor from an old drill press I had in the shop. Even the solar panel was a leftover from a jobsite. He's a brilliant kid."

"I'm totally blown away by this."

And I was. So blown away that when Connor put his arm around my shoulders and tucked me into his side, I let it happen. It was such a natural fit that I leaned in to his body and just let him hold me. My sinuses tingled. Damn, I was turning on the waterworks again. *Stop it, Bev!*

"Thank you for supporting Jacob. This means the world to him. Thank you for all you've done for my family. Thank you for taking a chance on me."

He leaned down and kissed my forehead. I was sure a few of my students tried to get a picture of their divorced chorus teacher out with a man at last. "Never a problem for me, Bev. Our boy did really good."

"*Our* boy?"

I stiffened at the snotty voice behind. Something I hadn't noticed was Doug's arrival. I looked up to see Mattie and Jacob making a beeline to me with Sarah and Abby following. Abby's head was swiveling around, and I guessed she was looking for any of her friends so she could escape the stigma of being at a middle school event. Sarah locked her attention solidly on Connor's hand clasping mine. She grinned from ear to ear.

"Mom! I can do a handstand all by myself! Watch me!" Clearly Mattie had already been into the donuts. If the chocolate smear around his mouth wasn't enough of an indication, his antics were.

"Mom, Autumn's over there with her parents. Can I go talk to her?" Abby had become a lot more subdued since the night of the party disaster. She hadn't mentioned Ashton's name in quite a while. I didn't mind it in the least since he no longer attended the school. Rumor was his father transferred him to a military school to finish out his year.

"Yes you may. You're still grounded, so don't even think about asking for mall time later."

She rolled her eyes and huffed, "Whatever," before escaping.

"Hey, look! I won first place!" Jacob was glowing.

I leaned down and hugged him tight to my shoulder. "Yes you did, sweetheart. I am so happy and proud of you." I kissed the top of his head as he squirmed for me to let go.

"Stop, Mom. You're embarrassing me."

Oh Lord, I have another teenager!

Doug frowned. Mandy wasn't around for a change. She kept such a tight leash on him, it was a wonder he didn't choke. "Who the hell is this, Bev?"

Connor's grip on me didn't slacken. He kept me right where I was while he reached out a hand to Doug, like he had to everyone else so far. "Connor MacAteer."

Doug looked at the hand like it was a snake before he grasped it. "Douglas Archer."

I saw Connor flinch at the contact and then watched Doug wince. I got the impression they were doing that handshake domination squeezy deal. I knew Doug would be on the losing end of that, as Connor was a strong man from all the physical work he did on a daily basis. Doug had sat behind a desk most of the time during our marriage, and I wasn't sure that he was even still working much, if at all.

"Connor! Hey, Connor, come see this one. It's a robot solar system that shows how time works. Come look!" Jacob had been into the sugary treats as well and was tugging on Connor's arm with frantic excitement.

Doug dropped the handshake first. He put a big smile on his face and gestured to the slowly turning screw. "Nice job on the project."

"Yeah, Connor and me worked on it a lot. It's a robot that transports water."

My usually chattering son fell silent in front of his father after that simple explanation. Jacob could spend days talking about nothing but his latest invention, an idea for an invention, the science behind it, and whatever else his smart creative head thought about. None of that showed now, and my son stood still with his eyes to the ground. The look on Doug's face was pained, and the smile was obviously forced. Awkward was the least word I would use to describe the quiet.

Connor became the only thinking adult and filled in

the silence. "Nice to meet you, Doug. Jake, want to show me where that solar robot is?"

Jacob lit up a bit. "Yeah, it's over there. Come on! It's really cool. It has a *bliggety-blah* that hooks into a *blah-blah*. And a second *blah-de-blah* in the *bliggle-blah*."

"Huh. That's almost like the first *bliggety-blah* we tried on the *blah-de-blah*."

Their gizmo talk got me moving at last. "Gah! Okay, you two foreign-science-language-speaking-nerdy-type people, go make goo-goo eyes at the solar system robot thingy. I'll stay here and speak to Doug for a minute or two."

Jacob took off. Connor hesitated. "You okay, *a mhuirnín*?"

I still had no idea what he called me, but it sounded nice. "Yeah, I'm good. Go be a science geek. I'll catch up in a minute."

Connor reached down and kissed my temple before going after Jacob. The gesture sent a thrill down my spine, and I had to stop myself from sighing like a lovestruck high schooler. *OMG, I hope this warmth never gets old.*

"Who the hell is he, Bev?" Doug's voice broke through my Connor fog.

"My neighbor. He moved in last fall and has been helping me with repairs and stuff."

"What kind of stuff?"

"The yard, the plumbing, Jacob's fancy water system. That sort of stuff."

"What else?"

"What do you mean, what else?"

"Are you dating him?"

By now, a few people were watching us to see what drama was unfolding. I kept a cool voice, but I was seething inside. How dare he question me about my private life when he had replaced me as quickly as possible with a live-in Barbie doll? "You can ask me anything about the kids, their school, their grades, their health, whatever it is you want to know, but anything else is nunya."

"What?"

"Nunya. As in nunya business."

"Beverly, I have a right to know who's spending time with my children."

Oh, hell no! He did not just go there. "And you just met him. You want to know what he's been up to with the kids? Just take a look at that." I pointed a stiff finger at the turning water screw as the water continued to burble along.

"I've always been the one to help Jacob with his science fair project."

Jeez, did he just whine? "Well, you weren't around. You told him you were too busy when he asked; therefore, Connor stepped in."

I had to admit he looked a little defeated and dejected when I threw that at him. I almost felt sorry for him.

Until he came back at me with a jabbed finger and outrageous accusation.

"This is your fault. You should've called me and told me about it."

My fault? How in the hell did he come up with that bit of logic? My temper rose to new heights, and I wanted to blast him so badly, but Mattie was still buzzing around us like a bee, and Sarah had glued herself to my side. It was not in me to push this kind of drama in front of them. They didn't need to see the ugly that their parents were starting, and if it meant swallowing my anger and pride, I'd choke it down somehow.

"No, it's not."

Sarah's words did what I couldn't do, and that was break Doug's focus on his anger at me. He blinked like he had forgotten she was even there. Maybe he had.

"It's not Mom's fault you didn't help Jacob. *You* left *us*. It's *your* fault."

I wondered if that was the way it looked when little David beat up big Goliath. Doug stepped back like something hit him. Sarah had been Doug's champion all through the separation and divorce, but Daddy's girl was no longer playing games. From the time she was born, Sarah had been bold and had no qualms in sharing her opinion. She was a smart and tough kid.

I opened my mouth to say something, but I didn't have any words. Sarah was right. It was his fault, and it looked like that particular truth had smacked him right in the face. His mouth opened and closed a few times. I guessed he didn't have any words either.

"Mom, I'm hungry. Can I have another donut?"

Thank God Mattie was oblivious to the tension in the air. "How 'bout a bagel instead?"

"Can I have cream cheese too?"

My little Mattie. So easy to please. I reached for my

wallet to hand him some money, but a twenty-dollar bill appeared in front of me to hand to him. Connor was back and his arm was around me again, tucking me close. "Get two more for your mom and me, please. Sarah, Jake, go with him and get something else if you want it. If you see Abby, ask her too, and come back if that's not enough money."

"Coolio!" The boys took off, weaving their way through the crowd. Sarah hugged my waist, then pursued her brothers, leaving the three of us alone. Doug watched them go, his mouth open as if he still couldn't comprehend his youngest daughter's sentiment. Reality could be a real bitch.

At least Connor was in control. "We got a problem here, Doug?"

He turned to face us, and I got a look at my ex. A real look. No matter what he had in his bank account, he was still going bald, and the hair he had left was grayer. His face was jowly, and he looked old for his age. Defeated was another word I would use.

Before he could form a sentence, Melanie showed up with a man in tow.

"Isn't it awesome? Connor, you and Jacob did such a great job on engineering the screw thingy. My goodness, first place! What an awesome deal! I heard Mr. Barnard say he was so proud of Jacob's work, he's gonna recommend this for the regional science fair. Might have a shot at state. Wouldn't that be something?"

She hugged me and then Connor with super-exuberance and completely ignored Doug. She was milking this moment for all it was worth, and I stifled a giggle. I loved my PITA BFF.

"This is Maxwell Pruett. Max, this is my best friend, Beverly, and her man, Connor."

He reached out a hand. "Nice to meet you."

Maxwell? I wondered what happened to Gabe and Ian. "Nice to meet you too." *Ah, hold up! "Her man Connor?" Damn, Mellie! Lay it on thicker, why don't you.*

"Beverly, I'd like to have a word with you." Leave it to Doug to pour a little rain on my parade. Or at least try to.

"Is that really necessary right now?" I was in a happy place, still reveling in Jacob's success and thinking about Melanie's words. The last thing I wanted to do was "have a word" with my ex-husband.

"If you can manage to tear yourself away from this man and be an adult for a few minutes that would be good."

Uh-oh. Please say he didn't say that to me.

"Be an adult? Exactly what do you mean, 'be an adult'?"

He scowled and flipped a hand in the air. "Come off it, Bevvie, you know what I mean."

I let go of Connor's hand and stepped toward my ex, crossing my arms in front of me. "No, I actually don't. Please explain it to me."

He huffed as four pairs of eyes shifted to him. "I saw you getting cozy with another man at New Year's, and you're here doing the same thing with a different one. It makes me wonder where your morals are and what our children are being exposed to."

Yup, he said that. The fucking bastard said that out loud, to me, and in front of my best friend and Connor. How did I ever share a life with him?

A flash fire of absolute rage went through me, but before I could take a breath and spit out flames, Connor stepped in front of me, cutting me off and going toe-to-toe with Doug.

"You get I'm hearing you say this shite, yeah? It must be your arse that's talking, 'cause your head ought to know better. The kids will be back soon, so it's time for you to go."

Melanie jumped into the fray as well. "What the fuck, Dougie? Hypocritical much? If you're so goddamn concerned with moral behavior, perhaps you should have thought twice before you fucked over your wife and kids and left them for a trophy girl closer in age to your daughter than yourself, then moved her ass in to live with you."

GAH! All right, Bev, time to shut this down. "Doug, you have no right and no leg to stand on when it comes to moral indignity and you know it, so I suggest you can the holier-than-thou routine. Connor's right, the kids will be back soon, and they do not need to hear or see this crap. This is Jacob's special day. He's worked hard for it and does not deserve anyone messing it up."

Connor stood in front of me but still let me lead. He was shaking, and I guessed it was in anger based on his clenched fists. "I think you owe the lady an apology."

The stare down between the two men stretched for several minutes. Doug was shorter than Connor by several inches, and he appeared to be weaker physically, if the growing soft tire around his middle was any indication. Connor was lean, strong, and had a thick, dominating aura around him. Doug backed down. He clearly wasn't happy, but he had no choice.

"Sorry for the slur, Bev." His tone didn't sound apologetic at all, but it was what I got as Sarah and Mattie skipped up to us, paper-wrapped bagels in hand.

"I got a plain one for Connor and a cimmamon one for you, Mom."

"Cinnamon."

"That's what I said. Cimmamon."

Sarah handed a bagel to Connor, and he murmured his thanks. Both kids seemed to be unaware of the tension between the adults, or at least if they did notice, they ignored it. I decided it was best to do the same. "Where's Jacob? Did he get a bagel? Did you see Abby?"

Sarah pointed somewhere to her left. "Over there with Mr. Barnard. I gave him one, but he was busy talking. Abby's sitting with Autumn at the concession tables."

I glanced where her finger indicated, and sure enough, there was Jacob, gesturing with his food instead of eating it. The older man was nodding and talking back, making circular motions with his hands. I bit into sweetened bread loaded with cream cheese and marveled again at my genius little boy.

"I see no one needs me, so I guess I'll just go."

I turned back to Doug at his words. I remembered him saying phrases like that during our marriage, and the thought occurred to me that they sounded like he designed them for guilt trips.

"I'm so tired from working all day. I just don't have the

energy to take out the trash or clean the house."

"I have a really bad headache. You just go on to the movie without me. I'll stay home and suffer."

"I wish my job had a summer vacation break. I have to work all the time."

That last one had always bothered me most. I spent my summer breaks doing lots of neglected house projects, child care, the required professional development classes, and a lot of piano subbing for those people who actually left town for vacations. Summer vacation meant time for extra work with a week off for Disney World. Doug's snide remarks got to me at one point. Now he just sounded petulant.

Sarah spoke without looking up. "Okay. Bye, Daddy."

No "I love yous" or "see you soons," just "bye, Daddy."

Mattie didn't even bother to say anything. Doug visibly flinched. I wondered if he was finally getting a clue that his children were learning to live a life where he didn't exist. He turned and left without another word.

Melanie eyes bugged at me as she mouthed, "Oh. My. God!"

Maxwell had stayed silent and was fidgeting around, clearly uncomfortable.

Connor took a big bite of his bagel and addressed the group. "I don't know about you, but I would like to see some other displays and then go for pizza. Bagels are an okay snack, but I'm gonna want some real food soon. Anyone else got a better plan?"

Mattie jumped up at the thought of his favorite food group. "Pizza!"

"Are you my mom's boyfriend now?" Sarah had finished her bagel and had planted herself in front of Connor.

He swallowed and addressed her directly, just as he would an adult. "Your mum and I have to work it out, but the short answer is yes. I hope you're okay with that."

She was for a quiet moment and then, in classic Sarah fashion, asked, "Are you going to leave?"

He squatted down to get on my girl's level and look her straight in the eye. "No."

Short, sweet, and to the point. *Heart. Going. Melty.*

Melanie leaned over into my ear. "If you don't want him, I'll take him."

I leaned back. "Not an effin' chance, baby. " *I've totally completely fallen in love with my neighbor.* "He filled up my gas tank. I'm keeping him."

CHAPTER 17

The kids weren't fazed at all from the new addition to our lives. In some ways, he had already become a part of us ever since the night he moved in next door. After the science fair, he became a nightly fixture in the house, ate dinner at my table, played games with Sarah, and helped Mattie with his homework. He worked with Jacob in the shop and passed the test of ultimate fire by taking Abby and a handful of her friends to the mall on a Saturday afternoon, post grounding. After that particular afternoon, he came back to the house and his first words to me had been "You owe me a year's worth of pies, *a rún mo chroí."*

Dating me meant being around the kids. Redbox movie nights and popcorn fights, school plays and presentations, even church attendance, he was there for all of it. He came over for breakfast early on Sunday mornings and cooked pancakes and sausage for everyone, then sat with the kids during the service while I played. Mike heartily approved with a wink and a thumbs-up from the choir loft.

The other consideration was the alone time I got with Connor. When it was all said and done, I wanted sex—lots of it—and we took every opportunity we could find. We had to carefully plan when we could get our privacy, but when we managed, it was an explosive time discovering all I had been missing.

I found out what it was like to bend over a woodworking bench and be taken from behind, Connor gripping my hips and pounding in hard while I tried to stifle my scream of pleasure.

I found out what it was like to have quiet phone sex after the kids had gone to bed.

I found out what a "nooner" was during the lunch break of a teacher workday when the kids were at club meetings. I was at home alone, and Connor snuck away from work.

I found I liked giving blow jobs in the car on the way back from a movie date where we actually went to a theater instead of renting.

I found out how good it was to have Connor go down on me for a quickie orgasm when we hid in the bathroom at his place. Adding to that was the thrill of getting caught by the kids while they stayed occupied with their own activities.

There wasn't much that could stop my perpetual good mood. Melanie was super supportive and thrilled I finally had a boyfriend. A relationship with a real man, not the fake version I had during my marriage to Doug. Connor was always there for me, always there for my kids, no matter what. This was what partnership was supposed to be.

Still, I had to wonder how long it would last. How long

Connor would want to be with me, the kids, and all the baggage that came with us. Specifically, Doug and the drama he caused. Now that I was with someone, suddenly he was more interested in seeing the kids and made a bigger effort to keep his times with them. That could have been a good way for him to reconnect with the children, and it did give Connor and me more time to nurture our own relationship. The problem was he made no secret that he didn't like me being with Connor. Sarah told me several times that he grilled them about Connor's work, where we went, what we did, what we said. I was furious at his intrusion into my private life, but Connor laughed it off.

"Let him bark, *a chéadsearc*. We have nothing to hide. He's finally figuring out he lost something good and can't get it back."

It came to a head the night of Doug and Mandy's wedding rehearsal dinner. He wanted the kids there for the big overblown extravaganza, and they had already texted me to complain about it. Mandy had bought them matching suits and dresses she insisted they wear. Abby had sent me a selfie picture of her and Sarah in poofed-out purple skirts, big sausage curls tied up with ribbons, and facial expressions of acute discomfort. Sarah was kinda cute in a little girl way. Abby looked ridiculous in patent leather Mary Janes.

I showed the picture to Connor as we headed out for a night of popcorn, peanuts, and Asheville Tourists baseball. He frowned even as he laughed. "Looks like they've been drinking vinegar. Tell them I said hi and chin up. They only have one more day until they get home, and I'll treat everyone to pizza and a movie at Asheville Pizza and Brewing Company. Deal?"

I typed the message back and watched as the three dots bounced.

Sarah: **Deal. Abby says she wants pineapple this time.**

Me: **What? And ruin a perfectly good pizza? Sacrilege!**

Sarah: **She says Chris likes it like that.**

Me: **Who's Chris?**

Sarah: **She says he's a boy at school. A band nerd and he's cute and likes pineapple on his pizza.**

Here we go again! I looked up at Connor as he put on his jacket. "Brace yourself. Sarah says Abby has a new love interest. Enough to want to commit the crime of adding fruit to pizza." I slipped my phone into the front pocket of my trusty school hoodie. My hair was in its usual ponytail, and I wore my stretchy mom jeans.

Connor opened the door to his truck with a loud creak. "What's wrong with that?"

"No. You're not one of them, are you? An alien who likes pineapple on pizza?"

"I'll take pineapple over anchovies or black olives."

"Seriously? Black olives?" I happened to agree with him on the anchovies, but it was too much fun to tease him and get teased back.

"Yup. Black olives. I don't like the way they look."

"What if I like black olives?"

"I'll get a pie half with black olives and half without."

"Sarah likes only cheese pizza, Mattie is all about

pepperoni, sausage, and extra cheese, nothing else. Jacob likes veggies, including black olives, but not mushrooms. Abby will only eat pepperoni and mushroom. Now she wants pineapple in the mix."

"So we'll order what everyone wants and take the leftovers home."

"That's a lot of pizza."

"We have a lot of family."

Warm fuzzies welled up in my heart at his words. I leaned in to kiss him as I got in the truck. "You're a good man, Connor MacAteer, and I'm so very lucky to have you in my life."

"I'm the one who's lucky. Now, are we done with the pizza debate? I'd like to get to the game before they start the seventh inning."

I blew him a raspberry and settled back to fasten my seat belt.

He mumbled something about being a smartass and how it might get me a tanning later. I don't think I ever smiled that big in my life. A little flare shot up in my stomach at the thought of what that would be like. Perhaps going a little *Fifty Shades* wouldn't be so bad.

Life drama just had to happen, didn't it?

My phone rang as Connor was backing out of the driveway. I saw it was Doug calling, and mom senses hit the pit of my stomach. I answered my phone and put it to my ear. "Hello?"

"Hi, Bev. Um… Mandy and I… well… we need some help."

"The girls already sent me pictures of their dresses."

"Huh?"

"I can't help you with them."

"Well… uh… no. It's not the dresses. It's Mattie, he… um… he had an accident."

The sound of Mattie crying hard and Abby's frantic voice hit my ears. My heart rate increased, and I could feel a different kind of heat build in my gut.

"What happened?"

"Um… well… Mattie eats a lot, and we're not serving dinner until seven. So… well… we have a bunch of canapé trays, but Mattie wanted pickles and…."

I may have dented my phone case I gripped it so hard. "Doug, what happened?"

"Mattie pulled a big jar of pickles over on himself. It broke, and he has a bit of a cut on his head."

"By the sound of him, it's more than just a bit."

"Well, you know head wounds bleed a lot, and—"

"Why the hell haven't you taken him to the emergency room?"

"All of Mandy's family are coming soon, and I'm meeting some of them for the first time. I really need to be here, and the emergency room takes so long…."

Red. I was seeing red. Nope. I was seeing magenta, crimson, and scarlet. Hell, I was seeing shades of red that hadn't been discovered yet.

"Are you asking me to come to *your* house to take *our* son to the emergency room because it's *fucking inconvenient* for your *fucking girlfriend*?"

The truck jerked to a stop, and I could see Connor turn toward me. I rarely dropped F-bombs. I saved them for the times when I needed to make a point. Big ones. Doug knew this but still chose to keep going.

"Ah… well… um… yes."

"You piece of shit. You're a total fucked-up piece of shit!" I was yelling loudly. "I swear, Douglas Archer, if you don't get off your ass, grow some fucking balls, and get your son to the emergency room, I'll spend every penny I have to take my kids away from you permanently!"

"Bev, there's no need to use that kind of language."

"Fuck you, Doug!"

I hung up and wished I could throw the phone to the floor. Worry for my son mixed in with white-hot rage at my ex-husband. My ears roared, and I was afraid if I let it out, it would consume everything around me. Connor parked on the street and leapt out, slamming his door hard in the process. The loud bang broke my fury enough to follow him.

"Doon't waste your time callin' him back. Weel take your van. The kids are comin' hoome." The look on his face, the accent, and his sharp movements told me he was angry himself.

We made it to Doug's fancy house in a fraction of what it normally took. Connor parked my van in the middle of the circular driveway next to a Lexus. An older couple had just arrived and was in the process of handing the key to a parking valet. They were dressed formally, like they were heading to a prom rather than a rehearsal dinner. *I guess that's a thing in a rich person's world.*

"Excuse me, ma'am, but I can move your—"

"Don't bother. We won't be here that long." I brushed off the young man's outstretched hand as I bulldozed my way through. The valet and the couple stepped back in fear from my growl, and I stomped up to the front door. Connor was right behind me.

I didn't bother to knock.

Doug met me, his face anxious. "Now, Bev, there's no need to cause a scene."

"Get out of my way, Doug. Where is Mattie?"

"It's not as bad as you think… and… what the hell is he doing here?"

Over it! Done!

"WHERE THE HELL IS MY SON!" The rafters shook with my roar.

"Kitchen. He's in the kitchen. Please keep your voice down."

"Fuck that!" I was really starting to enjoy saying that word.

I found Mattie sitting at the kitchen table with Abby holding a blood-soaked towel to his head. He was still crying softly and wiping at the snot dripping from his nose. Later, I might think about the luxury appliances, granite countertops, and expensive custom fixtures. Later, I might think about the designer clothes my kids had on. Later, I might think about all the people who witnessed the show. At that moment, all I could think about was my child's pain.

"Mommy!"

My heart tore in half.

"It's okay, sweetheart. Mommy's here. I got you."

I held my baby boy and carefully lifted the towel from his head. The cut was not "a bit" by anyone's standard. It was about two inches in length and extended from the corner of his eye up into his hairline. Stitches were a definite.

"How's your vision? Can you see okay? Nothing blurry or seeing two instead of one?"

"No, it just hurts!"

His cry ripped my halved heart into quarters. Mattie had spent most of his life collecting little hurts. This was his first big one.

"Okay, Mattie-boo, let's get you to the hospital."

"Will I have to have a shot?"

"Probably. But it's only to numb you and make the pain go away."

"Is Connor coming too?"

I glanced up at the man standing behind me. Sarah had burrowed under one arm and Jacob under the other. He addressed Mattie directly. "Absolutely, boy-o."

"I'm scared."

"I'll stay with you the whole time."

"I wanna go home."

"Me too," Jacob announced from his safe spot next to Connor. He was wearing an outfit that matched the one Mattie wore, a dark purple three-piece suit. Sarah was in her poofy frills dress, her expression one of disgust under the tear streaks. "Can I come home too?"

I looked at Abby in question, and she nodded.

"Connor and I only have the van. It may be a while at the hospital."

Sarah shook her head. "I don't care. I don't like it here, and I don't like *her*."

Jacob sniffed. "Yeah. If she would've let Mattie have his snacks, he wouldn't have built the chair tower to get to the pickle jar."

There was more there for me to pick through, but I had to get Mattie to the hospital and didn't have time to process anything else.

Connor had been around us enough times that he knew the drill. "All right then, lasses and laddies. T-minus five. If you have stuff here for the weekend, we'll come get it tomorrow. Right now we have to go."

It was amazing how bonded my kids were. They would argue with each other to their last breath over who farted at the dinner table, but if something hurt one of them, it was all hands on deck. Connor scooped up Mattie and carried him through the house. Strains of a string quartet wafted through the long hallway, and there were a lot of guests milling around who stopped to watch the spectacle of Connor and me taking a bloody kid to the front door. I heard a few gasps of "oh my" and "my word" as I tromped over the glazed tiles.

"Oh, thank God!" Mandy trilled as she hurried over to us in the foyer. "The caterer's been waiting to get in the kitchen for ages. My schedule is all messed up now! Did the blood on the floor get cleaned up?"

I didn't think about it. I didn't hesitate. My arm flashed

out, and I punched Miss Silicone Boobs right across her face. Not a little slap, either. I roundhoused her hard. She cried out as her nose crunched and she went down hard.

"Stupid, self-centered bitch! Guess the maids have a little more blood to clean up, huh?"

I shook my bruised knuckles as we marched out the door. If my last action had legal consequences, bring it.

Jacob's eyes got round as he passed Mandy blubbering on the floor with Doug squatting awkwardly to comfort her. "Wow, Mom. Epic!"

The van still sat where Connor parked it. Jacob and Sarah scrambled to get in the far back, and I sat with Mattie in the back seat. Abby got up front. Mattie was still upset and sniffling but calmer. Connor was shaking when he got behind the wheel, and his level of control impressed me. I was sure he had been fighting the impulse to either put a fist through Doug's face or through one of the walls.

He got us to the hospital in record time. I didn't think a police siren would have stopped him.

The wait to see a doctor wasn't as long as I thought it would be. Maybe the sight of a blood-covered little boy and his very determined mother had something to do with it, but in no time they whisked him to the back and he was getting stitched up. Connor stayed with the other kids in the waiting room, and I caught sight of him handing some dollar bills to Sarah, probably for the vending machine. The doctor was a young woman, probably an intern, but very good at putting Mattie at ease. She didn't blink at his explanations.

"How did you cut yourself?"

"The pickles cut me."

"Must have been a big pickle."

"It wasn't the pickle itself. It was the pickle jar. I dropped it when I pulled it off the shelf."

"Why didn't you get out of the way before it fell on your head?"

"I couldn't. I was on the ladder."

"The ladder?"

"Yeah, I built a ladder to get to the pickles."

"You built a ladder?"

"Uh-huh. I took a chair and put a stool on it and then a box and climbed up to get the pickles."

This conversation took place while she covered the area with a numbing spray before she gave him a shot of Novocain. She put twelve stitches in my son's head, and I winced at every one of them.

"There ya' go, buddy. You'll have a nice scar to show off to the ladies someday."

He lit up with joy. "A scar? Coolio, I've never had one of those before."

"And I'd rather you not get any more." She plastered several strips of Med-tape over the row and wrote a prescription for a topical antibacterial cream. "Keep it clean, and you'll need help with washing your hair for a few weeks. No more building ladders. If you want pickles, you need to ask someone to get them for you."

"I did. Mandy said no."

The doctor made a weird face, and I jumped in. "You can get pickles at home, Mattie-boo. I think we've had enough excitement for tonight. Let's get us all home."

"Did you go to the game and have pretzels?"

The big soft pretzels were Mattie's favorite whenever we went to the ballpark. "No, we didn't make it to the game at all. Your dad called me, and we came straight to get you."

"Why didn't Dad take me so you didn't have to miss your game?"

My anger had reduced to smoldering ashes. Still there, but I wasn't ready to fan those particular flames. Especially in front of my eight-year-old. "I don't know why, sweetheart, but I'm glad he called me. I would've been here anyway, right next to my little Mattie-boo with the coolio scar." Ruffling his head wasn't a good idea, so I settled for a squeeze.

"Does Connor like pretzels?"

"I'm sure he does."

"With mustard or salt?"

"I don't know, but you can ask him and I bet he'll tell you."

"I'm hungry."

Tears rushed out of my eyes faster than I could contain them. "Me too, precious. Me too."

The doctor left, and a nurse came in with a clipboard of forms for me to sign. Mattie climbed off the bed and dashed over to look at his head in the mirror. He poked at the tape and made faces. "Zombieee!" he rumbled at himself. "Think Connor will get us pizza now instead of Sunday?"

God, I love my kid! "We'll see what we can do."

Connor was pacing—yes, *pacing*—in the waiting room.

Jacob walked next to him in his purple finery. Abby and Sarah sat next to each other with a few open cracker packs and soda cans on the table in front of them. They were sitting in two chairs, but their skirts took up the space of four. I wanted to laugh at the sight, but before I could, all three kids rushed us with Connor bringing up the rear.

"Did it hurt?"

"How many stitches did you get?"

"Was it a big needle?"

I didn't say anything. I didn't have to. Connor folded me up in his strong secure arms and just held me. "It's okay, luv. Our boy is just fine."

Me? I clung to him. This man who had quietly become my rock, my anchor, my best friend, and my firm support. In that moment, I admitted to myself that I loved him. I loved Connor MacAteer and had for a long time. I couldn't imagine a life without him in it.

"Hey, Connor, can we get pizza?"

Mattie's voice cut through the emotional fog I was in, and I felt Connor's chest vibrate as he chuckled. "Already called it in, boy-o. We'll grab it on the way home."

"I like pepperoni and sausage and lots of extra cheese."

Connor winked at him. "Got ya covered. Ready to go?"

I sighed as I released myself from his arms. "I have to go check out and settle up. The insurance will cover most of this, but I'm sure there will be something left on the bill."

"Doug will cover that bit, won't he?"

I gave him my best you're-kidding-me-right look. I didn't want to say anything since the kids were in earshot.

"Talk about it later. Let me go do what I need to do."

I went up to the counter with my entourage loudly in tow. Sarah and Abby debated about pineapple on pizza, much like Connor and I did earlier. Mattie peeled off the tape to show his brother where his coolio scar would be. The woman at the checkout desk rapidly typed on her computer, probably to get us out of there as quickly as possible so the noise volume would drop.

"I checked your insurance and your deductible benefits. We need a deposit of twelve hundred for now until the insurance company pays out. We'll send a refund or a bill for the balance once the insurance settles."

Holy shit, that was a lot, but what else could I do? I was reaching for my credit card when Connor's debit card suddenly appeared. He tucked it into the machine and let it do its thing.

"What did you just do?"

He punched in his PIN. "It's only a deposit. I'll cover this, and when Doug pays, he can pay me back."

I whispered under my breath to try and keep it from the kids. "Doug's probably not going to pay."

Connor met my gaze with his strong one. "Oh yes, he will."

"Mom! Jacob says he doesn't like black olives anymore."

Connor grinned at me as he palmed the receipt. "A man after my own taste. Argue later, Bev. There's pizza waiting for us."

I kept my mouth shut. We drove by the pizza place, and Connor took Jacob in with him to carry the pizza boxes.

We had six people in the car and three large pies to feed us.

The aftermath was simple. We went home, ate our preferred slices, and played marathon Clue. Mattie's battery ran out early, probably due to stress and the painkillers the doctor had given him. It was late when Doug finally called to check up on Mattie. To his credit, he first asked if Mattie was okay. Then he asked if the children would be coming back to attend the wedding.

OMG, how was I ever married to this man? "Gee, Doug. Let's ask them, shall we?" I put the phone on speaker. "Hey, kids, are you going back for your dad's wedding tomorrow?"

The three who were still awake yelled toward the phone.

Abby was texting someone, her thumbs a blur on the phone screen. "There's no point in going anyway. We're not in the wedding party. We're just supposed to sit on the side and stay out of the way."

Jacob whined. "Do I have to? I wanna stay home and play games with Mattie."

Sarah gave her opinion. "I hate that stupid dress!"

I took the phone off speaker and put it back to my ear. Doug decided to throw a tantrum. "Beverly, those are my kids too! I'm getting married tomorrow, and I expect them to be here."

"You can come get them in the morning, but I won't make them go if they don't want to."

"I can't come get them! I don't have time. You'll need to bring them early."

"Not my problem."

"What the fuck is wrong with you? You come here all

high and mighty with your *boyfriend*"—he spat out the word like it was something foul—"and then have the nerve to punch Mandy in the face. You're lucky she's not going to press charges."

I stepped out on the porch so my kids wouldn't hear me, or at least I hoped they couldn't. I wouldn't put it past my little snots to try to listen at the door. "There is nothing wrong with me, asshole, but there is something seriously wrong with you. Mattie has twelve stitches sewn into his head. *Twelve!* Why? 'Cause your fucking girlfriend wouldn't let him have any snacks for fear of him getting that ridiculous purple suit dirty. The co-pay for the emergency room was twelve hundred dollars. A hundred bucks a stitch! You want to press charges? Try it. I'll be glad to explain in court how you couldn't be bothered to take your injured child for treatment."

"I hope you don't expect me to pay for it."

His statement stunned me into silence. No surprise that I was right, though. He wasn't going to pay.

"I just spent nearly forty grand on this wedding."

Silence over, and to hell with being quiet! "You spent forty thousand dollars on your wedding and can't afford to pay for your child's medical bill? Unbelievable! You've gone out of your way to please that Barbie doll wannabe and ignored your kids for the past year. Now you suddenly want to show them off at your big-ass wedding in big-ass skirts and big-ass purple suits. You want them there so bad, you can try to come get them, but unless you're prepared to take them kicking and screaming, you'd best stay away and enjoy your goddamn wedding! I'm sure Mandy has plenty of makeup!"

I took a breath to blast him again, but the phone was taken from my hand. I regarded Connor's face as he put the phone to his ear. He listened for a moment while he stared into my infuriated eyes. He was just as angry as I was, although his voice didn't show it other than a thickened accent. "I'll thank you tae never call Beverly that again, in my presence or no. You can keep actin' like an arse, or you can man up and be a father. The children are nae comin' back, and isna Beverly who you owe money to. It's me. I paid Mattie's hospital bill."

He paused as he gazed down at me. "How does that feel knowing another man took care of your child? I'll tell ya now, I'll be doin' it again. I'll be there for all the sprains or cuts or stitches. I'll be there for recitals and science fairs and football games. I'll be there when they graduate high school and college. And if I'm so lucky to pay for their wedding, I'll be standin' up for the lads and walking the lasses down the aisle."

I couldn't tell if Doug was saying anything or not. Connor concentrated for a minute and then burst into loud laughter. "Go for it, ya *gobshite*. I'm not opposed to a little scrapping now and then, and I'd not wager on who's going to kick whose arse. You might want to rethink having a matchin' black eye while you wait for your little bride. You want to bring police? Thasna a problem. From the days I've counted, this isn't really your time anyway, remember? Bev switched weekends so the children could be at your wee wedding. Didja' nae check your own calendar, *cábúnach*?" His eyes lifted heavenward. Abby would be proud of his eye roll technique. "It means worthless fuck."

My thought train careened around my head on a wild emotional roller coaster. I couldn't believe I had been married to a man who was that detached from his own flesh and blood. It was okay if he fell out of love with me—I was an adult—but the kids? That was mind-blowing to say the least. The signs had been there, but I never truly believed he was that self-centered as to throw the children under the bus. Then there was Connor, declaring he would be in our lives long-term, through thick and thin. My heart swelled. My brain spun. I didn't know how to handle this.

Connor fortunately did. He pressed a button, closed the phone, and looked at its face. "Isna the same satisfaction to hang up a cell phone than to slam it down."

He swiped a hand over his face. "Jesus, Mary, and Joseph, he's a real horse's arse. Come 'ere, luv."

I stepped into his firm hug. "Did you mean it?"

"'Course I meant it. That man is a *gobshite* and doesn't deserve to be called a father. A man makes children, it's a lifetime job. You don't get to pick and choose."

I shook my head against his broad chest. "No, I was asking about the other bit. The cuts and sprains and recitals and walking down the aisle bit. Did you mean that?"

"I meant that part too. You and your family are a big part of my life. One I love dearly, and if you left, it would leave a huge hole that canna be filled. It's a real challenge to take four teenage girls to the mall, but I'll gladly do it if it makes Abby happy. Jacob is a smart one, and I love his creativity. Sarah is just brilliant. Seeing her shine is a great privilege. Mattie, well, you can't help but want to be around him. He brings happiness no matter what he's doing, even if it involves pickles."

He leaned back and tipped my chin up with two fingers. "And there's you, *mo shíorghrá*. I'm a simple man with simple needs. I don't need fancy clothes, fancy houses, or fancy cars. What I need is to spend every day working alongside you and every night making love to you. You're more precious to me than my own life, and I would sooner go without myself than ever see you suffer. When life gets tough, I'm not going anywhere. It all boils down to one thing: I love you. I love everything about you. Being with you fills me with joy, and I'll do everything in my power to make you happy, even if I have to go on a blasted dating site to make it happen."

Connor loved me. He really did, and I had plenty of examples. Mowing the grass so I didn't have to, taking on my kids when I needed him, sharing meals together, and for the love of all that was holy, the man bought me a tank of gas!

I spluttered out an "I love you too" before reaching up to kiss him. It was sweet, sealing the deal that this was a long haul kind of relationship. I thought I had found the love of my life a long time ago, but I was so totally wrong. There were no conditions here. Connor loved me. *Just as I am.*

"Connor! It's your turn. We've been waiting like an hour!" Sarah's whine meant she was getting tired, but her competitive streak wouldn't let her give up until the game was over.

Connor laughed against my lips and hugged me close again. "I think it was Hermione in the library with the sleeping spell. Be nice to actually win for a change. Our girl is too smart sometimes."

Our girl. Oooo, heart all melty!

"So what does Mowsheergrah mean?"

"*Mo shíorghrá.* My eternal love."

Ooooo! More melty!

"Mom! Jacob took the last Twinkie!"

I slammed my forehead into Connor's sternum. "You sure about this?"

He laughed. "Yes, I'm sure about Hermione. Now let's get in there so I can finally claim a victory."

Chapter 18

It was still dark outside when Connor came down the steps. I had already put the pan of Jimmy Dean's Best in the oven and was wiping off the counters when his two arms came around me from behind. "Morning, beautiful."

I turned for a quick good morning kiss and immediately got interrupted.

"Mom, what's for breakfast?"

Mattie, of course.

"Bacon and egg biscuits are in the oven as we speak."

"Can I have coffee too?"

"Absolutely not. Where are your sisters?"

"Abby's in the bathroom, Sarah's in her room. Why can't I have coffee?"

"You're kidding, right? No way am I adding more fuel to the mix today. With all the sciency stuff and you caffeinated out of your mind, it's likely we'll start a nuclear event."

Connor chuckled in my ear. "You could get him some decaf."

I turned and gave him my best no-nonsense voice.

"There will never be a time when I will even entertain the idea of decaf coffee in my house, rented or otherwise."

He gave a belly laugh and let me go to move to the cabinets. "You're a real corker, Bev. Biscuits almost ready?"

My stomach quivered at the sound. *Get it together, Bev!* "Just about."

I watched as he opened the cabinet and got out a mug. He poured himself a cup and handed Mattie an oven glove before the little booger could burn himself pulling the hot pan from the oven. Sarah bounced down the steps, followed by Jacob and Muttface, the four-legged addition to our family. The shelter had listed him as a mixed breed, and in my opinion, he had all of them.

"Hi, Connor," Sarah greeted.

"Mornin', lass. Ready for breakfast?"

"Uh-huh." She got the jugs of milk and orange juice from the fridge while Connor pulled down several glasses. He poured a second cup of coffee and added cream and Splenda to it while the kids settled at the bar to eat. "Abby down yet?" he asked me.

"I haven't seen her this morning. She's probably avoiding me since I said she had to come with us instead of staying in Asheville over at Autumn's and hanging at the mall all day. It's a big deal that Jacob's project made it to the state level, and it's not going to hurt her to come support her brother. She keeps up that attitude, she'll be grounded until graduation. *Mattie's* graduation. From college."

Connor laughed out loud that time and handed me my cup. I took a healthy swig of the coffee and started moving around the room, straightening up the couch cushions and picking up the dirty cups and other debris from the trails my kids seemed to leave behind them wherever they went.

"Dearest children of mine, you possess one mouth each. Why is it that every drinking glass available gets used between the three of you on a daily basis?"

"I forget which one is mine, so I get another one."

"Ewww! Drinking from the same glass over and over? Gross."

"Doesn't this place have a dishwasher?"

Connor took the armful of stuff from me and dumped it into the sink. "Seems to me there are three perfectly good dishwashers here."

My kids looked at him in confusion. Sarah was the first to get the joke. "You mean us, don't you? Washing dishes by hand? Yuck!"

Connor nodded, his face full of humor.

"That's nasty!"

"You gotta stick your hands in goopy water with old food stuff floating in it."

"Cool beans!"

I looked at Connor's smiling face. "How much can I pay you to take them for the day and let me stay here?"

He shook his head in mock horror. "Not a chance, *mo shíorghrá*. I'm still recovering from the regional fair."

Jacob sprayed a bunch of crumbs across the area I had just wiped. "Yeah, Mom. You gotta come see if I won something else besides a participation ribbon."

I gave an exaggerated sigh. "Oh, the sacrifices I make

for my kids. Hand me a biscuit, and someone go light a fire under Abby."

The State Science Fair was held in Raleigh, which was a four-hour drive or better from Asheville. We had rented an Airbnb house instead of a hotel and decided to make a whole weekend of it. The Museum of Natural Sciences hosted the event this year. Connor and Jacob spent yesterday afternoon setting up the Archimedes screw while the rest of us toured the museum. I had to keep Mattie from climbing the dinosaur skeletons. Judging would take place this morning, and we would be there for the duration. It was going to be a very long day, but I'd already made plans to have someone sub for me at the church, so tomorrow we planned on more museums or the Pullen garden. As a family. Plus one.

Melanie came from her room, which was on the main floor. She, of course, was dressed to the nines and was in full makeup. The house had five bedrooms. The boys took one, the girls took another. Connor and I decided that separate bedrooms would be a good idea in front of the kids, partially because of an already impressionable teenager and a soon-to-be teenager. That left one bedroom, and Melanie invited herself along.

We also made the decision because Doug was making custody and child support noises, and neither of us wanted to give him any fuel. After this past year, I finally got my case in front of social services, and the people there loved to sue deadbeat dads. In Doug's case, with the amount of money present in his bank records, his negligence in seeing the kids, and the night of the hospital emergency, the legal people were rubbing their hands together with glee. My ex was toast.

"Coffee. Must have coffee." Her exaggerated plea for caffeine sent Jacob and Mattie into peals of laughter.

"Hey, Mom, Auntie Mel is just like you in the morning."

"Pbbbbt!" I splatted a somewhat wet raspberry in their general direction.

Connor poured Melanie a cup and handed it to her. Mattie ran into the kitchen area on socked feet. Connor caught him, then flipped him upside down over his shoulder. "Here, wake up your sister." Mattie screamed in delight and pounded his feet against the ceiling. "That should get Abby moving. Don't you fart on me like you did last time, boy-o."

I looked at Melanie, who regarded Connor with sparkling eyes. "Children. I have five of them now."

Somehow, we managed to get everyone fed, put Muttface in the outdoor kennel, and load up the van relatively on time. Abby and Melanie were discussing fashion trends, Mattie and Jacob were thumb wrestling in the very back, and Sarah was playing a game on Connor's phone.

Connor was driving when my phone chirped. Doug's name popped up, and my stomach plummeted.

I hadn't heard much from him other than an angry threat to sue for full custody. I didn't really take him seriously. I thought it was more posturing over his hurt ego than a desire to raise the kids himself, but I knew people sometimes carried on out of spite. Before I answered, I glanced in the mirror to see everyone occupied.

"Hello, Doug."

"Uh… hi, Bev. Um… I'm over at your house, and… well… no one is here."

"No, we're not. We're spending the weekend in Raleigh for Jacob's science fair exhibit. He made state, remember? This is my weekend anyway. You gave up yours to do that two-week honeymoon cruise."

"Oh. Yeah, that's right. I just thought that maybe you'd be home."

Damn, he sounded confused and a little depressed. Something was going on. I glanced over at Connor, who had a concerned frown on his face. His eyes darted to the mirror as mine had to see if anyone had noticed my conversation.

"I'm… uh… well…," Doug sputtered, then got quiet.

"Spit it out."

"She left me."

Whoosh, not expecting that. "She what?"

"She left me. We got home from the cruise last week, and she left me last night. Said she was tired of playing stepmom, the kids embarrassed her, *I* embarrassed her, and a bunch of other stuff. I got served with papers yesterday afternoon, and by eight, she was gone."

"Um… I'm sorry?" I had to phrase that as a question while choking down the bark of laughter that threatened to come out. I wasn't sure if I was sorry or not, but it sounded like that was what I was supposed to say.

"She gets half of everything. I have to sell the house and the cars. I'll be lucky to break even. I shouldn't have let that money go to my head. I thought our marriage—yours and mine, I mean—was stagnant. I felt trapped, and this was my way out of a humdrum boring life. Now I wish with all my heart I hadn't given that up."

What am I supposed to do with this? "I'm not sure what you expect me to say. Again, I'm sorry it didn't work out between you and Mandy, but not to be a super B about it, it's not my problem."

"I just thought…."

"What? Oh my God." My lip curled, and Connor noted my expression by reaching over and placing his hand on mine. "Please tell me you weren't thinking we were going to get back together."

"Well… um…."

"No."

"How 'bout we meet for lunch or something next—"

"No."

"Can we just—"

"No." I risked another glance in the back to make sure my phone actions weren't being observed. So far only Connor paid any attention, but he only heard my half of this conversation and didn't look too thrilled with it. "Not gonna happen ever in this lifetime or the next. That ship has sailed. That bridge is burned. That egg cracked. If I had more clichés, I'd say them. Get me? What we have left between us is the four lives we created. You want to focus on them, I'll talk to you. Anything else is nunya."

"I can't believe you won't even consider it."

Seriously, who the hell is this man?

"I'm happy. I'm happier than I've… you know what? I don't have to justify a thing to you. I'm done. Call me about the kids. Fight the custody and child support shit if you really want to drag the kids through more drama. You do you. You always have. Now I'm going to go see how my son's science project did at the state level. Good luck, and have a nice day."

I ended the call and settled back in my seat. I caught Melanie's eyes look up in the mirror. My BFF wasn't stupid, and I was sure she heard enough. Connor had a death grip on the steering wheel, and I reached a hand over to his forearm.

"It's all good, Mowsheergrah. I'll tell you later when little ears aren't so close in proximity."

He relaxed and gave me an easy side look. "*Mo shíorghrá.*"

"That's what I said."

"You say it with a Southern accent."

"You say it with a Jersey accent."

"*Ceanndána.*"

"Try again?"

"Means stubborn."

"You love me anyway."

He took a hand from the steering wheel and placed it over mine. "Aye, that I do."

We reached our destination, already teeming with school-aged science nerds and their parents. Row upon row of electric gizmos, biological gadgets, environmental whatnots, and lots of other thingies that lit up and made noise. Connor and Jacob went to check on their screw display while I got the rest of us settled.

"Abby, you can retain your coolness vibe by hanging

with Melanie. Sarah, you can go with them or stay with me. Mattie, you're either by my side or with Connor. No running through the aisles, no sticking your fingers in anything, no climbing on the barricade ropes, no fighting over whose project is the best. If you have to pee, do not announce it to the world. The concession stand is our safety spot. Everybody ready? Break!"

"We want to see Jacob's screw again." Sarah was standing next to Melanie, deciding the coolness vibe applied to her as well.

"Third row over. Let's go, and then you are free to roam."

Our entourage made it to the display only to find the screw wasn't turning. Connor was messing around with the motor, and Jacob was hovering over him.

"Is the *blah-blah* still attached?"

"I think it's the *bliggety-bleh*. See the loose *bleh-blab-blah*? Take the Phillips head and tighten it."

I held my breath as I watched my son take a screwdriver and stick it into the open motor casing. I was fully prepared to watch him fly across the room when he got zapped with a bazillion bolts of electricity. Hmm... bolts? Volts? Something like that.

Instead of the movie-worthy scene playing out, the giant screw started turning, and water began to move from one tank to the other.

Connor closed the metal plate. "Something rattling in there. Bev, can you stand at the other end and catch whatever it is? I don't want to take a chance on it backing up and burning out the motor."

I did as he asked and held my hand under the cool trickle. A moment later, a small hard object fell into it. "How did a ring get caught in your screw?"

Oh. My. God. Did I really just say that out loud around a bunch of middle schoolers? I held up the piece of jewelry. It had a wide white gold band engraved with curlicues and a single faceted diamond that sparkled from its recent tumble. It was rather pretty.

Wait. A ring? Holy shit!

I raised my eyes from the simple shiny stone. Connor was still on his knees and watching me. The younger kids were fidgeting next to him, like they needed to pee really badly. Melanie had a smirk on her face, and I knew she had been in on the plan.

"What do you think, Bev? Care to make a family of five into a family of six?"

Tears hit my eyes. "We're already a family of six, but we can definitely make it official."

Jacob jumped up and down. "The ring in the screw was my idea. It worked, didn't it?"

"I'm planning the wedding," Abby announced.

Sarah pushed her lower lip out and crossed her arms. "I am too!"

Mattie tried to do a backflip and ended up crashing into Melanie. "Ugh, take it easy, kid. We still have a science fair to get through. I think your mom's gonna win the big prize from floating on cloud nine right now."

Mattie paused and looked at me to see if I was still on the ground. I grinned at him, went up on my tiptoes, and waved my arms like I was a bird. Connor got up and took the ring before I dropped it and pushed it firmly on my left hand. "Want to tell me aboot yer phone call?"

Whoops! Irish accent coming out.

"Nope. I just want to bask in the glow for a bit."

His eyes grew soft, and he leaned down to kiss me.

"Ewww! He's gonna kiss Mom, like, right on the mouth!"

"Gross! Old people kissing."

"They do that in movies."

"They get paid for kissing in movies."

"It's still gross."

Basking done. "All right, you heathens, show's over. Go find cool stuff to do for the next hour."

Melanie, Abby, and Sarah walked away, debating on wedding colors. Jacob engaged in conversation with a judge who was regarding his project, clipboard in hand. Mattie gave up on the backflip and tried a cartwheel instead.

"I know it's not the same as candles and flowers, but Jake's idea seemed more like you. I meant it, Bev. I'm here for the long haul. There are two rocking chairs I've started making back in the woodshop that will go on our front porch. I'm not a rich man, but I never had to spend a lot when I was working the family business on the road. I saved quite a bit and bought the duplex last week. My side has a bigger kitchen, utility room, one full bath and one half bath, and a bigger family area. Your side is about the same but smaller rooms and only one bathroom. I drew up plans to remodel the inside so all the kids have their own room, and I can make them bigger. We'll have a nice kitchen, living room, and dining area. I might fit in a game room too. Unless you have an objection to this and want a new house altogether, I can have my brothers come in a few weeks to get started."

He took my hands. "If you want the girls to plan a forty-thousand-dollar wedding, I can give you that, but for me, I'll be happy with something small. Just you, me, the kids, Melanie, and my brothers and sister's family."

I smiled into his face. "I'm good with simple. Did you say you have *two* bathrooms? I love you, Connor MacAteer!"

"And I you, Beverly Archer."

Mattie appeared and wrapped his arms around both of our waists. "Me too. Mom, I'm hungry."

Epilogue

"Mom, did you pack sunscreen for me?"

"I get the big yellow towel this time."

"You had it last time."

"No I didn't."

"Yes you did."

"MOM!"

I gritted my teeth and shoved three more towels into Mattie's backpack. Between the drilling, hammering, sawing, and the shrill cries of my arguing children, my stress level hit highs previously unknown to man. *Only twenty more minutes. Only twenty more minutes. Nineteen. Eighteen. I swear if Doug calls to say he'll be late, I'll have a brain hemorrhage.*

School was out, graduations done, and life lapsed into summer mode. Doug had gotten better about his time with the kids. After Mandy left him and took half his money, he finally got his head out of his ass and was trying to reconnect with them. He stopped the court fight about child support and signed over full custody to me. This would be a long road, as neither the kids nor I completely trusted him, but all of us were willing to make the effort. Including Connor.

Summer mode was usually pool time with the kids, hikes, art camps, catching up on house projects, and the like. This year's season started off with a bang. Literally. Connor's brothers had shown up earlier this week in a gigantic RV and were pounding on the door just as the sun was rising.

"Come on, ya lazy feck. We're burnin' daylight."

I met Owen, Garrett, Patrick, and Angus in my worn-out blue robe, Bach head slippers, and massive bed head. Connor had already started the renovations in the house, and they had come to help. Tarps, power tools, construction scraps, and stuff I couldn't identify were strewn all over both sides of the house. The kids were heading off to spend a full week with their father, partially because of the dangerous construction happening and partially because all the bedrooms' walls were being torn down and reconfigured. Connor and I still had a somewhat intact bedroom, but everything else was in serious disarray. Connor kept saying they were making great progress, but all I saw was a big fat mess.

"Mom, someone's coming down the street!" Sarah was camped out in the window, watching for Doug. Her yell was accompanied by a loud roar pulling up outside of the house. Only one thing could make that sound.

Eva, my sister-in-law, had arrived, and I hurried to greet her. "You got an extra helmet? Quick, hand it to me and I'll climb on. We can make a run before they notice we're gone."

She laughed and hugged me as she dismounted from her motorcycle. She whipped off her helmet, revealing a head full of ginger hair and green eyes that matched her brother's.

"Stud is right behind me with the girls. It was my turn to ride and his to drive. I'm here to help while he takes the girls to the Adventure Center for the day. Betsey came too with her grandkids."

The other MacAteer men came up and hugged their sister.

"'Bout time you showed up."

"Married life is makin' you soft."

"Where are me bonny nieces?"

A van—that's right, *a van*—pulled up behind the RV, and none other than Thor, the gorgeous thunder god himself, emerged from the cab. Two towheaded little girls followed him, and he lifted a third from the car seat in the back. A woman with bright, dyed red hair got out on the other side with two older children. I'd heard about Betsey, the matriarch of the Dragon Runners MC, from Connor, but she was much more in real life. Her perfect hourglass figure was poured into tight jeans, high-heeled boots, and a sparkly off-the-shoulder top. Grandmotherly? Not in the least.

"Hey, y'all! I got a couple coolers a' barbecue in the back row. Got greens and homemade corn bread too. We'll have us a good dinner later tonight. I hope you have a bathroom that's working, 'cause I got to pee like a racehorse." She gave me an air smooch and a wave with her long red talons before clacking into the house.

I looked at Eva. I met her when Connor and I got married.

No big church thing or reception; it was a simple ceremony done in my pastor's living room. The kids and Connor's sister's family were there, along with Mike from the church, who volunteered to give me away. Connor's brothers decided to come down and celebrate with us when they came for the house renovations.

We watched as Betsey strutted into the house. Eva met my eyes with a smile and a what-can-you-do shrug. "Betsey, meet Beverly. Beverly, meet Betsey." Eva buckled on an impressive tool belt. "All right. Where do you need me?"

"Got several jobs going." Connor's voice rumbled in my ear as he hugged me from behind. "Bedroom walls are coming down, and new ones need framing and wiring by this afternoon. Insulation and drywall if we can swing it. Patrick and Angus are working on moving the furniture to get that started once the kids go off with their father. Owen and Garret are finishing the new kitchen cabinets and countertops. The kitchen sink still needs to go in, and I'm working on that right now. Kids' game room and the living room are done but need trim work. Master bath is done and needs it too. Medicine cabinet and towel bars need to be installed, and the linen closet needs the door hung. Take your pick. Plans are on the work table."

She nodded and went to work. I was amazed at how well and efficiently the brothers and Eva worked together. A big well-oiled machine that in the few days the brothers had been there had accomplished so much. It would go even faster with the kids away and Eva now here. It had been a real challenge to keep Mattie and Jacob away from the tools.

"I need some help in the fall. Our house needs another bedroom added before Christmas." Eva bent over to peruse the plans.

Stud paused in his kid-watching duties to regard her with a questioning eye. "We have four already. Why…?" The man went pale. "Again? Cactus, please, baby, make this one a boy. I love my girls, but I'm beggin' you, I need someone else with testosterone in the house."

She just smirked and donned a pair of safety glasses. "Karma, Studly Muffin."

She picked up several long boards of lumber and carried them back to the woodshop to start cutting. Stud just stared, slack-jawed, until one of his daughter announced she also had to pee.

Eventually all the kids lined up outside, mine with boxes and backpacks for a week and the rest with a pack for a day. Doug pulled up—late—and my four hooligans loaded up with a chorus of "bye, Mom, love you, bye, Connors" and whatever else hit their head. Betsey came back out of the house declaring the work looked good. She gave Connor and me big hugs before she barked orders at the rest of the kids and Stud to get moving.

I got in on the work action as well. I didn't know a thing about construction, but I could fetch waters, hold boards, hand tools to people, and basically be a go-fer for the day. The MacAteer family kept going until the sun was making its way to the horizon and Betsey made everyone stop for a fantastic barbecue dinner with all the fixings. Several motorcycles showed up, and it became a real party. I met someone called Ditchdigger and another called Chevy. Both were members of the local Dragon Runners MC chapter and were there to pay respects to Stud and Betsey and help where they could. Mike did a drive-by in the late afternoon and kept the kids entertained, giving Stud and Betsey a break. Melanie came by in the evening for food and social time.

"Those are Connor's brothers?" She nodded toward the group of men nearby.

"The ones without the Dragon thingie on are."

"It's called a cut."

"Cut what?"

"It's like a vest but… you know, never mind. I'm going to play eenie-meenie-minie-moe."

She "moe'd" on Garrett. I could tell by the tone of her voice she was on the prowl. Maxwell bit the dust, and she'd been without male companionship for several weeks, which was rare for her. I watched as she fluffed her hair, licked her lips, and baited her hook. "Be careful there, Mellie. If he's anything like Connor, he may not bite. He's supposed to go back to Jersey next week."

"Then I'll have to give him a big send-off." She winked at me and sauntered over to the group.

I sighed. Melanie was a grown woman, but I still worried about her lifestyle.

By the end of the day, the kitchen, game room, den, five of the six bedrooms, and two bathrooms were completed. Some finish work was still needed, like painting and some trim work, but the house was livable, and I could start making it into a home.

Connor and I tumbled into bed, both of us exhausted. The smell of plaster and wood shavings permeated the air as I snuggled into Connor's side. The kids texted me about their father's house, how they had to share rooms there as he had been forced to downsize. He still had some money left but not enough to continue his lavish lifestyle. He also had to go back to work. I had a hard time coming up with any sympathy.

"Kids okay?" Connor sleepily rumbled in my ear as he pulled me close.

I draped an arm across his hard stomach. "Yes. Abby is complaining that Doug won't let her go to the mall, and Mattie says there aren't enough snacks, but otherwise, everyone is good. They'll survive."

"We can always go get them if they want to come home."

"I know, and they know too, but let's wait as long as we can. I would love a few days with just us since we didn't get a honeymoon."

"We'll take one sometime. What do you want?"

"A cruise where there are no beds to make, food to cook, or dishes to wash."

"Deal."

I stroked my hand lower over his hard abs. After watching the amount of physical work the whole crew did, I knew exactly where those muscles came from. "How tired are you?"

His chest lifted as he chuckled. "Tired enough for you to do all the work."

I grinned as he pulled back the covers. He only wore boxers, so freeing him from the cloth was easy. He was already hard when I took him in my mouth.

"Oh, Bev… yes." He placed his hands on my head and shoulders, running his fingers through my hair as I sucked him. "I'm nae gonna last long, *a mhuirnín*."

I released him and quickly climbed on top. His hands moved to my hips as I eased myself down on him and began rocking back and forth. *Damn, he felt so good!* I leaned back, and the pressure inside me shifted to my favorite spot. My movements became harder to control as I worked myself on him. One hand left my hip, and I watched as he put his thumb in his mouth to wet it before slipping it down to press against my clit. That was all it took, and I exploded. He followed me with his own yell of release, and I felt his warmth flood my channel.

"Ah, Christ, Bev. I'm looking forward to a lifetime of this."

"Me too. Let me up so I can clean up, and I'll be right back."

Once I was back in the bed, my brain drifting toward sleep, he surprised me with a statement.

"Garrett and Owen asked me tonight about the business. They're both interested in settling in one place, and they like Asheville."

I went on alert. "Melanie put Garrett in her sights tonight. Does she have anything to do with it?"

Connor looked over at me in surprise. "She did? Jesus, Mary, and Joseph, we got ourselves another drama comin'."

"What do you mean?"

"Owen's got a thing for Melanie. If they both like her, it will be interesting to see who wins."

"You know she goes through men like disposable razors. Once they lose their edge, she's gone. I'd hate for either of your brothers to get hurt."

"I can't tell them what to do any more than you can tell Melanie what to do. Our job is to be friends and support them no matter what happens. Who knows? Maybe something will work out, and two of them will find something like what we have."

God, how I want that for my BFF.

"I love you, Connor MacAteer."

"And I love you, Beverly MacAteer. *A stór mo chroí, mo shíorghrá.*"

"I have no idea what you said, but whatever it was, back atcha."

I fell asleep to my husband's soft laughter.

Gaelic Terms and Meanings

A chara	Friend
Bhean ólta	Drunk lady
A mhuirnín	My darling, my dear
A rún mo chroí	My heart's beloved, my darling
A chéadsearc	My first love
Mo shíorghrá	My eternal love
Ceanndána	Stubborn
A stór mo chroí	My heart's treasure
Cábúnach	Worthless fuck
Gobshite	Idiot

ACKNOWLEDGEMENTS

This story was one of my favorite to write; so much of the book is real to me on a personal level. I've been a single mom, working nonstop to put food on the table and keep the lights burning. I've had cheating partners I had to support. I've been on blind dates to at least get out of the house and meet people. It's hard. It's a struggle. I can personally relate to Beverly's life, as much of my own in reflected in hers. Finding a good man is still possible and there are Connors out there, but they may not be shining white knights. They may come covered in wood chips and driving a pickup truck.

A big note of gratitude to the lovely women who helped me get this book done. Brittany Alexander, Kristen Scearce, Randi Creamer, S Aronson, Rebecca Allman, and Virginia Gaylor. Thank you so much for your details. Shout out to Becky Johnson, Donna Pemberton, Olivia Ventura and all the other ladies of Hot Tree Publishing. You'll always have my gratitude for taking me on and helping me grow.

Thanks for reading *Run With It,* MacAteer Brothers book one. I do hope you enjoyed Connor and Beverly's story. I appreciate your help in spreading the word, including telling a friend. Before you go, it would mean so much to me if you would take a few minutes to write a review and share how you feel about my story so others may find my work. Reviews really do help readers find books. Please leave a review on your favorite book site.

Don't miss out on New Releases, Exclusive Giveaways and much more!

LIKE ME ON FACEBOOK:

WWW.FACEBOOK.COM/AUTHORMLNYSTROM

FOLLOW ME ON TWITTER:

TWITTER.COM/ML_NYSTROM

FOLLOW ME ON GOODREADS:

WWW.GOODREADS.COM/AUTHOR/SHOW/17103715.M_L_NYSTROM

VISIT MY WEBSITE FOR MY CURRENT BOOKLIST:

WWW.MLNYSTROM.COM/

I'd love to hear from you directly, too. Please feel free to email me at WWW.MLNYSTROM.COM/CONTACT or check out my website WWW.MLNYSTROM.COM for updates.

OTHER BOOKS BY ML Nystrom

If you loved *Run With It*, you might enjoy the other sensual, sexy, and romantic stories and books I have published.

DRAGON RUNNERS MC SERIES:
MUTE

STUD

BLUE

TABLE

BRICK

About the Publisher

Hot Tree Publishing opened its doors in 2015 with an aspiration to bring quality fiction to the world of readers. With the initial focus on romance and a wide spread of romance subgenres, Hot Tree Publishing has since opened their first imprint, Tangled Tree Publishing, specializing in crime, mystery, suspense, and thriller.

Firmly seated in the industry as a leading editing provider to independent authors and small publishing houses, Hot Tree Publishing is the sister company to Hot Tree Editing, founded in 2012. Having established in-house editing and promotions, plus having a well-respected market presence, Hot Tree Publishing endeavors to be a leader in bringing quality stories to the world of readers.

Interested in discovering more amazing reads brought to you by Hot Tree Publishing? Head over to the website for information:

WWW.HOTTREEPUBLISHING.COM